HEREDITARY POWER

THE GATEKEEPER'S CURSE SERIES: BOOK THREE

EMMA L. ADAMS

To be notified when Emma L. Adams's next novel is released, sign up to her author newsletter.

1

"The Winter Gatekeeper's back." With those words, Hazel ended the phone call. "The Winter Lynn house is locked down again. Nobody can get in."

"But—which Gatekeeper?" I asked, since nobody else came out with the obvious question. *Not Aunt Candice. It can't be her. I banished her beyond the gates of death.*

Hazel shook her head. "I don't know."

"Evil Aunt Candice is back?" said Morgan. Our older brother, psychic sensitive and necromancer, was the one Lynn who hadn't been around in June when our distant relative had tried to murder us.

My heart sank. "It can't be her. Who told you she's back?"

Hazel slipped her phone into her pocket. "That was Lou from the necromancer guild in Foxwood. I asked her to watch the place while I was gone. Someone has claimed Winter's territory again."

A moment passed. "That... it might be good news, if Holly's come to finally take over as Winter Gatekeeper."

And if not? There was only one person who could have

1

claimed Winter's gate, and I thought I'd banished her into the afterlife for good.

"It's more likely to be Holly," Hazel said. "Maybe she heard the Courts pretty much threatened to declare war if she didn't come back. I'll go check it out."

"I wouldn't," I warned. "If it *is* you-know-who, you're in no condition to fight her."

Not to mention, she's dead. But if anyone was tenacious enough to sneak back into the land of the living, though, it was our deceased and distant aunt.

"We dealt with one ghost today. I can..." Hazel trailed off, pressing a hand to her forehead.

"You okay?" I asked.

"Yeah. The spell that knocked me out was damn strong. I'll be fine when we get to the house."

I hope so. The ghost we'd fought and barely beaten had nearly killed Hazel, and tried to use Morgan as a puppet to steal my talisman. All of us were exhausted, even River, my half-faerie, half-necromancer... I wouldn't say *boyfriend*, but if I'd been able to complete my necromancer training, he might have been.

At least, until about five minutes ago, when he'd revealed he'd known all along where our missing mother was. The Summer Gatekeeper had disappeared in the most dangerous region of Faerie: the Grey Vale, a death trap even to Sidhe, while on a quest that couldn't end until she completed it. I understood why he'd kept the truth from me, since faerie vows left no room for flexibility, but the betrayal stung all the same.

"We already told Lady Montgomery we were on a rescue mission," I said to the others. "Let's make it official. Send Arden into the Summer Court to warn them, and then..."

"Go after Mum," finished Morgan.

River shifted on his feet, the merest betrayal of his disapproval. Okay, I was well aware that Hazel was the only one of the three of us with any level of faerie magic—not counting River himself, of course. But I wouldn't leave Mum to suffer alone. Whether the Winter Gatekeeper was back or not.

Hazel snapped into Gatekeeper-in-Training mode. "Right. I'll clean up if someone has a spell handy. Morgan?"

"Why do you want to clean the place?"

"Because my housemates will ask awkward questions if they come back and find evidence of blood magic in the living room," I answered for her, heading for the stairs. "I'm going to grab some spare clothes. I'll be down in five."

I ran upstairs, removing my torn and bloodied necromancer coat and shoving it into a rucksack along with some spare outfits. I left my suitcase, scribbled a quick note to my housemates explaining I'd be back in a week or two, and checked on the book I kept in the pocket of my hoody. Small, square and unobtrusive—you wouldn't think it was a talisman that contained the power to control life and death. The curling symbol on the cover, which belonged to a faerie language I couldn't read, gleamed softly with white light, and its power resonated in my hands and in the mark on my forehead. The mark of a Gatekeeper who didn't guard the gates of Summer or Winter, but of Death itself.

Powerful curiosity brimmed within me at the sight of new text on the pages, but if I stopped to read it now, I'd lose track of time. *Find out which Winter Gatekeeper is back first, deal with the book later.*

I found the others downstairs, surrounded by the smell of cleansing spells. No blood or necromantic residue remained on the walls or carpet.

"The first spell turned the walls pink," said Morgan. "Damn Corwin… you ready, Ilsa?"

I nodded. "Hazel, where did you cross over from the Ley Line, anyway?"

Her brow wrinkled. "Ah. I can't remember... it's all fuzzy thanks to that bastard's spell."

"You must have used a Path, right?" I said. Oh no. The Lynn house rested in a liminal space on the Ley Line, the invisible line through the middle of the country which marked the place where the three realms of Faerie, Death and the mortal world overlapped. Only the Summer and Winter Gatekeepers or their heirs were capable of controlling the way in and out of the family home.

"I can help," River offered. "I'm familiar with the Line, since I used it to cross over from Faerie a few weeks ago."

I glanced at River. He didn't flaunt his magic most of the time, but it was difficult to forget he was half-Sidhe. His pointed ears and faintly glowing green eyes were clear enough markers, though his human side lent him slightly rugged features, tousled fair hair and a more muscular frame than most half-bloods. He wore his necromancer cloak, arms folded across his chest, and the grim exhaustion of his expression seemed to be expecting us to throw him out. Collectively, the three of us could probably toss him outside for not telling us the truth about our mother's captivity, but he was in the employ of the Summer Court, he knew what might be going on over there, and I'd rather have him as an ally than an enemy.

"If I invite you to come with us," I said to him, "do you swear not to lie to us again?"

Unlike Sidhe or other faeries, half-bloods weren't obligated to tell the truth at all times, which was how he'd managed to deceive us for so long. Morgan and Hazel looked at him, too, the former with disdain, the second with anger mingling with distrust. River's arms dropped to his sides as he straightened to his full six-foot height, and looked between us. "If your siblings don't have a problem with that."

"I don't give a shit, to be honest," Morgan said. "I'm no

more welcome in the Lynn house than he is. And we need allies."

All eyes turned to Hazel. She scowled. "Look, I'm already outvoted. We need to move if we're gonna rescue Mum. It's hardly the first time he's lied to us."

River's jaw twitched a little. "Very well. I promise not to deceive you, as much as it's in my power."

"A vow would hold you to your word," Hazel observed.

River looked at me again. "Is that what you want, Ilsa?"

The way he said my name threatened to undo the calm I'd managed to maintain since he'd revealed he knew where Mum was. If I asked him to swear to tell the truth—*really* swear to, on pain of literal death as per the terms of faerie vows, then… would he go through with it? It'd be a sure-fire way to tell how sorry he actually was. On the other hand, I hated the Sidhe's manner of forcing obedience, and besides, only people with faerie magic were able to force someone to swear a vow. He'd have to make the promise to Hazel, not me.

I met his stare. "No. I'll trust you to keep your word. It's up to you to decide how much that's worth, not a spell."

His gaze flickered away from me before I could read the emotion within it. "With your permission, I'll accompany you back to the Lynn house. As for the Ley Line, I can take you there."

"As long as it's nowhere near that bloody graveyard, I'm good," Morgan said.

I didn't want to place my trust in River, not when he'd so recently betrayed us, but we had few options, and if the Winter Gatekeeper had really taken back the other Lynn house, we needed to be ready to defend ourselves. Neither she nor Holly could directly harm anyone with the surname 'Lynn', which covered all of us except River, and he wasn't exactly a pushover, either. We had strength in numbers.

The four of us left the house, and River took the lead, walking down the road. The grey Edinburgh sky showed no signs of the battle that had taken place less than four hours before, ripping the boundaries of the worlds apart. Ghosts were common enough here that Edinburgh was the only major city in the UK to have a large organised necromancer guild. Morgan, River and I were still official members, despite having acquired permission from Lady Montgomery to go chasing after the missing Summer Gatekeeper. It still blew my mind that she hadn't locked me up when I'd told her the truth—or some of it, anyway.

"How are you tracking the Line?" I couldn't help asking River. "Is it because it's your home?"

His shoulders tensed, and there was a long pause before he answered. "No, but my vow binds me to the person I swore it to. It's another type of magic to regular faerie magic, and while it's faint here, I can still sense it."

"Huh." The spirit realm looked uniform to me. I couldn't sense the invisible spirit lines criss-crossing the city, let alone the major line cutting through the centre, where the faeries had tried to break out entirely too many times in the last few years. "So you're always aware of it?"

"In some way."

The whole time we'd been together, he'd known. Not just in the sense that he was lying to me with every word, but via an actual link to the faerie realm. I swallowed down angry words, too tired and worn down to start another argument. I'd chosen to let him help us, and we'd deal with our issues once my family was reunited.

Eventually, a faint shimmering on the road ahead caught my eye, the only hint of the invisible line separating our world from Faerie and the space between. Hazel moved to take the lead. The circlet on her forehead—borrowed from

Mum, but infused with her own inherited magic—glowed a little.

"This is it," she said. "It feels… off."

"Probably cause of that bastard's spell," Morgan said. "C'mon."

We walked right into that shimmering light, Hazel in the lead, a green glow spreading from the symbol on her forehead beneath the circlet, marking her as Gatekeeper of Summer. As we moved in behind her, Edinburgh's cobbled streets became a field running parallel to a long fence, circling a manor house.

Hazel staggered sideways into the fence. Then she gasped.

Clouds marred the usually perfect sky over the Summer house. No sunshine shone onto the flowers blooming all over the garden, the evergreen trees hunched together in gloomy clusters, and the smell of decay crept in, unheard of in our garden. The house itself looked… sad. Empty. It usually gave the impression of being packed with people even when only Hazel and Mum lived there now, and both were absent a lot of the time, because Summer's magic kept it alive. Hazel tripped over the threshold, dropping the keys into a bush.

"Hazel?" I said. "Are you okay?"

"Yeah. I'm just—drained." She lifted her head. "My magic should be functioning here. But it isn't."

"Something's wrong." I retrieved the keys and unlocked the door myself.

There were no humming noises, no signs of the ever-present magic which kept the house running. Just eerie silence, and the faint smell of decay. I switched the light on and found the source—several large house plants had died.

"I swear it was fine when I left." Hazel made it to the living room, where she proceeded to collapse onto the sofa. I entered behind her, scanning the paintings of past Lynns, the bookshelves crammed with old trinkets. Normal… yet so quiet. At least the lights were working. The only time I'd ever seen the house's magic fail was when the spirit barrier around Winter's house had broken, causing their magic to spill into our territory. But if that were the case, it'd be colder. The house was mildly warm, same as usual.

Morgan stood awkwardly in the doorway then shuffled in, warily, as though expecting Mum to leap out from behind a door and turn him into a deer. Morgan had only just come back into our lives after running away eight years ago, when Hazel and I were fifteen and he was seventeen, and Hazel had barely forgiven him for that. It hadn't entirely been his fault—his psychic sensitivity had been untrained and he'd never told anyone about it, leaving him vulnerable to ghosts convincing him to pursue ridiculous stunts. But his leaving had left a gaping hole in our family, and none of us knew how Mum would react to his sudden return.

I crossed the room to the bookcase and found the last picture of the three of us, lying flat where Mum had left it after that awful summer eight years ago. Blowing dust off its surface, I flipped it upright.

"Hey," Morgan said from behind me. "I didn't know Mum kept that."

"She has the others in a box in the spare room." I cast a brief glance at River, who remained by the door in his blood-stained coat. He'd once expressed an interest in seeing my childhood photos, though I was kind of glad that this was the only one on display. It'd been taken on mine and Hazel's fifteenth birthday, and featured Morgan and me having an intense tug-of-war over the book I was reading while Hazel stole all the birthday cake. Morgan snickered and held it in front of Hazel's face. She feebly lifted her head. "Good god, what was I wearing?"

"Mum's best Court gear, I think," I said. "She let you steal the circlet, remember?"

She gave a faint laugh and pushed herself onto her elbows. "Yeah. Forgot about that. You look just like her."

"Who, me?" I said, surprised. Hazel was always the one people compared to Mum—probably because they saw the two of them side by side all the time. I didn't even think we looked that much like twins, certainly not as much as we did as chubby, awkward teenagers in the photograph anyway. But it'd been so long since I'd seen Mum in person that my memories were blurred.

"Sure." Morgan returned the photo to the shelf. "You look just like she does when she comes back from the Court ready to do some damage."

"I feel more like a nap." My whole body ached from being thrown around by ghosts. I'd healed my worst injuries using a witch spell, but blood stained my hand and arm where I'd cut it in a risky attempt at blood magic.

"No kidding." Morgan removed his bloodstained necromancer coat and threw it over the back of the nearest armchair before sinking into it. He took after Dad more than Hazel or I did, though we shared the same Lynn dark brown eyes. He'd grown his hair out in the years since he'd left, and while he'd lost a lot of weight since he'd run away, he looked much healthier than he had when he'd shown up gaunt and sleepless on my doorstep a few weeks ago. "I'll take a nap, you come up with a plan. Someone has to."

"I'm going to shower, for a start," I said, grimacing at my bloodstained arm. "Can one of you throw those rotting plants out?"

I walked upstairs to the bathroom, where I rinsed the blood from my hands in the sink before climbing into the shower, yelping when ice-cold water doused me from head to toe. Summer magic was entirely responsible for keeping the house heated, too, apparently. I scrubbed off the blood the best I could, then dragged a brush through my matted hair, scowling at my reflection in the mirror. My eyes remained dark brown, not tinted green with Summer magic, while my tangled hair was more or less the same shade as my eyes. Except for the mark on my forehead, which gleamed a little, but not bright silver like Hazel's did. I'd kind of hoped having a faerie mark on my forehead might at least do a little to make me look magical and interesting. Instead, I just looked tired and pissed off.

I pulled my spare clothes on, looping the necklace-shaped spell around my neck. The mark on my forehead vanished, fading into the background. Ghosts could still see it, but nobody else could. Which suited me just fine.

I returned downstairs to find Hazel passed out cold, while River and Morgan sat in separate armchairs in the sort of uncomfortable silence of two people forced to interact who had absolutely nothing whatsoever in common with one another.

"I threw out the plants," said Morgan. "Your boyfriend says there's no Summer magic here at all."

I opened my mouth to argue with the word 'boyfriend', then decided it wasn't worth the energy and sank into the remaining armchair.

"Your defences are out," River said. "However, the salt barrier is still intact, and there's an iron barrier circling the house, too."

I glanced at Hazel. "She must have set it up herself. I haven't been home much since June. Guess she got the idea from you."

He inclined his head. "It'll keep out the dead, at least. This magical drain isn't the result of a spell, otherwise I'd be able to detect it."

"But Summer magic can't switch off," I said. "It's supposed

to remain in balance, no matter the season. Unless… no. It can't be to do with Mum, either. Or Hazel. The magic depends on the Court, not the Gatekeeper."

"Precisely why I think we should speak with the Summer Court," River said.

"Hasn't anyone found Arden yet?" I asked. "That's not my job. I hate the little bastard, he isn't going to listen to me."

Morgan snorted. "You think he even knows who I am?"

Hazel lifted her head. "Shit. Maybe he's serving Holly."

She might well be right. Arden served both Gatekeepers, though he'd failed to mention that slight detail until he'd already passed on pertinent information on our family to the Winter Lynns, not to mention framing me for murder. Sure, he might be as much a slave to the faerie Courts as any of us, but I didn't like the idea of depending on him for anything.

"Arden," I called. "Oi, Arden. We need to send a message to the Summer Court."

Silence. Suspicion brewed inside me. "You know… maybe I should go to Winter after all."

Hazel pushed into an upright position. "Not without me."

"Hazel, you need to recover your strength. Maybe go to the grove. I'm just going to look at Winter's house. I can use my spirit sight to check who's there without even walking up to the doors."

"I'll go with you," River put in.

I pressed my mouth into a line. I didn't want to be alone with him, especially now, but of the others, he was best equipped to handle anything we might run into. "Okay, then."

"I'll watch from the house," Morgan said. "If there's anything seriously nasty out there, I can come and help."

"Sure. We won't be long." I already had the talisman in my pocket, but I added some knives, salt and iron filings to my weapon arsenal before leaving the house. River carried his own talisman, a faerie-made sword gleaming with runes carved on its hilt. Its silver sheen usually carried an emerald tint, but it didn't now. "Is your magic working okay?"

"It's difficult to tell," River said. "I haven't been using it as often as I should, and considering the presence of the dead sapped my magic, I'd have to get closer to Summer to check."

His tone was polite. Non-confrontational. That was the worst part about his betrayal—we'd had no time, and there'd been too many people around, for us to confront the matter head-on. Besides, there was nothing more to say. He'd had his orders and obeyed them. It wasn't like he'd never disobeyed a faerie vow before, and if he'd honestly wanted Hazel and I to know the truth, he'd have found a way to tell us. Okay, we'd have probably gone charging off into the Vale to rescue Mum despite her supposedly not needing to be saved, but still.

For now, I'd hold him to his word. Forgiveness would come in time, if at all. The important matter was dealing with the house—and finding out if Winter was responsible.

The fence alongside our garden didn't stop when it reached the forested area at the garden's end, hiding the gate to the Seelie Court. As the trees thickened, there was a shift where they turned from evergreen to snow-covered, and our territory became Winter's. The shape of the Winter house appeared on the other side of the fence, facing away from us. The house had been abandoned for nearly four months, and I'd begun to worry her daughter, Holly, wouldn't return before the Winter Sidhe's deadline. But if the wrong Gate-keeper had come back, we were in serious trouble.

River strode on, blade in hand, pausing out of sight of the house. I took in a breath, and tapped into my spirit sight. Greyness flooded the world, bleaching out all colour, as I searched for signs of life. Living spirits shone bright, dead ones were paler. In cities, it was confusing to tell them apart, but out here, the only living beings within reach were the two of us. I pushed outward with my mind, extending my awareness in the direction of the Winter house. Within, there was an unmistakable glow. I moved closer, my heart beating fast.

The glow... I took a few steps forward in the waking world, honing in. Definitely a living spirit.

This time, there were no spirit barriers, and no Winter Gatekeeper—aside from Holly Lynn, my cousin. But was she friend or foe this time?

I turned off my spirit sight. "Holly." I looked to River, who nodded.

"It's her." He continued to walk alongside the fence. "She's not using necromancy. There aren't even any redcaps around."

"Probably because the house has only been in one piece again for a day."

When I'd killed the Winter Gatekeeper, the house had been in ruins. But Winter magic ran here as strongly as Summer magic was supposed to run in Mum's house, and had clearly repaired the damage. The house's stark white walls and the smooth snow-coloured lawn made our non-functioning magic look all the more suspicious.

River caught my sleeve in his hand as I opened the gate. "Are you certain?"

"She can't harm me." Thanks to an argument between Aunt Candice and Mum, no Lynn could inflict damage on one another. Besides, Holly hadn't been hostile when we'd parted. More like heartbroken. She'd tried to stop her mother's deranged spirit from escaping, but it'd cost her dearly.

I approached the door and knocked before I changed my mind. Several seconds passed. Tapping my spirit sight on, I honed in on Holly's spirit. She hadn't moved.

I knocked again. No response. The curtains were drawn. It wasn't that late, though I felt like several lifetimes had passed in one single day. I was worn down, far from ready for a confrontation... but I knocked one last time all the same.

"CAW."

Arden swooped down and landed on my head. I jumped off the doorstep, catching myself against the wall. "Dammit, Arden."

"Nevermore."

"You're damn right. Why isn't she answering the door? For that matter, why are you serving her?"

"I serve only the Gatekeepers."

"Thanks for nothing, then," I spat. "You knew, too, didn't you? You know where our mum is." I ignored River's warning hiss. I didn't care if Holly heard. "Is she draining our magic?" I demanded.

"No," said the raven, fluttering his feathers. "If I were you, I'd ask your Court."

I swore under my breath. "You're the only one of us who *is* capable of asking Summer, on our behalf. In fact— that's exactly what we need. An audience with the Seelie Court."

"Caw. I will provide."

He took flight in a flutter of feathers. "I meant *after* you explain what the hell's going on, Arden."

The door flew open, and Holly scowled at us. "Haven't you people done enough?"

"Oh," I said, awkwardly. "Hi. Yeah, we came here to see if it was you who'd come back, and not... someone else."

Her eyes narrowed. "No, my mother's beyond the gates

where she belongs. I've come back to take my rightful place as Gatekeeper."

"Er… good. I think." Awkward silence, much? I'd basically killed what was left of her mother… who'd tried to kill me and my sister, and almost succeeded. Pretending to forget either of those things was impossible for both of us. Holly herself looked about as exhausted as I felt, her dyed black hair in disarray and bags under her bright blue, Winter magic-tinted eyes. "So you got your house back. Did that happen when you accepted the magic?"

"Ask your sister what the ceremony involves." She scrubbed a hand over her forehead. "Look, I'm tired as hell and I've been running around for the Court all day, so if you don't have anything useful to say, come back later."

"You've been to Winter?"

"That was implied, yes."

Damn. They actually had forgiven her for betraying them. That, or they'd had no choice, because if Winter didn't have a Gatekeeper, war would break out with Summer.

The spirit I'd defeated had seemed to think Summer and Winter were on the brink of declaring war on one another anyway… which was another issue I'd kind of forgotten, considering all the other crap we'd had to deal with. Holly and I might not be outright enemies or even rivals, but it wouldn't do to forget our respective Courts hated one another.

"Okay," I said. "Just wondering, since it's been months since you were here last. Is everything… normal here?"

She raised an eyebrow. "Is anything about this shit normal?"

"Point taken. I mean, the house was in ruins, your magic was pretty much gone. You didn't have any trouble taking it back, or…"

Her eyes flashed bright blue and the air went even chiller than usual. *That's a no, then.* Months might not have passed at all. The house was as white as the snow coating the trees, sturdy and upright and gleaming with magic. It wouldn't do to confide our own weakness to her, and hell, if the answers were within the Summer Court itself, it definitely wasn't Winter's business. I was too tired and drained to run an interrogation on someone who hated my guts.

"No," she said, through gritted teeth. "This delightful curse of ours ensures that I'll wield this magic until I die, and so will my children. Nice seeing you again, Ilsa."

She closed the door, firmly. I raised an eyebrow at River. "I've had worse family reunions."

"Her territory isn't draining yours," River said. "If the source is in Summer, they ought to respond to Arden's request quickly."

"I know they did last time, but it *was* nearly the end of the world. Mitigating circumstances."

I shook my head at the door and turned away. As we walked through the field alongside the fence back towards home, I gave the Winter house one last glance over my shoulder. Normal. As though it hadn't lay neglected for months. Holly lived there all alone. It was kind of sad, really. Her mother hadn't left much of a legacy behind. No wonder she still seemed to nurse a strong resentment towards the Lynn curse, and our common ancestor.

"Is it true?" River asked. "The curse passes directly through the bloodline. Does that mean Hazel's children...?"

"In theory, but I don't think the curse is that specific. As long as both Gatekeepers belong to the Lynn bloodline, it doesn't matter if they're the Gatekeeper's own children. I'm sure there have been incidents in the past of one of them dying young, or even switching sides if one branch of the family didn't have kids." I shrugged. "So Holly might choose not to have any children in order to beat the curse, but then if Hazel or I do… they're liable to be hauled off to Winter."

River didn't say anything for a long moment. I stole a sideways glance at him, wishing I hadn't brought up the subject of children, or even marriage. It wasn't as though I'd ever thought much about the subject. I'd barely begun to live *my* life, let alone someone else's, and Mum's hands-off parenting approach was down to her having one foot permanently in the Seelie Court.

"Is that why you can't move away from the Ley Line?" River finally asked.

"Wouldn't surprise me. Any reason?"

"The terms of the vow," he said. "They're not usually *very* complicated, in words at least."

"Why does that matter? It's not like we've ever found the person who actually bound us. Unless there's something else you didn't tell me."

He shook his head. "No, of course not. Does the title automatically pass on, then?"

"What, when the Gatekeeper dies?" I forced my thoughts to go in the direction of the deceased Winter Gatekeeper rather than the unthinkable. "Yes, it does, but it doesn't have to happen that way. If the Gatekeeper decides to retire, then they can choose to voluntarily give up the circlet. The Sidhe encourage it, to be honest. They want the Gatekeepers to be at the peak of their power and strength."

We came within sight of the Summer house. The smell of burning drifted from an open window. "Shit." I didn't see smoke, but picked up the pace all the same. "Tell me it isn't fire imps."

"It's not the faeries," River said.

It wasn't. I found Morgan in the kitchen, a burned pan in

the sink. At least it wasn't actually in flames. "Hazel went to shower. She wants someone to cook, so…"

"You decided to set the kitchen on fire." I sighed. "Look, we might not have functioning magic, but honestly." I opened various cupboards looking for something edible. "It's not like we can call for takeout to be delivered here."

A thoughtful look crossed his face. "If we're still linked up to Edinburgh, technically…"

"You're not supposed to use the Paths for that," I said. "Mum would be appalled."

"She also wouldn't want us starving to death."

I rolled my eyes at him. "Don't be melodramatic."

"What's going on?" Hazel said from the doorway.

"Our brother thinks we should use your highly secret and dangerous magic to order a takeaway delivery from Edinburgh. Did you leave the Path open?"

"Yes. You're right, Mum would kill us. Let's do it."

I sighed. "You have zero faith in my domestic skills, don't you?"

Everyone looked at River. "Can you conjure up a decent meal using your faerie magic?" asked Hazel.

"Unfortunately not. I'm a bodyguard, not a chef."

"Two votes for the Path. I'll make the call." Morgan left the room. "Is the house phone still in here?"

"Yeah, it is," I said. "Is drawing more people to our house a good idea?"

"Humans are fine," Hazel said. "Did you sense anyone at Winter's place, anyway?"

"Holly," I said. "It's her. Not… the other one." Like a weird superstition, I couldn't bring myself to say her title aloud. Like our distant and deceased Aunt Candice was listening.

"Oh. So she did take the job." Hazel nodded. "You spoke to her?"

"Tried to. She said she got accepted to train as Gatekeeper and something about a ceremony that you'd know about. Didn't really want to talk much."

"Damn. Did she drain all our magic to rebuild her house?"

"Nope," I said. "Arden was there as well, but he flew off to ask the Court for an audience rather than coming back here with me. He implied that Summer might know why our power's being drained."

All eyes went to River again. He frowned. "It's the first I've heard. I haven't actually been in Summer since I resolved my last mission, which is why I don't have a direct invitation to go back. But the magic around the gate doesn't seem to be functioning any more than your defences are." River took a step towards the door. "I can take up my old bodyguard job, if you like."

"There's no need," I said. "Three of us are necromancers who can pick up on any intruder who isn't a wraith."

Wraiths couldn't be detected until they were directly on top of us, but the salt barrier ought to keep them from getting close to the house. Few enemies could even find our house thanks to its rootless nature, hovering in the gap between worlds. But Hazel looked uncharacteristically nervous. She wasn't used to being underpowered. I'd spent enough years in her position to feel sorry for her despite the small vindictive part of me who thought having a day without her magic might make up for years of her being the only Lynn sibling with any at all.

I pushed the thought away. Hazel had never been smug about being the one chosen and not me, though admittedly, she'd also been mostly oblivious to how shitty it'd been to be mistaken for her, or worse, targeted by the Gatekeeper's enemies. Morgan might be the oldest, but once it'd become clear he wouldn't have magic, he'd mostly been left alone.

Being the Gatekeeper-in-Training's once-identical twin had been hazardous and depressing at once, depending on the day.

Morgan sprawled on the sofa, opened a beer bottle and took a swig. "What? It's been a long day."

"Yeah." I fell into the armchair next to him. If I half closed my eyes, I could pretend this was like old times, when the two of us had watched movie marathons while Mum and Hazel were off serving the Seelie Court or doing magical training. Of course, Morgan himself was usually running around causing trouble, but things had been a hell of a lot less complicated then.

"Don't mess up the house," Hazel said. "We're leaving it exactly as we found it, for when we bring Mum back."

Nobody argued about how impossible that seemed, though Morgan wore a sceptical look, and River, the only one of us who hadn't sat down, shifted imperceptibly backwards.

Hazel looked sharply at him. "Is there anything you haven't told us? Where exactly was she?"

"I told you everything I know. Your mother wouldn't tell me the nature of the quest she was sent on, and it's difficult for me to say *where* she was when the Vale arranges itself according to the person who enters. I didn't spend long there, only enough for her to give me the order to come and guard the Gatekeeper. I knew nothing of your family before we met—I didn't lie."

Nope. You just omitted information. But re-treading the same arguments would get us nowhere.

"Mum knew about the book," I said. "Either Grandma told her, or—hell, she knew Great-Aunt Enid. That must be it. But she didn't know it'd choose me." My head hurt. "Was it Summer who destroyed my house after all? Or Holly's people? She didn't want *me* to get hold of the book. Arden, though…"

"I think he did want you to get hold of it," said Hazel. "He didn't want a war, no more than we did."

I sighed. "Yeah, well. Looks like we might be getting one either way."

3

Despite my exhaustion, being in the same bedroom where I'd once been attacked by a wraith didn't encourage restful sleep. After waking from my seventh consecutive nightmare, I walked downstairs to find Morgan sitting in front of the blank TV screen, like he used to do when I couldn't sleep as a kid and came downstairs to find him wandering drunkenly around after being kicked out of the village's only pub at midnight.

"Hey." I sat down at the other end of the sofa, pulling Grandma's old hand-knitted throw over my legs to warm them.

He grunted. "This place hasn't changed at all."

"It's run by the Sidhe. They don't like change much." It must be seriously weird for him to be back at the house, even with Mum absent. I looked out the window, spotting River sitting on the porch. He'd accepted Hazel's offer of a guest room and then gone outside to act as bodyguard anyway, apparently.

"Not for long," he said. "The Sidhe don't give a crap what happens to us, even Mum."

"I know that," I said. "God only knows why they sent her into the Vale, if not to avoid putting their own lives in danger. We're immune to magic, not wraiths, or skin-eating faeries, or—"

"Stop it," he said. "Knowing that won't change anything. She can survive it. *We* might not."

His tone was such a total contrast to his usual bravado that I stared at him. "What, you seriously don't think we should go after Mum?"

"Frankly, I think she'll toss me out of the Vale herself."

I shook my head. "No, she won't. Not when she finds out we single-handedly saved Edinburgh. Give it a chance."

"I don't think so." He paused. "Might be this new power, but I get the feeling I'm supposed to do something else with it. Something in this world, not Faerie. Same with you. That talisman of yours isn't faerie-made, is it? Humans made it. Our ancestors."

I couldn't get used to Morgan speaking coherently, let alone making so much sense. "Guess it's true, but the Sidhe gave us this magic, and it's their symbol on the book. They were definitely involved, even if it isn't their magic."

"Yeah, that part makes no sense. You can't trap necromancy in a talisman... can you?"

"If I knew that, I'd know how they do it to Summer and Winter magic," I said. "I don't think it's true, though. Summer and Winter Sidhe... their own life is effectively tied to their talisman. If they lose their talisman, they're weakened. But that's because their power comes *from* the talisman. Necromancy—if anything, it comes directly from the spirit world."

Which meant there was a good chance it wouldn't function in Faerie at all. River had said it wouldn't, back when I hadn't known that was the type of magic I had. *Shit. That could cause problems.* It shouldn't surprise me that death magic didn't work in a realm where nobody died, but the Sidhe *could* die. Which meant their immortality had never been permanent to begin with.

Morgan cleared his throat. "You should know… Hazel went out earlier."

"What do you mean, 'earlier'? It's barely light outside."

He glanced over his shoulder at the window. "Think she went to the grove, but she told me she'd throw me over the fence if either of us tried to follow her."

"Dammit, Hazel." She probably would, too. Unlike the two of us, Hazel had had personal combat training from experts used to going up against faeries and could throw a man twice her size over her shoulder. Losing her magic had hit her pretty hard, and she was probably taking the house's magical drought as a personal insult.

"She's fine, Ilsa. Oh, and your faerie's awake."

"He's not a faerie. Or mine." My gaze went to the window before I could stop myself, to be greeted with the view of River just out of sight, blade in hand, cutting down invisible enemies. He moved so swiftly and gracefully, it was impossible to see him as human. Morgan snickered, and I glared at him.

"Don't let me stop you admiring the view," Morgan said.

I threw a cushion at him. "I'm going to make coffee."

After an appropriate amount of caffeine, I felt a little better, even though it looked like the only food we had in the house was stale bread and leftover takeout. I skimmed through the talisman book to avoid looking at River. The curtains were partially drawn and he probably didn't know I could see him. That, or he was tormenting me on purpose with memories of his hands on my bare skin, his muscular body pressed against mine. *And lying about my mother the whole time.*

"I've never seen you mope over a guy before," Morgan observed.

"I'm not moping. I'm reading this book."

"You're projecting like hell."

I backed away from him on the sofa. "Stay *out* of my head, Morgan. I thought you had the mind-reading thing under control."

"I do. You're the one whose mental shields are totally screwed. You kept waking me up with your wraith nightmares all night."

"I'm not psychic. Aren't you wearing the iron band?"

"It fell off while I was asleep." He ran a hand through his hair. "I can pick up on you and Hazel, just nobody else. Oh yeah, and she's back."

The door slammed open and Hazel stomped in from the hall, dripping melting snow all over the floor.

"Are you okay?" I rose from my seat, alarmed.

"Obviously." Hazel kicked her shoes off. At least she could walk in a straight line today.

"What were you thinking?" I said. "If those redcaps were still around—"

"They weren't. No evil Aunt Candice, no monstrous redcaps. I don't think Holly even has servants. Pity that. No wonder Arden was hanging around to keep her company."

"What did she say to you?"

"Told me to piss off," Hazel said. "I went for a look at the Winter gate."

"And?" said Morgan.

"And her magic's working. Ours isn't. I don't get it."

"Mine works fine," River said, entering the room behind her. "But my source isn't tied to this house."

No. It's in your talisman. Which must be hidden close by, since he wasn't carrying it. He'd clearly just showered, his blond hair damp and falling into his eyes, and he'd changed from his necromancer coat to a light shirt and trousers that looked faerie made. He'd effortlessly switched from necromancer mode back to faerie mode, and once again, I couldn't help observing how easily he seemed to fit into both worlds.

"Neither is mine," Hazel said. "It's from the Court." She touched the mark on her forehead, biting her lip. "If anything happened to Mum, it'd get stronger, not weaker, because I'd inherit the magic. The circlet is still clearly marked as hers."

She'd been wearing Mum's spare one for weeks, but even the heir's magic had nothing on the Gatekeeper's. Worry grew inside me. If Mum was losing her power in a similar way, did that mean she was more at risk in the Vale? *We need to get her out.* But to do that, we needed—

The window blew open and Arden flew in, a scroll clamped in his beak. He landed on Morgan's head, who yelled in alarm, wildly snatching at the raven. Arden let out a *caw* of laughter, and took flight again.

Morgan swore, shaking his head. "Damn bird."

"The ingratitude," said Arden, landing on the bookshelf and spitting the scroll into Hazel's hands. "You have permission to meet with the Seelie messenger at the gate."

Hazel scanned the parchment and looked up. "Genuine. Do the messengers know what's going on here?"

"Caw. Only one invitation to Faerie. I'd advise you to take it. Walk to the gates by noon, or lose your chance."

Hazel looked at me. "The messengers… they're usually fairly clueless about secret Court matters. Whenever I went to the Court with Mum, I'd stay with one of them. So at least I know that part of Faerie. I'd guess River does, too."

"Your family?" I asked him.

He nodded. "I can't say they'll know any more than we do about the mission your mother was sent on, but I can ask."

"Who *did* send her there?" I asked.

"She wasn't able to tell me," River said. "The vow she was under was typical of any Sidhe one, and I can't say I know who'd have the motive to send someone into the Vale. If I'd known what exactly she was looking for, I might have been able to guess."

I sighed. "Then we'll find the person in charge of the family curse."

"Lord Kerien is the messenger who deals with humans," said Hazel. "I know a few other names, but I won't get a proper introduction until I ascend to Gatekeeper. And... well. There's the slightest chance that they'll refuse to speak to anyone except me."

Of course, the rest of us were effectively invisible to the Sidhe most of the time, and even River hadn't been able to convince them that the wraiths posed a threat to the Court. *Then I'll make them listen to us if I have to.* The Sidhe might have an irrational hatred of mortals, but they'd sit up and pay attention if they realised just how much danger they'd been in when the Winter Gatekeeper had attempted her coup. We'd yet to see the fallout from that, and I was kind of curious how much information the messengers had passed on to the rest of the Sidhe.

"The summons does lead right into the Court, doesn't it?" I asked. "I'm not wandering around Summer's forest."

No human with any sense would wander outside of the main Court into the notoriously bloodthirsty borderlands. Admittedly, the Court itself was no better, since the Sidhe were more likely to turn humans into deer or make them into servants. Unfortunately, while most magic bounced off the Lynn family's defences, the powerful magic of the Summer Court might be an exception. Even the Sidhe themselves weren't entirely immune to its effects. Otherwise they wouldn't be able to kill one another.

Shit. Did they all know they could die for real now? Ivy Lane had known, and she was human, but heaven knew how she'd stumbled across that information. I wouldn't be bringing it up unless I knew for certain.

"Apparently, we just walk through the gate," Hazel said. "I assume we're all included in the invitation." She looked at Morgan first, who scowled.

"I'm not staying behind," he said. "Don't you—"

"I wasn't," Hazel said. "But… remember everything Mum said about the Sidhe. If you were listening. I'm Gatekeeper-in-Training, which means they have to treat me with some level of respect, but the same doesn't apply to any other human."

"We're magic-proof," said Morgan. "It's fine. I *have* been there before, remember?"

So had I. Most Gatekeeper events were restricted to Mum and Hazel only, but all three of us had attended the ceremony in the Summer Court shortly after Hazel's magic had awakened. I'd been twelve at the time, while Morgan had been fourteen. Thanks to the haze of magic in the ceremony, all I remembered was a lot of flashing lights, and a total sensory overload. Which pretty much summed up Summer.

Hazel gave Morgan a look. "You nearly caused an incident by jumping into the fountain to chase mermen, if you've forgotten."

"Ah." He grinned. "Yeah, I forgot."

"And Ilsa stared at the orchestra for twenty minutes until Mum dragged her away."

"I did? I don't remember much."

"Faerie music does that."

I grimaced. "Okay. Maybe we should add earplugs to the packing list. Are we allowed to carry iron?"

"Technically, no," Hazel said. "Not in visible weapons, anyway. A jar of iron filings, you could probably get away with as long as you don't spill it."

Morgan looked at River. "So you're allowed to carry your sword?"

"It's faerie-made," he said. "Does your mother have any faerie-made weapons?"

"No, she probably took them with her," Hazel said. "Witch spells don't work there either. But it's okay. I have my magic."

I won't. The book shifted in my pocket as though in protest. I'd have to bring it with me, and hope I wouldn't be punished for carrying a non-Sidhe talisman.

"Then let's move." Hazel made for Mum's workroom, and I did likewise. Salt and iron filings didn't feel like particularly useful weapons, but who knew, maybe my necromantic magic *would* work. It wasn't like the book carried the usual type of necromancy.

"Are we supposed to dress up if we're visiting royalty?" asked Morgan, indicating his T-shirt and faded jeans. Neither of us had any faerie-made clothes like River and Hazel did. Both of them wore knee-length coats embossed in green and gold, the colours of the Summer Court. River could easily pass as minor royalty. Given the tangled family trees of Summer's royals, it wouldn't surprise me if he *was* a direct descendent of the Erlking. Fear clawed its way up my throat. I didn't belong in Faerie. They'd know that, and they might well target me for it.

"Chill," said Hazel. "Once we're through the gates, I'll throw a glamour on both of you. River's wearing one."

I shoved my fear into a dark corner. *Mum. We're doing this for her. And they don't know I'm Gatekeeper.* My talisman was equal to theirs, easily. It glowed faintly in my pocket, almost like it wanted to reassure me.

Hazel approached the gates. Tall and overgrown with ivy, it looked like a metal gate from a distance until you got close and saw that the spikes were actually made of sharpened tree branches, almost grown out of the forest itself. A curtain of moss grew all over it, giving a neglected air, but the same symbol as the one on Hazel's forehead topped the gate, gleaming faintly. My heart beat faster against my ribs.

"Before we go," Hazel said, "let's cover some pointers. Don't look directly at the Sidhe. Don't speak unless you know for certain they won't retaliate. Don't do anything reckless, or wander off alone… anything else?"

"Yes," said Morgan. "Are we allowed to mention the Vale? Because that's our goal in all this. We find out where Mum is, and get there."

"Only a Sidhe can," River said. "We'd need to have a Sidhe actually accompany us into the Vale if we went there, and the odds of finding a volunteer are slim to none."

"So you went there with a Sidhe?" asked Morgan.

"No, I went there on the word of a vow," River said. "Your mother sent a message to my father requesting assistance, and I chose to take the job. Once I accepted the agreement, the vow activated, and I was transported into the Vale."

Damn. A chill raced down my back. Vows… despite our family curse, I hadn't had nearly enough experience with Faerie's most deadly and unforgiving form of magic. A single word could throw you around like a puppet on strings.

"So you went into that place alone?" said Morgan. "See, it *is* possible to survive there."

Hazel turned to River. "So you saw Mum, and then —left?"

"She ordered me to leave," River answered. "I understand it looks like I left her to die there, but she told me only to protect the Gatekeeper's heir. Then she ordered me to return to Faerie and go to your house immediately. My vow kicked in, and I was pulled back into Faerie before I could do anything more."

"Did you tell anyone?" asked Morgan suspiciously. "In the Court?"

"Obviously, I told my father I had an assignment in the

mortal realm. I had no other assignments, so they didn't ask too many questions about it."

"I thought your skills were in high demand," said Hazel.

River scowled. I knew what he was thinking—the Sidhe had never taken the threats of the wraiths seriously no matter how many times he warned them.

"The Sidhe and I had a slight misunderstanding a few months ago," he said. "Not enough to get us thrown out, but if you hear the name Lord Daival, stay far away. He's the client who was keeping humans in cages, and he didn't like that I freed them."

"No way," Hazel said. "Humans? You actually set humans free from a Sidhe?"

"He'd hired me on a job and didn't give me specific instructions not to go near them," said River. "I wasn't about to leave them there, but since it was my father who helped me smuggle the humans out of the faerie realm, he's likely to be displeased about me bringing you with me."

Ah. Crap. Should have figured even the Gatekeeper would have trouble finding allies in the faerie realm. River was seriously lucky he hadn't suffered worse punishment. Like exile.

"If he won't kill us, that's a step above most Sidhe," said Hazel. "And—wow. I can't believe you did that. Who *is* your father?"

"Lord Torin," River said. "If not for his connections with the human councils in this realm, I doubt I could have got away with it."

"No shit," said Hazel. "It's not actually legal to keep humans as prisoners, but nobody ever bothers to enforce that rule. You hear that, Morgan? Be careful."

"Got it," he said. "I'll be on my best behaviour."

"You'd better." Hazel approached the gates. A golden glow lit up her forehead, and the plants growing on the gates awakened, also glowing with green Summer magic. Light spilled across the path, and the gates opened with barely a whisper.

A leafy path beckoned, flanked with tall trees. I took in a deep breath, and went after my sister into Faerie.

4

The forest path looked like any other, until the others filed in behind me, and the gates closed. Then the magic hit me like a jackhammer to the face. Brightness shone from the trees, which seemed a hundred shades of green all at once, ignited by the blazing sun overhead.

I looked down and saw my clothes had transformed into an outfit similar to Hazel's. As she turned to check we were behind her, the golden light shining from her forehead damn near blinded me.

"You all okay?"

"Sure." The forest smelled of earthy magic, like River's own magic turned up to max. He was glowing, too, bright green magic gleaming along the blade of his now-unsheathed talisman. He'd mentioned he carried it openly here, as a show of strength, and with the way he and Hazel stood, hiding Morgan and me from view, it was probably our best arrangement to look powerful and intimidating. Morgan and I, mundane humans without a mark or visible weapon to protect ourselves, were entirely vulnerable.

Morgan scuffed the forest floor with his heel. "Why am I the only one without shiny special effects?"

I touched the mark on my forehead. "Crap. The witch spell stopped working."

River looked at me, concerned. "The Sidhe likely won't recognise the mark, but maybe you should hide it."

"Might get me confused with Hazel again," I said wryly, arranging my hair to cover the mark. That hadn't happened in years, as the magic she'd gained had altered her appearance to mimic the Sidhe. Her hair had lightened to honey blond, glowing in the golden light of her magic, while she tanned easily, unlike me. But it was the way she stood that made my insides ache with a familiar jealousy. She was tall, and strong, and for all the world like a princess or queen marching through her court.

Here, the Sidhe wouldn't respect anything less.

"This way," Hazel said, striding down the forest path. My eyes watered with the scents of growth and magic, the warm breeze stirred my hair and made me long to run breathlessly through the woods, like a small woodland creature—*oh no*, I did *not* want to be a deer. I scowled at everything in the most human-like manner I could manage, releasing a breath when the path ended, opening into a sunny glade the size of a small village. Birdsong drifted on the faint breeze, which was just the right temperature to balance the suffocating warmth. I fought the urge to inhale, pushing aside images of bouncing through fields. Bloody magic.

"Where are we?" I asked quietly.

"Holdover territory." Hazel sniffed. "Dicks. If they wanted to speak to us right away, they'd have brought us directly to the ambassadors' place."

Morgan made a strangled noise, arms outstretched. "I can't fly..."

"Don't," Hazel said. "Someone's spinning a spell. If you

think too hard about the sky, you'll turn into a bird, and I don't have time to chase you around."

"For me, it's bounding through fields," I muttered. "It's okay. I've got it under control. Shouldn't our shield deflect this?"

"It's subtle magic. Some prick doesn't want us here."

She strode into the middle of the clearing. "I asked for an audience with the ambassador."

"And you'll get one." A man appeared in front of us—no, a *Sidhe.* If the pointed ears weren't enough of a clue, the magic pouring off him would be. His eyes glowed bright green, his skin was golden tan, and he wore a regal-looking coat with gold cuffs. He carried a glowing staff carved with runes and entwined with glowing purple flowers. Some primal instinct in the depths of my mind screamed at me that he wasn't human. I'd almost compare the sensation to my ability to tell whether someone was human or not when in the spirit realm. That same sense recognised this being as *more than human. Dangerous. Horribly, murderously beautiful and terrifying.*

Don't look directly at them, Hazel had said. Oops. My eyes watered, but looking away from the Sidhe would only give him more cause to believe we were pathetic humans.

"Who are you?" said Hazel. "I asked for Lord Kerien."

"He is otherwise occupied. I am Lord Raivan, ambassador for the Seelie Court designated to handle all cases involving humans and half-bloods."

He didn't sound particularly thrilled about his role.

"You know who I am, right?" said Hazel. "I'm the future Gatekeeper of the Summer Court. Do you even know about the Gatekeepers?"

"I know of them."

Hazel groaned. "We don't have time for this. Someone's decided to drain my family's magic, and I was told the Court has the answers. And can you tell the person trying to turn my siblings into woodland animals to cut it the hell out?"

All the air seemed to leave the clearing. Hazel took a step back, gasping, and I forgot to breathe. The green magic swirling around the Sidhe lord brightened to a glare, while the impulse to bound through the field was replaced by the instinct to run far, far away and hide.

"You speak with little respect, Gatekeeper's daughter."

"That's because your Court sent my mother on a suicide mission," said Hazel. "Unless she's here. Where is she?"

"I have no idea about your mother, Gatekeeper's daughter. It's not my job to handle your family."

"That's why I wanted to speak to someone who knows who I am," said Hazel. "Why's our magic not working? Isn't it tied to the Court? Arden said you can help us."

His gaze passed along our group. "Some areas of our territory are experiencing a magical drought. Perhaps the same has affected your house. We have yet to determine the cause, but we have every intention of eliminating it." His tone implied we'd be wise not to mention it to anyone outside the Court.

"In that case, may I ask your permission to traverse your territory in order to pay a visit to Lord Torin?" said River smoothly.

The Sidhe looked at River as though he'd only just noticed he were there. It didn't surprise me. They'd treated me the same for years, and I couldn't imagine living as a half-blood in this place. At least he probably couldn't feel the side effects of Summer's magic as strongly as the rest of us.

"Do you have permission to visit Lord Torin?"

"Yes, as I'm his son. Your nephew," River added.

Lord Raivan's mouth tightened and he waved a hand. Immediately, the clearing disappeared, to be replaced by a meadow filled with blooming flowers. I opened my mouth and closed it again. I hadn't even picked up on the resemblance between the two of them, though admittedly, I was still having difficulty focusing on the Sidhe lord's face.

River led the way down a side path between low fences. On one side was a large pleasant-looking house, which he approached through a gate.

"Your uncle's nice, isn't he?" said Hazel.

River shrugged. "Some Sidhe don't like being associated with those who have mortal children. He's better than most."

"Because he hates us too much to capture us and put us in cages?" I said, rolling my eyes. "Tell me your father will have something useful to say. He knows where Mum is?"

"Yes, but only because I told him. However, I was here on his territory when I received the job, so he's the person most likely to know more about it. This territory is one of the safest places for visitors in the entire Summer Court. At least my uncle didn't send us through wild territory." He approached the door and knocked.

A small creature with bark-like skin opened the door. *Wow. They have a brownie. They must be loaded.* Not that it was a surprise. In Faerie, magical power meant wealth, and the Sidhe had no shortage of both.

"Greetings, River," said the brownie. "And who are they?"

"The Lynn siblings. The Summer Gatekeeper's children."

"Ah." The brownie gave us an appraising look. "You wish to speak to the master? He's in the orchard."

"Thank you, Quentin." River walked into the hallway. After a moment's hesitation, Hazel followed, with Morgan and I close behind.

"Orchard?" whispered Hazel. "This place is fancy. Is this where you live when you're here, River?"

"Yes. Half-bloods aren't permitted to own land or property in Faerie, so only those of us with family willing to accommodate us are in service to the Court. Several of my half-siblings sometimes live here, too."

I'd forgotten he'd once implied he had siblings, because his father was probably hundreds of years old and had doubtlessly been with more than one mortal. As generous as his offer sounded, I couldn't forget that the Sidhe had intentionally put their half-blood children into a position of inferiority and dependence on their generosity. And mercy. River must have thought working for the Summer Court was worth the indignity. Then again, he *had* got a free talisman out of it, which were usually off-limits to non-Sidhe.

We walked through a bright conservatory into the garden, where River led the way to a wooden gate. Beyond, a number of trees bearing fruit that shone in bright shades crowded us. Their strong aroma urged me to pick the fruit and bite into it. I could drown in the smell, which probably meant it'd turn me into a deer. I bit the inside of my cheek, my nails digging into my palms. The smell of apples brought back memories of the half-Sidhe I'd dated as a teenager, who'd seduced me in a grove of his own creation. The memory did a pretty good job of neutralising the effects of the spell, because now I wanted to throw up instead.

"Don't touch the fruit," River said in a low voice. "It tends to have unpredictable effects on mortals."

Morgan replaced the apple he'd picked up, then jumped when a tall Sidhe male with River's pointed ears and fair curly hair appeared. He wore a finely made shirt and trousers, which I supposed was the Sidhe's idea of casual clothing. Like River, he carried a sword strapped to his side. The weirdest part was that underneath the glowing effects of faerie magic, he barely looked older than River did. Yet he'd likely lived for centuries.

"Son," he said to River. "I wasn't expecting you to return so soon."

Ah. Faerie time travel. It'd been weeks since River's return, but time passed differently here, with mortal years going by in the blink of an eye to the Sidhe.

"There have been developments in the mortal realm," he said. "I have brought the Gatekeeper's children with me, as they have questions they need to ask a trustworthy Sidhe."

"Apparently they haven't heard the stories," said the Sidhe. "Not a one of us is trustworthy to mortals, and they should do well to remember it."

"Didn't you knock one of them up?" said Morgan. "Or several?"

"Ignore him," Hazel said quickly. "I'm Hazel Lynn, the heir to the Summer Gatekeeper's title. I'm told that you might know where our mother currently is, and who sent her there."

"If you came here, my son likely told you her whereabouts himself. The Vale is not a safe place for you mortals, even less than here."

"No shit," Morgan said. "Let's assume we know the Vale is dangerous and we're gonna rescue her anyway."

The Sidhe turned to him. "Rescue? My son tells me the Summer Gatekeeper seems to be coping admirably in hostile territory."

"But our magic is fading," Hazel said. "We *need* to find her. It'd help if we at least knew who sent her there. River said she's visited your house."

"Yes, some time ago," said Lord Torin. "As for the Court's magic, I heard rumours of a drought, but I can't say it has reached me here."

"So if *you're* okay, everyone else must be, too?" said Morgan. I half wished he'd shoved the apple into his mouth after all.

The Sidhe cocked an eyebrow. "Who exactly are you, mortal?"

"Morgan Lynn. Necromancer. Means I deal with dead people."

I quickly stepped in. "Who might have sent our mother into the Vale?"

"If you follow her, you'll likely lose your lives," said Lord Torin. "But the last person known to have spoken to the Gatekeeper was Lady Aiten."

Hazel took a step backwards. "We saw her. Recently. She answered my last request for help from the Court. You mean to say she knew all along? She didn't even try to answer my questions."

She must mean the Sidhe who'd questioned me after the Winter Gatekeeper's death, one of the three who'd come into the mortal realm.

"You're not likely to get answers from any Sidhe by showing up on their doorsteps," said Lord Torin. "An early death, perhaps."

"This concerns peace within the Courts and outside them," Hazel said. "If the Summer Gatekeeper goes missing, what happens if outsiders attack? The former Winter Gate-keeper attempted a coup once already and nearly destroyed the Courts in the process. You must have heard about it."

"Nothing can destroy the Courts," said the Sidhe calmly. "Do not think I am unaware of your family's role as peace-keepers. Lady Aiten will be attending an event later today, at the house of Lord Niall. That's the only time she *might* agree to speak with you. But I don't need to warn you of the dangers such events pose for mortals." He gave Morgan and me a disparaging look.

Morgan bristled, but Hazel stepped in. "Thank you," she said. "Any clues about a way to contact our mother would be greatly appreciated."

He gave a brief nod of acknowledgement and turned to

River. "I warned you not to ask for my assistance in helping humans again."

River looked at his father defiantly. "I kept my word. They asked for assistance of their own free will. I assumed the Summer Gatekeeper was welcome on the territory closest to the council on Earth."

"The Summer Gatekeeper is, of course," he said. "Humans, however, are nothing but trouble. Lord Daival is still dealing with the fallout from his... livestock escaping."

River's body stiffened, his hands clenching at his sides. Coldness spread through me despite the heat. Livestock? He was talking about humans. And River looked like he wished he'd decapitated the Sidhe he'd stolen the humans from. I didn't blame him.

"You people really do have no souls," said Morgan.

Lord Torin turned on him. Magic flashed, and Morgan yelped, jumping backwards as thorns sprouted from his hands.

"Enough!" River said sharply.

The thorns vanished, but the Sidhe's expression remained furious. "Son, you have an open invitation here. So does the Gatekeeper. Not these... others." His gaze skimmed our group, lingering on me this time. My throat went dry.

"Sorry!" Hazel said. "We've had a seriously rough week, and our mother might be dying. He's never been around Sidhe—you know what, we'll go over here."

Hazel all but hauled Morgan away, and I made to follow —but a thorny plant blocked my way. I took in a breath. Showing weakness might get me killed, and the Sidhe had apparently picked me out as a target. Lord Torin hadn't moved, but his magic flowed through every plant in this garden. Sharp thorns gleamed, and fruits dripped deadly juice onto the grass.

I met his stare, aware that he'd be able to see the mark on

my forehead, and would draw his own conclusions about what it meant. It wasn't like being looked at by River, though they both had the same intensity to their green-eyed stare. Like they were paying attention to nothing else. With the Sidhe, it was outright terrifying.

"Yes?" I said, relieved my voice sounded steady.

"You're not as loud as your fellow humans," he observed.

Yeah, that's because this is awkward as hell. I was kind of dating your son, for a while. Also, I can't stop picturing you with Lady Montgomery and it's seriously weirding me out.

Aloud, I said, "I have nothing to add. We need to find who sent Mum into the Vale. If she's tethered to them by a vow, they can invoke the same vow to bring her out of the Vale, right?"

"Did my son tell you that?"

"I worked it out." From something River had said, but he didn't need to know.

"You're a perceptive mortal."

"I'm choosing to take that as a compliment." *Go on. Mention the mark. You want to.* There was no other reason for him to stare at me that intently. I was an unknown element. A curiosity. "If you don't mind, I'd like to join my siblings and make a plan. Will the person who cast the vow likely be present at this event today?"

"Many Sidhe will." He tilted his head. "My son mentioned you."

Ah. Crap. I hadn't thought Lord Torin even knew my name, as I hadn't told him. But he must have figured it out somehow. Sidhe were way too observant.

"Yeah, I was the unknown person the Summer Gate-keeper sent him to guard," I said. "I'm grateful that he helped keep me alive." What the hell, maybe I could help River regain the respect of the Sidhe... but I doubted so. The word of a human with questionable magic probably didn't outdo the audacity of setting a bunch of mortal prisoners free.

"Yes, that mission led him on quite the chase," said the Sidhe. "Your magic is… interesting."

"How do you know? I'm not Sidhe."

"No, and yet… that mark. Very curious."

"Yeah, it is." I kept looking into his eyes, knowing he wanted me to look away. River wouldn't let him hurt me, but depending on anyone in this realm was a risky move. Besides, this man might be less awful than most Sidhe, but he also referred to humans as *livestock*, and had probably ignored River for most of his life. As for Lady Montgomery? I'd bet that even if they'd parted on friendly terms, the Sidhe didn't get the concept of paying for child support. I never thought I'd feel bad for Lady Montgomery of all people.

"It's a pleasure to meet you, Ilsa Lynn," he said. "You may join your family."

Why did I get the impression he'd learned more from looking at the mark on my forehead than I had from our entire conversation?

"I take it we need to make preparations before going to this Sidhe event," I said.

"Naturally. Ask the brownie. I think he enjoys human company."

I figured that was probably an insult, but let it slide. I had to get the others alone to explain my plan—and I couldn't help wondering if the Sidhe would be as keen to refer to us as 'livestock' if they realised *they* were basically long-lived mortals now, too.

5

River and I found the others inside the conservatory. I sat down beside a plant, which immediately wrapped itself around my leg. Hazel zapped it with Summer magic and it withdrew.

"Bloody plants," Morgan growled. "One of them tried to strangle me."

"Be thankful it wasn't worse," River said. "If you intend to insult every Sidhe present, you won't walk out of this realm alive."

"Don't worry, I'll behave," Morgan said. "If nobody insults *me*. Or humans in general, come to that."

"Morgan," Hazel said warningly. "If you want to get into an argument, pick literally anyone except the Sidhe. I have one shot to get information on Mum. I can't waste it chasing you around."

"Nor me," I said. "I can pretty much bet that this Sidhe event won't be human friendly. Also, this." I pointed at my forehead. "Your father seemed to recognise it, River." I glanced over my shoulder, but if the Sidhe wanted to hear what we were saying, I doubted he'd bother to hide himself.

"He likely knew it for an Invocation," River said. "The language is intimately familiar to the Sidhe, as much as their own. Maybe you should obtain a glamour... Hazel, your magic should be stronger here. Mine is, too, but glamour isn't my strong point."

"You're saying I should put a fae disguise on those two?" said Hazel dubiously. "I *can,* but if any of the Sidhe so much as breathe in their direction, it'll probably fall off."

"It'll get us in," River said. "Hazel and I have implicit invitations, but you two... it's possible the Sidhe will make a fuss. I'll ask my father—"

"There's no need," growled a voice. The brownie had sidled into the room, unseen. "I will ask them myself. As a member of the Council of Twelve, I am allowed passage to speak with the ambassadors."

"Thank you, Quentin," River said.

Hazel stared at the brownie. "I didn't know the council was allowed here. Does that mean they're all in Faerie? Even the humans?"

"No," said the brownie. "I serve two families, one here, one in the mortal realm, and it is my duty to act on behalf of the Council of Twelve to ensure peace between our realms. Your mission's purpose is to keep the peace, therefore, I can ask for permission."

He bowed and left.

"Am I missing something?" I asked.

"Yeah, I didn't understand a word he just said," Morgan said.

"The council... the alliance between human and faerie realms," Hazel said. "That brownie must carry messages between here and the human council in the mortal realm. So he has the clout to get us into this event. Good enough."

"A council of humans and Sidhe?" I asked. "Would *they* know where Mum is?"

"I don't know which Sidhe are on the council, because it's new," Hazel said. "It only formed in the last year. But… hmm. Might explain why Lord Raivan's so prickly. He's stuck dealing with humans."

"So the brownie can get us in," Morgan said. "Good enough for me. Who's holding the event?"

"Lord Niall, of course," said Hazel, with an eye-roll. "It's always Lord Niall. They say he held a party all through the last war with Winter."

"I don't think so," River said. "Likely an exaggeration… but he does have a reputation. He doesn't care much for torturing mortals, but his guests might feel differently."

"Then we'll wear disguises," said Morgan. "Can I have some shiny special effects now?"

"I'll do my best," Hazel said, drumming her fingertips on her knees. "Better hope the magic in this place is enough to make up for the drought."

Great. So I have to dress up as one of them. For Mum's sake, I'd dress up as a troll, but when Hazel was done with Morgan and turned to me, I dug my heels in.

"If my glamour falls off, the mark's the first thing they'll see," I said. "I need to be prepared to fight or run. No magical dresses this time."

"I was thinking the same," Hazel said, to my surprise. "Okay. Let's see what I can do."

To my surprise, since the Sidhe didn't have strictly gendered clothing, nobody commented on my knee-length armoured coat and trousers like the Sidhe warriors wore. Being a glamour, the armour wasn't as thick as it looked, but hopefully it'd deter people from taking a shot at me.

The pointed ears were seriously weird, even though when I touched my ear, it felt normal under the illusion. And my glowing green eyes would make it even more likely people would confuse me with Hazel. All I needed was a horse and I might actually pass as a Sidhe. I'd ridden them a few times in the mortal realm but was long out of practise, and the horses the Sidhe rode definitely weren't made of the same stuff. They moved with the same eerie grace as their faerie kin, and I frowned when I spotted several of them tethered at the front of the house with Hazel beside them.

"We're riding?" I asked River.

He briefly stroked a coal-black horse's head, and lithely sprang onto its back. "It's quicker. It also might be more comfortable if you join me. The horses can tell you're human."

"No, it's cool." I climbed up behind him awkwardly. How many times could we be put in compromising situations in a single day?

"Come on," said Hazel, who sat astride a magnificent white steed which wouldn't have looked out of place as a Lord of the Rings extra. She wore a dress in shades of gold and lilac, her circlet gleaming with magic. Real flowers were twined in her hair, which spilled down her back in golden curls. Magic, but not an illusion like my own was. Behind her, Morgan slouched back on the horse, somewhat dampening the image. He wore his own Sidhe disguise with pointed ears and jet black hair grown out past his shoulders Sidhe-style, but he sat like a human.

"No galloping," he said. "I'd like to get out of this with my balls in one piece, thanks."

"Nobody wants to know, Morgan," Hazel said. "Let's go."

The horse took off in a gliding motion that momentarily convinced my body we'd actually left the ground. I grabbed River's coat for balance, too startled to yell. The ground slid away, the movement more like flying than riding. In the space of a few seconds, we left the garden behind, and there was nothing but trees on either side. I heard Morgan swearing loudly behind me.

"Holy shit," I gasped into the back of River's coat.

"It gets easier," he said. "Just sit back and enjoy the ride."

"I've ridden fairground rides that were less hair-raising —" I cut off in a gasp as the horse performed another dizzying glide, this time landing in a field of flowers. Their perfumed scent only made me even more dizzy, and I was fervently glad I hadn't eaten in hours. "Please tell me it's almost over."

I felt his body vibrate with laughter beneath the death grip I had around him. A third glide brought us up to a thorny gate in front of another manor house, at which point two armoured Sidhe nodded to River and let us pass.

"Wait, we're in?" I shook my head. "Wow. Apparently Sidhe nearly falling off their horses is a common sight."

"You aren't going to fall off," he said. "At least, the way you're crushing my ribs indicates that's not the case."

Ah. "Sorry." I loosened my hold, barely lingering a second to enjoy the sensation of his hard muscles beneath my hands. I carefully climbed down, after which River led the horse to the stables in the manor's expansive grounds.

Bright flowers that didn't exist in the mortal realm exuded a smell that captured all my senses at once, while a thick forest surrounded the back of the manor. Long-leafed, unfamiliar plants stood on either side of the oak doors, which were wide open, inviting. Guests walked in and out, talking in the faerie tongue. I didn't know enough of the language to eavesdrop on whatever the Sidhe found to be interesting conversation topics.

Humans would call the Sidhe 'pretty', in the 'deadly rose with sharp thorns' or 'angry peacock' sense. They wore similar finery—long coats embossed in gold, with flowers, feathers and thorns being a popular feature. They generally kept their hair long, and wore elaborate headgear or plants woven into their long tresses. All had the trademark bright green eyes of Summer royalty, and their talismans were equally prominent—swords, crossbows, even an axe or two.

I'd worried a little about River, but he was far from the only half-blood present, and the sheer amount of magic in the air made the half-faeries look almost identical to the Sidhe anyway. He blended in perfectly, in shades of green and gold. His hair glowed, and so did his eyes. God, he was gorgeous. And untouchable, even though I still smelled faintly of his magic from being so close to him during our ride here. Or maybe the hair-raising horse ride and Faerie's ever-intrusive magic was more to blame. I'd never felt more like a mundane human.

We stepped onto a cobbled path, and I stopped to stare around. The manor was designed more along the lines of a garden than a house, with fountains and statues and tables heaving with faerie dishes. Blood red flowers glowed on the ceiling, gold and white on the walls, and a large tree sat behind it all, which appeared to have merged into the back wall. Doors on the east side led into a courtyard where yet more Sidhe gathered, and a band stood on a wooden stage, playing an eerie melody. My body swayed to it, and part of me wanted to dance, to grab River and press my body close to his again...

Nope. No transforming into wild creatures, no dancing, and definitely no breaking boundaries with River.

Brownies moved amongst the crowd, offering drinks. I glanced over my shoulder to make sure Hazel had Morgan under control. He wore a slightly glazed expression, but the illusion of green eyes cancelled it out. In fairness, I probably looked the same. It was impossible to know where to look to avoid being dazzled by the magic. Piskies flitted around, wearing flowery crowns, while a Sidhe took to the stage in the room's centre.

"Guests," the male Sidhe said. "Please welcome the esteemed Lord Niall, master of revels."

I snorted. "That's his official title?"

"He does know how to throw a party, I'll give him that," Hazel whispered, moving in behind me.

"No kidding," said Morgan.

A handsome male Sidhe wearing a gold crown on his silver hair stepped to the front of the stage, smiling broadly. He held a glass in his hand, probably containing elf wine. "It's an honour to host so many of the Summer Court's finest.'

Sure it is. Which of these Sidhe might have callously sent Mum wandering into the Vale, alone? Did any of them know or care that their immortality no longer existed, and war with Winter might be just around the corner?

"Might there be faerie-necromancers *here?*" I whispered to the others. "It's not like the Sidhe would know or care."

"It's possible," River murmured. "However, most half-bloods in the Court are in service to the Sidhe and would never betray them in such a way. They know what fate awaits if they do."

I tuned into Lord Niall's speech when applause rose from the crowd.

"Let the festivities begin." He spoke a few words in an odd tone, like a song or a prayer, and the hair lifted off my head as birds exploded into life from the ceiling, flitting over the crowd. Life magic, *creating* life.

Morgan shook his head, looking dazed. "What the bloody hell was that?"

"Magic," I said, equally shaken.

"Yeah," Hazel said. "What a waste. Invocations are the language of the gods. Most Sidhe don't dare use them at all, and what does that guy do? Summon a bunch of birds."

"I didn't know he planned to do that," River said. "It was rather foolish and showy."

"Seems like that's a running theme with that guy," I said in a low voice. "Let's not stay any longer than we need to. We have to find who sent Mum into the Vale."

"Lady Aiten must be in the crowd somewhere," River said. "She's likely to know, even if Lord Niall himself doesn't."

He took the lead around the room's perimeter. I followed, wishing I had an oxygen mask or something so I could inhale without filling my lungs with intoxicating magic. It made it hard to think clearly enough to form a plan, much less focus on the crowd and spot Lady Aiten. On my right, a glass door led out onto a wooden veranda. Eyes glittered from the bushes outside.

"Who are those?" I pointed to them.

"Borderland fae," River said. "They don't have invitations. Lady Hornbeam's soldiers, I'd guess."

"Who?"

"One of the ruling Sidhe of the borderlands," River said. "Apparently she has an army. It's not uncommon. Lord Niall doesn't, however. I think we can question him if Lady Aiten won't talk, provided that your siblings remember that those same words he just used can also strip the magic from a person, or drive them to madness."

"Don't worry. Hazel might be impulsive but she's no fool, and she'll keep Morgan in check."

A Sidhe I recognised walked past, wearing a scowl at odds with the jubilant atmosphere in the room.

"Oh hey, Lord Raivan," said Hazel. "Might I ask—?"

"I'm not here to assist humans," he said icily, and stalked away.

"Wow," said Hazel. "Someone needs a dose of elf wine."

"You're not drinking, are you?" I asked warily, remembering the last faerie event we'd both been to.

"Water." She held up the glass in her hand. "I don't think

Lord Niall is going to leave the crowd any time soon. Better hope Lady Aiten has something useful to say."

"She might have been the last person to speak to the Gatekeeper, but she might not necessarily have known about her quest," River said. "The Sidhe keep as many secrets from each other as they do from everyone else."

"Maybe, but... damn. I don't understand why she didn't give us a clue when she spoke to us before." Hazel stood on tip-toe, annoyance evident on her features. We Lynns weren't exactly short, but there wasn't a Sidhe under six feet tall, and picking out one of them was all but impossible. "Right. I think we should split up—"

"Nope," said River and I at the same time.

Hazel gave him an irritated look. "Cover one half of the room each. You take care of Ilsa, I'll watch Morgan."

"Not after what happened last time," I said. "You damn near died."

"What?" said Morgan, appearing to tune into the conversation for the first time.

"That's irrelevant," Hazel said. "I'm not drinking, and besides, these people won't attack the Gatekeeper. Meet you here in ten minutes."

She grabbed Morgan's arm and pulled him after her into the crowd.

I groaned. "I should have seen this coming."

"If she doesn't drink anything, she'll be fine," River said.

"Yeah, got it. How much wine does it actually take to get a Sidhe drunk, anyway?" From what I could see, they were drinking it by the bucket-load. Then again, Sidhe's metabolisms were faster than humans'. I'd never seen a Sidhe in that condition, which was probably for the best. They didn't bother to control their magic at the best of times.

"I've never thought to ask." He began to circle the room in the opposite direction to Hazel, and I walked alongside him.

Sidhe gathered in groups around the fountain, paying little attention to anything other than their own conversations. A bright green glow drew my attention to the sprawling tree at the back of the room, which gave the illusion that the whole house was alive.

As we passed one of the tables, a group of Sidhe walked past. One of them was the female half-faerie who'd come through Summer's gate to talk to us before. Tall and slim with olive skin and thick dark hair, she wore an imperious expression. Green shone from her eyes and from the crossbow strapped to her back. *There she is.*

I'd found the Sidhe who'd last seen our mother.

6

I gave River a sideways look. Hazel and Morgan were on the opposite side of the hall, and while I didn't want to lose sight of our quarry, I didn't particularly want to draw the attention of her companions either.

On the other hand, Lady Aiten knew about the book, and what I'd used it for.

I took in a deep breath, walking after her. River caught my arm, and I shook my head slightly.

"You're glamoured," he murmured. "She won't know who you are."

"Most people here are glamoured," I whispered back. "She'll catch on that we're following her eventually." I didn't slow, continuing to walk after her and her two Sidhe companions. Maybe the two who'd been with her before, in the mortal realm, maybe not.

"Excuse me?" I said. "Lady Aiten, I'd like to speak to you."

"I thought I smelled a human." Her contemptuous tone made me want to peel off my disguise and punch her in the nose, but as Hazel had cast the spell, the most I could do was glare.

"You know me. I'm Gatekeeper."

"Leave," she told the others, and the two Sidhe stepped lithely away. "Did you risk your life in the mortal realm for nothing? This is no place for a human."

"The person who sent my mother into the Vale seemed to think it is. Did you?" I pressed. "I'm told you were the last person to speak to the Gatekeeper before she left."

"The Gatekeeper did indeed come to inform me that she would be away from her duties for a few weeks. She didn't say where she was going."

"But you know—" Dammit, telling the Sidhe here about the book was out of the question. "You know what I did. What she gave me. Mum's the one who did it, and she's in danger. We need to find out who sent her on this quest so they can bring her back."

"That's not how it works," she said. "It's your mother's duty to serve the Court, as it will be your sister's duty when her time comes."

"But—can you at least give me a clue about who'd send her there?"

She gave me an appraising look. "Your mother works for the Court as a whole. All of us have the authority to ask her to help."

Not all of you. Most of them wouldn't entrust a human with any task at all, which gave me no clues whatsoever. But what might they need doing that they couldn't do themselves? That's the part that confused me. The Sidhe had it all, and what they didn't have, they could get, with magic. All the Gatekeeper did was keep the peace. So either her mission involved something that would further that goal, or something the Sidhe *didn't* already have.

Lady Aiten gave me a last cold look and walked away.

I sighed, turning to River. "Great. Another Sidhe off the

list. Where's our esteemed host?" I looked around and spotted Morgan staggering towards us.

"Do not," he said. "Do *not* go behind the curtain over that way unless you want to see what trolls look like naked."

"Oh god, you're wasted."

"I am not." He fell sideways into the table. "I've seen things I cannot unsee."

Hazel strode up, thankfully looking sober. "Lord Raivan needs to take a swift dive into the fountain. So much for the Sidhe's exquisite manners."

"No luck?" I asked.

"We couldn't find anyone to speak to, so I figured he might give us some direction. He told me to get lost. He's the wrong person to put in charge of human affairs."

"Is that his job?" I asked.

"I know why they sent him to meet us," she said. "It sounds like Lord Raivan was the person who told the Summer Court to vote on whether to let half-bloods enter the territory in order to claim their parentage. They voted to let the half-faeries in, but so many people kicked up a fuss that he ended up being put in charge of dealing with humans for the foreseeable future. He used to be a high-ranking ambassador. Poor thing."

"But did you learn anything?"

"About Mum? Nope. You?"

"No, but I guessed something," I said. "The Sidhe... look at them. They have everything they could ever want. So what she's doing must involve either getting something they don't have, or something to do with peacekeeping."

"From what Mum said, not many people even know who we are," she said. "Except maybe Lord Niall..." She trailed off as the curtain of ivy parted, and a male Sidhe walked past, stark naked.

"Fucking hell," said Morgan.

"That was Lord Niall," said Hazel. A thoughtful expression crossed her face.

"You have got to be kidding me," I said.

Hazel laughed. "The moron actually left his talisman behind."

"Please don't," I said. "Seriously…"

"Well, why not enjoy the party," said Hazel.

"Because the guests can transform into murderous psychopaths in the blink of an eye?"

I turned to Morgan, only to see him disappearing behind the curtain of ivy.

"Oh, for god's sake," I said. "Can one of you conjure up some common sense?"

"I'm going after him. Wait here." Hazel walked through the ivy curtain. A wave of magic followed in her wake, showing images of Sidhe naked and draped over one another amongst the trees.

"Damn, that's strong." I took a step backwards into River, who steadied me. His own eyes were hazy with magic, and pulling away from him felt like yanking the gates of Death closed. "We should probably walk away before we end up naked in the woods. No way will Lord Niall talk to her now."

"Actually, he seems somewhat distracted." He stood close to me. Too close. I smoothly stepped back, despite the pull of magic urging me to make terrible decisions. River had deceived me. Even if he was probably the least deceptive person within sight, I couldn't afford to forget it. "Your sister's glamour is wearing off. You're turning human."

"Shit," I said, ducking my head, relieved my hair was long and thick enough to hide my non-pointed ears.

"I highly doubt any of the Sidhe in the grove will notice," he murmured. "But if we stand here any longer, someone might spot you."

I moved behind him. "There. Nobody can see me."

"Except me." And now he was too close again. Where did all the air go?

"You don't sound like you mind that I look human."

"I prefer you like this." His lips were too close to my ear. "You have no idea how much."

Stop seducing me. I'm angry with you. Was angry. Whichever. Never mind that he'd been driving me insane through sexual frustration for weeks, which didn't go away after unwelcome revelations.

"I prefer not being lied to," I said, the words sounding like they came from the human beneath the faerie disguise.

His hand dropped. "I've told you the full story. There are no more secrets between us. It's up to you to decide whether to forgive me or not. The wording of the vow was such that I couldn't get around it."

"I know," I said, my eyes on my feet. "It's—I want to be angrier with you than I am, because it'd be more productive than being raging mad at the people responsible for *this*." I gestured at the room in general. "But that's *why* I can't be angry with you." It'd help if the faerie magic made it easier to articulate my feelings, rather than intensifying them.

I raised my head to look at his expression. His faerie-bright eyes were a combination of surprise and something else I couldn't place. "I deceived you. That's a fairly essential part of being Sidhe."

I shrugged one shoulder. "So is not having any sense of ethics. I'd rather save all my grudges for the dicks who messed with my family."

"Speaking of... maybe we should check on Hazel or Morgan."

"I was trying *not* to think about whether either of my siblings is screwing the guy we're meant to be interrogating. But you're right." What if Hazel had pushed too far and pissed off the host, or Morgan's disguise had worn off like mine had and he'd been caught by the Sidhe? "Ready to hold your breath?"

I pushed through the ivy, and magic hit me like a hammer to the skull. Hazy greenness filtered across my vision, stirring my senses, caressing my skin like a soft breeze. Right away, I spotted Morgan lip-locked with a silver-haired male who was either half-blood or Sidhe. "Wow. That magic is strong. Morgan doesn't even *like* faeries."

I more or less swayed onto the nearest path, River close behind me.

"Hazel?" I called. More trees passed by. More Sidhe in various stages of undress. Heat pulsed in the air and my glamoured clothes felt uncomfortably warm.

"There she is." River pointed. Hazel had her arms entwined around another Sidhe. I couldn't tell whether or not it was Lord Niall.

"Great." I looked away. "Which way is back?" The forest all looked the same. Left... we'd come from the right hand side. I walked that way, swaying, and River caught my hand.

I didn't know when I stopped walking and started kissing him, only that I couldn't stop. His hands were all over me, touching every inch of skin they could get at, and I wished I'd gone for a more revealing outfit after all. I gasped as his thumbs stroked my hips through layers of cloth, strong hands pulling me tight against him. A jolt of sheer wanting went straight to my core, and I shivered with pleasure as he nipped at the skin of my neck, then my ear. Every inch of my skin flushed from his touch as I drew his mouth to mine. I wound a hand into the curls of his hair, and the smell of his earthy magic made my nerves ignite.

"You're exquisite," he whispered, running his hands over my breasts underneath the thin fabric of my shirt.

My nipples tightened under his touch. "I want you."

His breath hitched as my hand brushed against his erec-tion. "Not here."

"I don't see why not." This type of magic only amplified the feelings already there, and every inch of me wanted him.

I sucked in another breath, and choked on the sudden smell of decay. Beneath the magic, something rotted, and a chill breeze broke through the intoxicating warmth.

It smelled of the dead.

River drew back, panting. Something was… off. Wait, the music. It'd stopped. And that smell…

Greyness swept across my vision. I saw two glowing lights. River's spirit, pulsing strongly, and mine, too.

Spirits weren't supposed to appear in Faerie.

River leapt back from me with an exclamation of alarm. All the colour had drained from his face. "Did you feel that? Either someone opened a way to earth, or someone used necromancy *here.*"

Shock jolted me back to my senses. *"How?"*

"I don't know." He shook his head. "It's not possible—it shouldn't be possible." He grabbed his blade, which had disappeared in a glamoured haze while we'd been kissing.

Wishing I had a proper weapon, I put my hand in my pocket and touched the book. Its power crept up my arm, invigorating, *wrong*. The magic had remained dormant since we'd come here. It shouldn't exist. Despite myself, I pulled out the book. The symbol on the cover gleamed white, and so did my hands. A whisper across my spirit sight made me jump backwards.

"There's a spirit here." I put the book in my pocket, turning to look for the way back.

Then the first wraith appeared, its shadowy form sweeping over the clearing.

Screams rang out as a chill breeze followed in the wraith's wake. Everyone here could see it. Hell—it'd probably been a

Sidhe while it'd been alive. I didn't have necromantic candles with me, which left me with one means of banishing it. I held up my hands, glowing white.

"Get over here, you bastard," I shouted.

The wraith turned on me. Its shadowy form descended, and bright green magic exploded into life. Thorns rose into the air, grabbing at every Sidhe they could reach. *Whoa.* No Sidhe had cast the spell. The wraith still had its magic, and now it was attacking its kin. Magic streamed from my hands, but much less bright than it was in the mortal realm. The wraith shook off my attack. Summer energy blasted into the wraith, thrown from a couple of Sidhe, but did no damage.

"Keep hitting it!" River shouted at them. "It's vulnerable to magic. Get it onto the ground!"

Necromantic energy blasted from his own hands, mingling with mine, but was it possible to banish a wraith from a realm which had no veil? The wraith fell back under the assault as several other Sidhe joined in the attack, but the thorns continued to rise, striking any Sidhe who came near. Bright faerie blood stained the pristine forest floor, and the curtain of ivy had been ripped away, exposing the panicked Sidhe running around the main room—and two more wraiths, hovering above the crowd. Piskies flew around, panicking, while the band fled the stage.

"Get out!" roared a voice. "Get *out* of my house." Lord Niall stormed through the room, pure anger twisting his face. He slammed his staff into the floor, and the whole house trembled.

They were going to utterly destroy this place if someone didn't banish those wraiths.

With a glance at River, I switched on my spirit sight. If the gate *could* be accessed here, I needed to get them out. I willed the book's magic to fill my veins with cold power, searching for the familiar spiked gate, but saw nothing but greyness and the burning shapes of the wraiths. Dark spirits, clawed and hideous, reduced to something less than Sidhe or human.

The Vale. They came from the Vale.

But—that's where Mum was.

River's attack smashed into the nearest wraith, sending it flying backwards. The other two flew over the crowd, as though revelling in the chaos they'd created. Sidhe fired arrows at them, which simply sailed right through their enemies.

"Magic is the only weapon that works," River called to them. Everyone seemed to be in too much shock to care about a half-blood giving them orders. "Watch it—they can use Sidhe magic against you."

Thorns burst from the ground, and green light exploded overhead as the Sidhe's magic collided with the wraiths'.

Hazel ran up to us, magic flowing from her own hands. Morgan stood alone, shouting the banishing words at full volume. His disguise had gone, like mine. I marched past the panicking Sidhe to Morgan's side and joined him in shouting the words of banishment. Necromantic power continued to flow from the book to my hands, combining with Morgan's own attack. River joined us, but even the collective power of all three of us wasn't enough to send the wraiths into the afterlife.

Bleeding Sidhe lay around us. Some of them might die— for real. Imagining how the Sidhe would react to *that* strengthened my resolve. The book's power pulsed through my veins. *It's not tied to one realm. It's tied to me, and it's mine.*

I drifted out of my body, still holding the book. White light shone from my hands, colliding with the nearest wraith. *Where the hell is that gate?*

"Get back into the hell you came from," I snarled, imagining the gates appearing, sucking the wraiths into the void. *Come on...*

A wrenching sensation tugged through my whole body, and darkness appeared beyond the wraiths. Not the gates, but something else. Death? Maybe. I shouted the banishing words, over and over, magic pouring from my hands like a faucet.

The darkness closed in, and the wraiths disappeared, leaving grey fog, and gleaming lights within.

Two things were apparent. The Sidhe *did* have souls... or spirits, at least... and every one of them had seen what I'd done.

I fell back into my body, staggering against River. Exhaustion blurred my vision, masking the Sidhe and dulling their voices to a continuous hum.

Lord Niall's voice broke through the haze. "There will be no further revels without extensive guards!" he shouted. "No *humans* will be welcome."

"*You're* welcome," said Morgan, but his voice was lost amongst the crowd. This time neither Hazel nor I stepped in to warn him. Because if I wasn't half-dead, I'd say the same.

"We have to go," I mumbled. "Guys... get over here."

Something was wrong, like I'd given more than the book's power when I'd used its magic. Almost as though it'd drained some of my life force away, too.

"Way to go," Hazel said to me. "That was—wow."

"They think you're the angel of death." Morgan snorted. "Hey—Ilsa. Crap. Are you okay?"

I tried to say *I think I'm dying,* but it came out as a croak. My legs gave out as the last of the book's power fled, and blackness rushed in.

7

I woke up on a soft bed, surrounded by the pleasant smells of flowers and muted Summer magic. And a familiar earthy scent. River sat in a chair beside the bed, his eyes closed. I tried to sit up. My body and head didn't like that. Dizziness swept through me, and I flopped back onto the pillows.

River stirred. "Ilsa? Are you okay?"

I groaned. "Try hungover with a side of migraine and a terrible case of 'got run over by a faerie horse'."

He pushed his hair back with one hand. "Then it's probably a good thing that you didn't wake up when we rode back."

"Please tell me I didn't throw up on you."

"No. You were completely unconscious. You worried me." He walked to me in his swift faerie manner and brushed a strand of hair from my forehead. My face heated at the memory of his hands on my skin in the forest, and I ducked my head, willing the images to disappear.

"The Sidhe… they saw me," I said.

"They didn't see it was you who banished the wraiths,"

River said. "They saw into the realm of Death, same as all of us, but they're not experienced in telling one spirit from another."

"Someone must have been to let those wraiths in," I croaked.

He passed me a glass of water, and I drank the whole thing in one go. How long had I been lying here? Long enough for dawn to break outside. Days might have passed at home, and anything might have happened back in Scotland.

"Yes," River said quietly. "Someone let them in. There was either an outcast or a necromancer present. Given the level of magic there, I'd guess a traitor."

"They opened the Vale." I swallowed. "I—I could have done the same, but I didn't want to send those wraiths after Mum. I can't believe the Sidhe couldn't take them down. What about those Invocations?"

"Their magic has little effect on the dead. Winter would work better, and I bet the attacker was counting on that."

"I saw them. In Death. Is that because they're no longer immortal, or…?"

"I don't know," River said. "I've never seen anything like that in the years I've worked for them."

"Are they—okay? I mean, nothing's come back and attacked them again?"

He shook his head. "No. Lord Niall ordered a search of the grounds, but we'd left by then. We weren't the only people glamoured, and the Sidhe know nothing of necromancy at all."

"Good," I said. "I mean, it's *not* good that the attacker might still be there. It's not like my spirit sight works as a tracker the way it does at home."

Out of curiosity, I tried to access my spirit sight. But the familiar greyness didn't appear. I couldn't imagine tracking would work when the Sidhe's magic muddled everything, anyway.

"You opened the realm of Death in Faerie," River said seriously. "The mortals' Death, no less. You're lucky to be alive."

"I don't think it was the gate I opened," I said. "I think… I don't know *what* it was. Not the Vale, either. What happens when Sidhe die, anyway? I mean, they have souls. I know that now. They must disappear temporarily even if they come back."

"I can't say I know," River said. "Did you see the Vale?"

"No. I'm not so sure I can open the Vale from here at all." I reached for the book, which was still in the pocket it'd been in before I'd been glamoured. "Just when I think it can't surprise me any more…" A new section had appeared in the back. *Faeries and death.* I briefly skimmed the page, as River leaned in to look.

"Death Kingdom," I said. "Oh—it's apparently in Winter. Not the Vale at all."

"It's where banshees live," said River, reading over my shoulder. "But what you did to the wraiths didn't open a door within Faerie itself, but somewhere beyond it. The 'Death Kingdom' is just a name for the far reaches of Winter territory. I went on a mission there once, and it's not like our Death realm. There aren't ghosts there."

"Hmm." I slid out of bed. I still wore my faerie-made clothes, though my glamour had long since faded. "Is there a shower here somewhere?"

"In there." He pointed to the en-suite bathroom. "No hot water, I'm afraid. Only the Sidhe have that luxury."

"I'll survive." The room was fairly cool, but the sun outside the windows indicated another scorching day.

The shower looked suspiciously like a human creation except without temperature controls. What did the Sidhe do, hop over the Ley Line to swipe the humans' inventions and then replicate them with magic? It wouldn't surprise me if they did. They hated us coming here, and had put even River into a position of inferiority, but I'd bet everything I owned that they'd expect to be treated like royalty in our place. They'd come over to the mortal realm and left us to clean up their mess, while even the lesser nobles here lived like kings.

The soap smelled of flowers. Big surprise there. I wondered if Winter's equivalent smelled of ice and despair, and decided I didn't want to know. After dressing in more faerie-made clothes—which, to be fair, were somehow both comfortable and flattering at the same time—I found River waiting outside.

"The others are in the conservatory," he said. "We have food that won't have adverse effects on humans."

"Thanks." I tugged a hand through my hair, which was still hopelessly tangled. "How long have we been here?"

"You've been unconscious for about twelve hours." He walked into a side room, while I spotted Morgan sitting in the conservatory.

"Hey," I said, scooting over to join him. "You okay?"

He scowled. "Bloody faerie water. I didn't have *one* drink and I feel like shit."

"Yeah." I collapsed into the chair next to him. "Where's Hazel?"

"No clue. Thought she was with you."

"No…" I frowned. "It's not like her to go wandering off. I was going to suggest finding someone else who might know what the hell happened yesterday. There was a traitor, or a necromancer, right there at the party. Did you sense anyone?"

"No. I wasn't paying attention."

I sighed. "I don't blame you, but a *Sidhe?* Really?"

He grinned. "I just wanted to see if they're as good as everyone says they are."

"What's the verdict?"

"Yeah, they are. Dicks."

I snorted. "Well, they certainly did a great job screaming and running around like headless chickens. You'd think they'd never seen a ghost before."

"They hadn't," River said, returning with a platter covered with faerie food—homemade bread, cheese, fruit. "They were lesser nobles. I've passed on my concerns to my father about the presence of a traitor, but the guests have long since departed. I doubt you'll be able to get into the inner Court with the added security."

"We'll see what Hazel says." I picked up a grape and bit into it. "How many days have we lost at home?"

"I don't know, but probably less than a week," said River, helping himself to a handful of grapes. "I wish there was an accurate way to check. I lost six months the first time I came here."

"Bet Lady Montgomery loved that," said Morgan through a mouthful of bread.

I tensed, ready to tell him to stop winding up River, but River himself didn't look particularly bothered. "She knows Faerie. I did warn her."

"How long have you lived here?" I asked.

"It's difficult to measure in our time. I've worked for the Court in some capacity for four or five years, but I was first invited here at eighteen. My father..." He paused. "He offered me the talisman as a gift, and it chose me. A good job it did, because we were attacked by borderland outcasts on my first visit. The Court offered me a job in exchange for helping them."

"That's how you got into bodyguard duty?" I asked. "I remember you mentioned the borderlands once."

"Most of my tasks weren't that high-risk. I was usually asked to safeguard magical objects or escort lesser fae through the outskirts of Faerie."

"So do you prefer that or dealing with the dead?" asked Morgan.

"I don't have a preference," he said. "I worked at the guild for longer. Your sister's back, by the way."

Hazel came into the conservatory, her expression distraught and her face pale. "The circlet... the light went out."

The light on her forehead had faded, and no green or gold glow surrounded her. Her magic had gone.

An icy chill spread down my spine, masking the warmth of the room.

"Shit," I said. "Is Mum...?"

"It doesn't mean the Gatekeeper has died," Hazel said. "Someone's taken the gate."

"What?" I stared at her. "The gate *here*? Who?"

"I don't know, do I? I can't open the gate without the bloody circlet," Hazel said.

River swore. "If your power's tied to the Court—I'll ask my father if he might be able to help."

He glided out of the room. Oh, boy. River had had to ask for more than enough favours on our behalf already, and it wouldn't surprise me if the Sidhe kicked us out by this point. The idea of the *house* being compromised... it wasn't thinkable. I had to do something.

"How can anyone have got into the garden?" Morgan asked. "Don't we have defences everywhere?"

"Not on the gate," Hazel said. "It's supposed to be a defence force all by itself, because its run by the Court's magic."

"So it died because the Court's magic is fading?" asked Morgan.

"If they have the gate, they have the house," Hazel said. "Mum has things in the house which I do *not* want anyone else getting hold of."

Hope it's not Holly. But Holly, we could handle. Ghosts couldn't take over a house, so who else might be attacking? Even most Vale creatures didn't have the intelligence—or the access, considering how well the house was hidden.

River ran back into the room. "There's still a link to your house from my last mission. We can leave through the garden."

"But can we come back that way?" I asked.

He shook his head. "No. I wish we could. I've asked my father to keep an eye on the Court and send a messenger to me if there's trouble, but his brownie has left on a mission for the council. You'll have to find another way back."

Leaving would put our quest to rescue Mum on hold—but if we let anything happen to the house, the Gatekeeper's entire position might be in jeopardy. Hazel's expression mirrored mine, and she must be feeling it worse than I was—after all, she would have done anything to fulfil her role as Gatekeeper. But when that goal clashed with keeping us safe, she'd go against it up until the point where her vow to the Court made it impossible.

"It might be a mistake," I said consolingly. "The gate leads back here anyway, if it turns out it's still there. Has anyone ever taken it before?"

"No," Hazel said, biting her lip. "That's the thing. It leads directly here. How many of our enemies need a direct route into the Summer Court?"

"We need to leave," River said, reappearing. "There are people at the door asking questions about the events at Lord Niall's party yesterday."

"Shit," I said. "The last thing we need is to be hauled off for questioning."

Actually, the last thing we needed was for some unknown villain to hijack the gate into the Summer Court while the Gatekeeper was potentially held captive in the Vale, but the universe wasn't inclined to let any of us catch a break lately.

We crept out of the conservatory, between thorny plants, until we were safely out of sight of the house. Then River paused, looking up at the sky. "Here…. I can sense the vow."

I didn't sense anything except the smell of faerie fruit and flowers, and the scorching hot sun burning my skin through my clothes. There was a whole world of magic cut off from me, and to be perfectly honest, I'd prefer to keep it that way. But was the talisman book so different? What it'd done to me yesterday—it wouldn't have stopped if I'd died. The void would have continued opening to swallow this realm whole.

River said, "I'm crossing over. Get behind me."

There was a flash of white light, and immediately, we stood on another lawn, one with rotting grass beneath a grey sky. Dead plants, decay, and…

"The house is still there!" Morgan said.

"It looks… normal," Hazel said, confusion furrowing her brow. "Nobody's inside. I don't get it."

I frowned. The Summer Lynn house stood the same as usual, down to the curtains of ivy growing on the walls. But beyond, the country road… didn't look right. No forests were behind it. Only fields of heather, and beyond, darker shapes silhouetted against the sky. Mountains?

"Guys," I said. "Look at the road. I don't think we're attached to the Ley Line anymore."

The house stood where it used to, countless years before someone had used a spell to detach it from the mortal realm. The Winter estate was nowhere in sight.

"Look on the bright side," Morgan said. "We're not homeless."

"Speak for yourself." I stared at the cloudy sky. "You

know, we can't access Winter's house from here. Or anywhere else on the Line."

"Or open Paths," said Hazel. "Oh, shit. We're stranded." Her gaze fell on the forest behind, which had once led to the Winter estate on the other side. There was no sign of Holly's house at all.

"Damn," I said quietly.

Summer's gate had vanished.

8

We looked around at the garden, the sky, the impossibly normal Highlands... and the missing gate. Not to mention the other Lynn house. Had Holly even noticed anything was wrong? Or was she somehow responsible?

"There are worse places to be stranded," I said, but I didn't really believe it. Someone had *stolen* the gate. It shouldn't just vanish. "Hazel, isn't your magic working at all? Can you sense the Ley Line?"

"I could never sense the Line. It was just... there." She removed the circlet from her forehead, her hand shaking and her lip trembling. She was on the verge of tears, which meant using one of us as a verbal punching bag. I didn't particularly want to be on the receiving end.

"Great," Morgan said. "I never gave a flying fuck about the house and even *I* know it's bad news that we're marooned in the middle of nowhere."

"At least we're next to the village, not on top of a mountain," I said. "This area's pretty free of wild fae, too. Probably because of Mum. Or Agnes and Everett."

"Aren't we right next to the graveyard?" asked Morgan.

"Our family mausoleum's closer." My throat went tight at the thought of Grandma. I'd never see or speak to her ghost again. "We can go to the village. Nothing escapes Agnes. I want to know how *she* got to Edinburgh from here."

"Flew, probably," Morgan said. "Wasn't there a rumour that she has a pet dragon?"

I rolled my eyes. "She might know who took the gate."

"Or Arden." Hazel walked off. "Hey, Arden!"

No response came. The raven seemed to come and go whenever he liked, which wasn't particularly helpful right now. I didn't even know if he'd still been in the Court while we'd been there. Maybe he was with Holly, but we couldn't reach her either.

"I don't think he's coming back," I called to Hazel, who scowled.

"Bloody menace of a bird. Some use he is." She strode over to me again. "The necromancers?"

"I can talk to them here," I said. "Since we're not in a liminal space any longer."

"Really?" said Hazel. Her voice cracked a little, and I politely pretended not to notice. "I don't think I've seen you do it before."

"That's because Graves froze you the first time I tapped into the spirit realm."

"He did?" said River. "That explains it. I was certain I sensed unusual necromancy, but I wasn't aware of your powers at the time."

"Yeah, I was surprised, believe me. Let's see what's going on in Death."

Greyness smothered my vision, and I looked around the spirit world. After the void of death I'd seen in Faerie, it was kind of a relief to see it.

"Hey," I called out. "Greaves. Either of you will do."

The older Greaves appeared, a scowl on his withered face. He blamed me for his accidental intrusion into the land of the living, since the first time I'd banished a wraith on the Ley Line, it'd somehow caused a necromancer Guardian to be unceremoniously yanked back to this side of the grave. As a high-ranked necromancer, he could probably leave whenever he liked, but since there was no longer a living leader of the necromancer guild in the village, the others likely needed the guidance.

"Lynn," he said. "What have you done this time?"

"Absolutely nothing. We went to Faerie and someone messed with our house. It's uprooted from the Ley Line altogether. Do you know how?"

"That can't happen from this side," he said. "I know nothing of Faerie, but I do know that it's not this realm's magic that binds your house. The cause isn't here."

Well, crap. "So where the hell is it, then?"

"You're asking the wrong person," said the old man. "Besides, the Ley Line isn't that far away. It's within walking distance, certainly. You'll find Winter there."

"I'm not looking for Winter," I said. "We're miles out in the middle of nowhere. We don't have a car, our mother's still missing in Faerie, and if anyone in either realm needs our help again, they're pretty much screwed."

"Then it's a good job you're here," he said. "Agnes's shop is on fire."

I switched off my spirit sight, alarm flickering through me. "Did something else follow us here?"

Morgan shook his head, having apparently been listening in. "Agnes is a powerhouse. Nobody can hurt her."

"Most people aren't stupid enough to try." I looked around for Hazel and saw she'd left the house door open. I ran into the hall, heart hammering. The house felt... normal. Several pairs of eyes seemed to follow me from the portraits lining the entryway, like the past Lynns were casting judgement on all of us for making such a monumental mess of things.

"Nothing's been stolen," Hazel said, sticking her head out of Mum's workroom. "What is it?"

"Someone's attacking Agnes's shop." I moved in behind her. "Are there any functioning weapons in here?"

"We blew through most of the witch spells, but there's no shortage of iron."

She handed me a couple of spells, but it was plain to see our supplies were dwindling. Like everything else in the house. If the Vale was attacking, we'd have to rely on our magic. Hazel herself was armed to the teeth and her expression was set with simmering rage. I'd seen that look on Mum's face a dozen times. Like when she'd found out about the local half-Sidhe bullying me, or when Hazel had been in trouble at school. The look she wore when she went to war for one of us. Hazel *would* do that, I knew. As I'd do the same for her or Morgan.

I didn't have time to change out of my faerie-made clothes, so I shoved a hoody on top, relocating the talisman to the inside pocket. "We're low on iron filings." I passed a container to Morgan. "Don't use them unless the threat's a faerie, okay?"

"Why are we risking our necks for her?" he asked, taking the container from me. "She jumped ship when we got attacked in Edinburgh."

"She also gave us spells free of charge that saved all our lives, in case you've forgotten. Besides, she's probably toasted the threat and the fire's made of their barbecued corpses." That seemed more likely than Agnes having any need of help. But when I walked out the front door and spotted a stream of smoke rising from the village, my panic came back. Seeing the village from the house at all seemed wrong and out of place.

River took the lead, moving with half-faerie speed, while the rest of us hurried to keep up. We might have iron, but none of us carried any necromancy props. I bloody hoped it *wasn't* a wraith. We didn't have time to take a detour to deal with the living necromancers. Their headquarters looked as though it was locked, anyway.

Sparks of light shone above the village as we ran along the rain-damp path, and a thin trail of smoke rose amongst the rooftops. Those sparks were awfully familiar.

"Faeries," River warned, conjuring magic to his own hands. Away from the Court, the green light wasn't quite as bright and flashy, but the sparks of green and blue light surrounding the transparent figures floating overhead looked like a fireworks display. *So much for the iron.*

People ran around screaming as the half-faerie ghosts flung handfuls of Summer and Winter magic, causing the ground to freeze or thorny plants to appear wherever they hit. Of course the little bastards had used glamour, so to anyone without the Sight, it looked like faerie magic was exploding from thin air. Calling on the book's power, I ran to meet them. White light ignited my own palms. I didn't care about exposing it to the world anymore.

A green-glowing ghost landed in front of me. "Gatekeeper."

"Go back to hell." Necromantic power poured from my hands, striking the ghost in the chest. He flew back, rage sparking in his blazing green eyes. *Someone* had no trouble drawing on Summer magic. But when he aimed an attack at me, the magical blast struck my shield and ricocheted into the air. I hit him again, knocking him off balance. From his clumsy movements, he hadn't had nearly as much practise moving around as a ghost as I had.

Morgan and River ran below the ghosts, both drawing on necromantic energy. The ghosts flew away from the panicking humans to target us instead, but thanks to three of us being able to deflect magic and River's ability to move swiftly and retaliate with necromantic attacks, the ghosts couldn't land a hit on us. Hazel marched in, ordering the crowd to break up and take shelter. I hoped they'd listen to her, because with raindrops beginning to fall from the sky, spotting the transparent ghosts became even more difficult. Freezing drizzle soaked through my clothes, numbing my hands. *Enough of this crap.*

I shouted the banishing words, blasting the nearest ghost with necromantic power. He vanished, but his neighbour descended, yelling in rage. Ghostly hands grabbed at me, tugging at the essence of me. "Come with us, Gatekeeper."

"Where, the Vale?" I asked through gritted teeth. "I'd love to meet the person you're working for."

"Oh, you won't," said the ghost. He kept tugging. I let him, and power built behind my hands, pulled straight from the book. "You're coming to the Vale so you can wander there forever, while we take back what's ours."

His hands latched onto my spirit and *pulled.* I let go, soaring out of my body, power blasting the faerie ghost onto his back. Grabbing his throat, I let him struggle, squealing in astonishment that I was attacking him as a ghost.

"Do none of your people know who I am?" I asked. *Damn. He's not faking.* It came as no surprise that the half-faeries didn't know how powerful the book was, but made it that much harder to guess the perpetrator. "Tell me who you're working for. It'll go easier for you. I can walk in and out of the Vale any time I like. Understand me?"

The ghost paled. "I—I don't want to die."

"You're already dead."

Tears spilled from his eyes. "This is all *her* fault. We're stuck here because of her, and now we can't come back unless we help *them*."

"Who?"

Fury sparked from his eyes. "Ivy Lane. She condemned us to this."

"What? How?"

He shook his head, tears spilling. He was really young, despite his ghostly state. They all were. *Ivy Lane? She did this to them?*

"I can help you move on," I told him. "It'll be fast. But you need to tell me what you know."

He sobbed again. "I've been stuck in the Vale for so long… I had to get out. There were other half-bloods, they told me to help them. They told me to bring you with me and I'd get to live again."

"They lied. You can't raise the dead permanently, not in the way you want. If it's any consolation, the Sidhe are the same."

The book's power filled me, the image of the gates appeared at his back, and he faded from view, disappearing beyond.

The spirit sight receded, greyness fading to be replaced with bright light and a burning smell. My heart lurched.

Smoke poured from the roof of Agnes's shop despite the rain, and River emerged with Everett leaning on him. Behind, Agnes stormed out, coughing and swearing at full volume. Relief filtered through. *They're okay.*

The remainder of the crowd dispersed pretty quickly when Agnes unleashed several firework spells into the sky. I saw the necromancers casting suspicious looks at me, but none of them seemed to want to get too close to the burning shop. Hazel stood talking to two of them, presumably giving them a human-friendly explanation. Even a village full of supernaturals had little chance of banishing faerie ghosts. It was seriously luckily none of them had been wraiths.

Everett stepped away from River, eyeing him suspiciously. "You certainly have a good sense of timing."

"The ghost of old Graves warned me," I said. "Are you and Agnes all right?"

"We've been worse," he said. "We have healing spells. The fire's out, but the spells need to… settle down."

Agnes snarled, throwing a spell over the house. The smoke dispersed. "You can all stop looking at me like you're expecting thanks for doing nothing," she growled at the remaining necromancers, who fled as far as possible from her condemning stare. "Useless, the lot of them."

"Who started the fire?" asked Hazel, striding over. "The necromancers said the ghosts appeared at the guild first."

"Bastards," said Agnes. "Those ridiculous sparks of theirs got into the shop and hit my entire display of elemental kindling spells."

"We can salvage the rest," Everett said consolingly. "It's not the first time the shop's been attacked."

"No, but it's bloody annoying," Agnes said. "Our house is two minutes from here. The faeries wouldn't have the nerve to torch *that*."

"We'll come and check." To my immense surprise, River moved to help her walk. He'd distrusted the old mage when we'd first met, even going as far as to believe she was working against us.

She shot him an aggrieved look. "Do you think me incapable of walking by myself?"

"You were attacked in a room full of volatile spells. Both of you are lucky to be alive."

"Is he always like this?" said Agnes, jerking her head at him.

She'd probably meant to say, *does he know what I'm capable of?* I answered both: "Yes. His mother is the leader of Edinburgh's necromancer guild and his father's a lesser noble in the Seelie Court."

"Royalty." She snorted, but allowed him to help her. River didn't appear to have suffered any injuries, to my relief. Nor had the others. Hazel checked on the houses as we walked, making sure the faeries hadn't left any damage, while Morgan and I checked the spirit realm. Quiet. Obviously, it wasn't a coincidence that the ghosts had targeted the village the instant we returned from Faerie, but they hadn't been an organised collective. They'd been angry, chaotic.

I'd been wondering if I'd see Ivy again ever since her unexpected appearance in the Lynn house, but if she'd left those half-faeries to suffer in limbo, maybe I was better off sticking with the handful of allies I had. I pulled up my hood against the rain, daydreaming longingly of the warm café in Edinburgh, secret dates with River, the closest to calm I'd known in a long time.

I sighed in relief when we entered Agnes and Everett's bungalow, the warmth of the fire driving the chill from my limbs. I hadn't been here in years, but it kind of amazed me how much junk Agnes and Everett had managed to cram into one room. There was hardly enough space for the four of us to file in, and a single armchair was the only spot free of trinkets and half-made spells.

Agnes marched to the armchair and sat in it as though daring the rest of us to challenge her. We filed in behind her, standing with our arms against our sides to keep from knocking things over. Everett cleared his throat and went off into the adjacent kitchen, switching the kettle on.

"Will one of you tell me where the bloody hell those ghosts came from?" Agnes said.

She was looking at me, but Morgan spoke first. "Out of the Vale, probably."

"Really." She turned her gaze onto him. "Are you certain?"

"Yeah. That's where they're operating from, I s'pose. Someone's giving them orders."

"They seemed to think they could come back to life," I said, wishing I had something to lean against. Using the book's magic again had left me feeling as drained as running two necromancer patrols back to back. "Sounds like that's what the enemy is promising them, anyway."

Agnes accepted a cup of tea from Everett. "You spoke to them."

"In Death? Yes."

Everett passed the tray of tea cups and biscuits to Morgan, who proceeded to surreptitiously conceal them on the already-crowded bookcase. Everett's baking was known to occasionally turn people into household objects, and it usually wasn't worth the risk. When River shot me a confused look, I whispered, "Trust me, it's not worth it."

The bookcase wobbled and Hazel moved in front of it as Agnes looked in that direction. "Er, so is your shop insured?"

Agnes scowled. "Well, I own the place, so it's not insured. Most companies don't offer magical protection for highly dangerous spells, let alone in places not on the map. But we can fix the damage."

Morgan said, "They used to say the shop is dragon-proofed."

"Dragons have better manners than faerie ghosts."

"I don't even know if you're being serious or not," I said. "Has this been happening since we left?"

"No, but I heard you caused a stir in Edinburgh after I left," said Agnes. "I have to apologise for leaving the way I did."

"Don't worry about it," I said. "Believe me, we have bigger problems. Someone yanked our house off the Ley Line and stole the gate from the garden."

Everett's eyes widened. "Someone stole the Gatekeeper's gate?"

His wife, however, looked as unperturbed as ever.

"Yes." Hazel's hands clenched at her sides, her knuckles whitening. "We went into Faerie overnight and everything went to hell. Now we're stuck here with no magic."

"If you need any spells, you're welcome to any from the shop," Everett said.

"And if you want to go to Edinburgh," Agnes said, "I do have a way. I'd have to make a few phone calls first, but I think they'd make an exception for the Gatekeeper."

"We might have to take you up on that offer," I said. The house might be unprotected, but the Ley Line went through the whole country. In Edinburgh, we had a whole team of potential allies. If only I could say the same for the Seelie Court. "But we need to find the gate first before we handle anything else."

Hazel caught my gaze and nodded, her grim expression a reflection of my own.

9

"I hope you have a plan," Morgan said when Hazel unlocked the front door of the Lynn house. "Because I think Edinburgh's a safer bet than Faerie."

"And I think the answers are in the Court," Hazel said irritably. "They must be. The Court—someone in Faerie stole my goddamned gate."

"It's not *yours*," said Morgan. "It's the Court's property."

"Then they should be lining up to help me." Her face was flushed and her whole body shook with rage. She was used to stepping up and taking charge, while I was used to standing invisibly in the background. So was Morgan, come to that, but he looked equally pissed off.

"Guys," I said. "Calm down."

Hazel shot me a glare. "Do you have any idea how much trouble we're in? Mum's supply of cash is gone. So is mine."

"What, you still use magically generated money?" Morgan snorted.

"The Sidhe don't know how to use human banks, obviously," Hazel said. "So they use magic to make the money appear in the house, in Mum's secure deposit box. The

85

money's always there. Except it isn't, because there's *no* magic here at all."

"Obviously," Morgan said. "We can survive a few weeks, and if it all goes tits up, we might not have to worry about that at all."

"Morgan, you're not helping," she snapped. "I'm not relying on charity, especially as this is my fucking job."

"No, it's our mother's job. And what's she done? Got herself kidnapped." He stormed into the living room, where River wisely glided out of the way. I was tempted to grab him and run somewhere quiet—like the library—but without the house's magic running, anything they broke would remain in pieces.

"At least I've never stolen from anyone," Hazel shot at Morgan. "From my *family*."

Morgan scowled. "I wasn't in my right mind back then."

"And you never freaking apologised."

"Guys!" I said.

"Who even fucking cares? Those were faerie antiques. It's not like she *or* the Sidhe were ever going to use them," Morgan said.

"Want to know why I care?" Hazel said. "This is my life. I have given my entire life to the Sidhe, and this is how I'm repaid for it. I nearly lost both of you." Her voice cracked. "And they don't care in the slightest."

"Haven't the rest of us been telling you that all along?" Morgan folded his arms. "This isn't news."

"Then stop blaming it all on Mum," Hazel snapped. "She was an only child, so she always knew she was born to this. She never had to pick her family over the Sidhe, because her family already served them."

"She wouldn't pick *us* over the Sidhe," Morgan said.

"Yes, she would," I interjected. "Both of you, calm the hell down."

River cleared his throat from behind us. "You have a visitor," he said.

The doorbell rang. I frowned and tapped into my spirit sight. *Holly?* It must be her. Who needed a security system when you had the ability to peer at someone's very soul?

Hazel walked to the door first, with the rest of us behind her, and pulled it open. Holly stood with a couple of books in her arms, her circlet gleaming bright blue. Full power. It hadn't been evident to me until now how like Hazel she looked, despite the generations separating each half of the family. She had the same confident stance, the same aura that drew attention even when she wasn't trying to. She'd dyed her hair black and clipped it to chin-length, which made her pale skin look paler and her blue eyes more startling.

"Hazel," said Holly, breaking the imposing impression. Her teeth ran over her lower lip not unlike Hazel when she was nervous. "I came to speak to your sister."

"Me?" My brows rose. "You told me to go away before."

"I know I did." She glanced over her shoulder at the garden. "What happened here?"

"Faeries," I said, like that explained anything. "Actually, I've no bloody clue. None of us have." Telling her Summer was in trouble wasn't a wise move, not now she was interacting directly with the Sidhe. But maybe she'd guessed. Who knew how much more information she had access to now she was properly immersed in Gatekeeper training?

"I came to help you," Holly said. "Believe it or not."

"Go on," I said warily. She showed no outward signs of hostility, but I wouldn't trust her until I knew she hadn't in any way been involved.

"Ilsa," she said, almost hesitant. "I... when I returned to the house, my magic restored it to the state it was in before the Winter Gatekeeper's magic destroyed it."

"Yeah, I figured. But that won't help us with ours."

"That's not what I wanted to say," Holly said. "My mother... when she was scheming, she ordered that bird of yours to bring her some books from *your* house. They burned with the house, but my magic brought them back." She held out a book, a thick ancient tome with a velvety red covering. "I can't make up for what I did, but I can at least give you this. I think it's how she found out about the Gatekeeper's magic, and it was what I used... you know, when I was trying to work out if the Gatekeeper's powers would be able to save her."

I blinked, startled, but took the book from her. It was surprisingly heavy. "Wow. Faerie magic's really something, huh." I should have thanked her, but it felt too awkward and strange. And I'd dearly like to know *how* magic had managed to restore something that had been completely destroyed. I hadn't really thought about how Holly was in the same position Mum had been in—as the only child, the only contender for heir, her role had been set before she was even born. Same as her own mother. Maybe that was why Aunt Candice had been so determined to break the curse.

Holly passed me a smaller notebook, too. "This is your aunt's diary. I didn't find much in there, but maybe you'll be able to get more out of it than I did."

"Great-Aunt Enid." I took the book from her, feeling her hand trembling. "Thanks. A peace offering, right?"

"I don't want to fight with you," Holly said. "I'm not my mother. And... I don't know what happened to your house. I'm sorry."

"I think there's a traitor who stole our gate," I admitted. "In Faerie. They have their magic to protect themselves, but... the village doesn't."

Her eyes widened. "They stole the gate?"

"When we were *in* Faerie," I said. I doubted she'd use the information against us, and it wasn't like we had a whole lot in the way of information anyway. "God knows how, but we're off the Ley Line. We have other ways to get around, but not to Faerie."

"Ah. I'm not allowed to let anyone through Winter's gate, and I don't think you'd survive it anyway."

"No worries. We'll figure it out."

The books in my hands called to me like a siren's song. With this information, I had a proper guide to the Gatekeeper's magic. *Finally.*

"If you need my help, just ask," Holly mumbled. The words sounded like they pained her to speak aloud, but I gave her a smile. It probably wasn't very sincere, but she gave me an equally false attempt at a smile back. And then she turned away.

"Hang on," I said. "How did you get here, from the Ley Line? Where is it?"

"Over the hill," Holly said. "My house is exactly where it always was. I didn't even know yours wasn't there until I went to check on the village."

"Have you seen Arden?" asked Hazel. "He's been missing ever since we went to Faerie."

Holly shook her head. "Sorry, no. I'll keep an eye out."

"Sure. See you around," I said.

And she left. Hazel closed the door. "Damn, Ilsa. What's in those books?"

"Answers. I hope." I took both books with me into the living room. "Let's see what the last Gatekeeper has to say."

The book, it turned out, wasn't a guide to the Gatekeeper so much as a tome of advanced necromancy. The sort of book that would have been kept in Lady Montgomery's office at Edinburgh's necromancer guild, out of the way. It wasn't a magical book, but a dryly written technical manual of how to do dangerous things like disconnecting from one's body, exploring the spirit realm without a tether, and removing a force possessing a living person. Nothing I hadn't done already, but it was nice to have an explanation for how it all worked.

Great-Aunt Enid's journal was less useful. Most of it was old letters written in her almost-illegible handwriting. In the back were drawings and odd words scribbled down. *Faerie... Gates... Ancients...* and no context. Helpful. Maybe she was writing down her thought process, but I'd need to read the whole book to make heads or tails of it. Morgan and Hazel seemed to have forgotten their argument and lapsed into silence, so I went to my favourite spot in the library and prepared to do some serious digging.

Even without the house's magic functioning, the comforting smell of old books embraced me as I read through the textbook. Apparently, I didn't need to open the whole gate whenever a spirit got loose—I could carefully let only one spirit through. As I'd done with the half-faerie. But the part I wanted to know about was how to use the Ley Line to travel as Ivy did.

The spirit lines are anchors.

I stared at the page. Anchors... like candles. So did that mean if I left my body while on a spirit line, I wouldn't go floating off into the void? I suspected most necromancers had absolutely zero control when they disconnected from their bodies, so I was one step above them in that I could actually control where I moved and how I extended my spirit sight. But master necromancers could go one step further and move anywhere they liked at will. They had absolute control. Their methods were also a swift ticket through the gates if they went wrong, but those who survived to become Guardians were able to use the spirit lines to travel great distances.

And so was the Gatekeeper... except I didn't need to be dead to do so. I could go wherever I wanted at any time.

I looked up, and jumped, seeing River's reflection in the window. "How long have you been standing there?"

"A while." He gave a tired smile and walked to the desk. Besides the textbooks was the sci-fi paperback he'd borrowed from me when he'd been here the first time, what felt like a lifetime ago. "I never did borrow the rest of those books of yours."

"Go right ahead." I stretched my neck. "I might need to put some of this into practise soon."

"Anchors?" he said, reading over my shoulder. "I didn't know that about the spirit lines."

"Where's the nearest one to here?" I asked. "Aside from the Ley Line, I mean."

"I assume there's a spirit line close to the necromancer guild, or your family mausoleum," he answered. "Why?"

"Because I can travel along spirit lines." I closed the textbook. "Any of them. I could get to Edinburgh from here without leaving the village. I can travel between key points. There's no risk of me leaving the line and risking being dragged through the gate."

River's fingers trailed over the back of my chair, and the earthy scent of his magic filtered through the old-book smell. My body remembered our encounter in the Sidhe's forest even if my mind wanted to focus on the present. We had few hours of daylight left, and if it was possible for me to use my ability to find the Gate—I had to try.

River shook his head. "That skill's Guardian material, and extremely dangerous. Key points closer together, maybe, but not that far apart."

"My talisman can do it," I said. "*I* can do it. Imagine what I can see from that side. Ivy did it, and she doesn't even have the book."

"Ivy?"

Ah. I hadn't told him. So much had happened since that

it'd quite honestly slipped my mind up until the half-faerie ghost had mentioned her name.

"I had a visitor, the day you first showed up here," I told him. "She looked like a ghost but wasn't one. Ivy Lane. That's what she said her name was. It was her who put the idea that we had to find the heir to Summer into my head, but I don't think she meant to—it was Arden who interpreted what she said in that way. It's not like I knew her, though she claimed we were distant relatives… and she had a faerie talisman."

His brows shot up. "She brought a talisman into *Death?*"

"Apparently. It's not like we had time to talk. I was convinced she was either working against us or a figment of my imagination, and I haven't heard from her since. But she travelled all the way up here from England, along the Ley Line."

River looked at me with disbelief etched on his face. "It shouldn't be possible."

"Trust me."

River's mouth drew down at the corners. "I trust *you.* But whatever powers this Ivy person has, it's not worth risking your own life."

"Then set up a tether," I said. "Activate some candles as a backup and watch me while I try to move around the spirit lines. Then it won't harm me if it doesn't work. I have to at least try. Maybe I can even get into the Vale."

"And can you guarantee you'd make it out?"

He had me there. "You know how important this is."

"I know your life is more important to me than whoever decided to leave this task to you." He spoke quietly, his head bowed a little, his fair hair falling into his eyes.

My throat closed up. "And if my mum did it? Just let me try. I'm trusting you to watch me on this side, okay?"

He gave a sharp nod. "Right. But the slightest sign of danger and I'm bringing you back into this realm. I don't think the person who made that book intended its wielders to have long lives."

"Great-Aunt Enid did fine," I answered.

"Did she ever have to do anything like you have?"

"Maybe. I'd need to read the rest of this to find out." I held up her journal. "But I want to try the spirit lines before it gets dark outside."

———

Once we reached the mausoleum, I had a look around to see if there'd been any new disturbances. None. Grandma's ghost had moved on, so there were no residents here, but the amount of iron built into the walls kept out hostile presences. River set up the candle circle while I skimmed to the last section of the talisman book. I already knew what I'd find there. This was the way into the Vale—by disconnecting from my body, and risking certain, permanent death from which there would be no return.

If Mum had known how dangerous it was, she surely wouldn't have passed the book on to me. But nobody from her own generation had claimed it, and from what I'd read of Great-Aunt Enid's journal, she hadn't told a soul.

I swallowed down my complicated feelings on Mum's decision, and walked up to the circle of twelve candles. River had spaced them out so I had room to sit between them. I climbed carefully into the circle, making the mistake of meeting his concerned stare.

"I want to do this," I told him. "And I trust you to hold the rope. Okay?"

"I won't let go, Ilsa."

He spoke the words with all the intensity of a faerie vow. If I'd had faerie magic, those words would have bound his soul to mine. My mouth dropped open, taken aback, and he kissed me hard. His hands gripped my shoulders firmly, saying more than words could. Then he let go and took a step back.

I slipped out of my body. He was there, too, a pale shape floating beside the circle of candles. I drifted out of the circle, towards the necromancers' place. A thin line appeared beneath my feet, faintly silver in colour. The same colour as the light around my body. I moved and my spirit did, zipping down the line.

I stopped abruptly, staring around. I'd ended up somewhere I didn't know, beside a grassy hill surrounded by forests and fields. Must be another liminal space. Some faeries had hidden in these spaces before the invasion. Nobody could harm me as a ghost, but hellhounds and other creatures were known to wander the spirit lines. Probably from the Vale. It was all connected, after all.

I could get to Edinburgh from here.

I turned south, and continued to drift. Occasionally, I spotted other spirit lines intersecting with this one. Edinburgh was easy to find—a tangle of lines, lit up like a beacon. No wonder it was such a hot spot for ghosts. Other spirits drifted around, and I faltered, not wanting to run into any necromancers. I'd have a job and a half explaining how I'd travelled so far from my body.

I floated back north into the countryside, then stopped, my skin prickling. Someone was following me.

"Hey, you. Wait."

I spun around. A woman appeared on the hillside, striding towards me with purpose.

10

"**S**peak of the devil."

Ivy Lane herself floated above the line, with the same confidence as she had when she'd walked through our living room wall.

Ivy paused before me, looking me up and down. "Believe it or not, that's not the first time I've been called that. I know you."

"Ilsa Lynn," I said. "Gatekeeper." There was no hiding what I was here in Death.

Her gaze went to my forehead, and her eyes widened. "No kidding. I guess it's my turn to ask how you got here."

"Let's just say there have been changes since we last saw one another," I said. "Turns out my family have necromancy in the bloodline, too."

"Well, that explains *some* things," Ivy said. "I was actually on my way to speak to your sister. Or your mother."

"She's not around." I weighed the odds, then came out with it. "Actually, she's in the Grey Vale, on the orders of the Sidhe."

Ivy's brows shot up again. "I should have asked more questions when we spoke before."

"Most of this is recent. This is the first time I've been here, for a start. How are you doing it?" Her body was outlined in blue light that hadn't been obvious when I'd seen her as a ghost before. My gaze snapped right to the source—the sword at her waist, glowing so brightly it looked almost solid.

Her eyes followed the direction of my gaze. "My magic is… different. You?"

"Same here."

The hint of a smile came to her lips. "I guess it's fitting that I ended up speaking to you and not your sister."

"Who sent you? I never had chance to ask."

"Nobody did. I came of my own volition." Her fingers traced the hilt of her blade. "A year ago, things went… wrong, in Faerie. Around the same time, I found out I had family. But I didn't know where you were, or who you were. The communication lines with Faerie were kinda screwed up for a bit. We're still rebuilding them. I had no idea there was anyone with such a close link to the Courts in this realm."

"Most of our business is in Faerie, not here," I said. "Mum's is, anyway. But things are screwed up now, too. That's why I'm floating around here looking for answers. Can I get into the Vale through here?" I indicated the pale silvery line beneath our feet.

Ivy gave me an appraising look. "Yeah, you can. You might not be able to get out. Necromancers who know Death really well can… Frank the necromancer did, but he's already dead."

"Who's Frank the necromancer?"

"A necromancer Guardian, and one of the Council of Twelve."

That rang a bell. "My mum knows the council. My sister doesn't, but she was due to meet them…"

"They're gathering in Edinburgh right now, actually. That's where my body is."

"Seriously? You're that close?" I stared at her. "Wait, is the necromancer guild meeting with them as well?"

Her expression twisted with incredulity. "Don't tell me you're involved with them, too."

"Yeah. If anyone's mentioned a raving mad ghost sending a supernatural fae monster to attack psychics, my siblings and I are the ones who stopped it."

Ivy shook her head. "I should have come looking for you sooner. When they called the meeting here, I came all the way from the Midlands with a group of mages, not to mention half a witch coven and a bunch of shifters and necromancers. You shook up the Ley Line all through England."

"The ghost did, technically," I said. "But she was working with half-faerie ghosts from the Vale, and some of them are still out there. They're plotting against both this realm *and* the Courts."

They'd also blamed Ivy for their predicament. But even here on the spirit line, with both of us transparent and floating insubstantially between worlds, she wasn't someone I wanted to cross. That blade of hers glowed brighter than the silver light. I couldn't take my eyes off it. The book stirred in my hand where I held it at my side, like the blade called to it, too. A silver glow spread up my arm.

Ivy's gaze went to the book. "So that's how you got here. I've never seen a talisman in that form before."

"You've seen others?" My voice rose in surprise.

She tapped her blade's hilt. "Aside from Helena? No."

I blinked. "You… named your sword? Or is it an official title? Mine doesn't have one."

The book stirred in my hand again. Ivy looked at it, frowning. "No, it's just a nickname. Do you have faerie magic?"

"No, but my sister does. We're both fully human, but only one person gets the Summer Gatekeeper's magic. Are you human?"

"I am," she confirmed. "But that book… how'd you get it?"

"Inherited it," I said. Something told me I could trust her, but part of me remained wary. "It woke up when our family was attacked by the dead."

I summarised what the Winter Gatekeeper had done. Ivy looked aghast. "Damn. I wouldn't have expected it of a human."

"The half-faeries who attacked us mentioned your name. They said you got them trapped in the Vale."

"Shit," said Ivy. "I should have known some of them escaped. There was a war… some half-faeries chose the losing side, because the enemy promised they'd get to be immortal. I guess this new enemy is probably doing the same. They don't take much convincing."

Well, damn. "Even though the Sidhe aren't immortal? It's true?"

"They aren't," Ivy said. "Yeah. Can't say I know how that Winter Gatekeeper found out, but given how the Sidhe are prone to murdering one another, I doubt it took long for word to spread throughout Winter."

"You… you saw how it happened?" A suspicion seized me. "You *caused* it."

"I didn't have a choice," said Ivy. "Someone tried to hijack the immortality source to create an army of immortal soldiers, so I had to destroy it. I'm trusting you not to share that with them, by the way. They think the villain did it. It's easier to have them believe one of their own was the cause. And it kind of was, because he pushed me into a corner."

"I… don't want to think of what they might do to you for that."

"It's not me I'm worried about." She ran a hand over her blade's hilt again. "I've had to put down a half-dozen schemes since, but this is the first I've encountered where they're using *human* necromancy. There's no way to permanently bring someone back from death… not in the sense that their body is already dead, anyway. You can reattach a spirit if the body is alive. You can heal a body from the brink of death or stave it off with certain types of magic. But unless the Sidhe had a backup plan, there is no way for immortality to return in the normal sense."

"Backup plan?" I said. "What was the first plan?"

"A cauldron of blood with the ability to create new bodies from scratch." She grimaced. "Turns out it doesn't hold up well to an Invocation."

"Is there any type of faerie magic you *can't* use?" I asked her.

She gave a wry smile. "I'm not supposed to have stayed here this long… if you're able to come and speak to the council in Edinburgh, I'll be there a while. I can tell you more in person."

"That's on the plan," I said. "Once we've figured out who sent Mum into the Vale."

"I wish I could help you," Ivy said. "There's no guarantee of being able to find a specific person in the Vale. And it sounds like the vow she's under might not allow her to return with you."

"I was afraid of that," I said.

Ivy's body had turned even more transparent, while her blade wasn't glowing as brightly as before.

"I'm fading," she said. "You're not, but… if this is your first time here, I wouldn't stay too long. My fiancé is pretty insistent about watching me. I take it you have someone watching over you too?"

I nodded. "I do. I'll come and find you later."

Ivy shimmered all over with blue light, then disappeared.

I turned around. I couldn't tell which way I'd come along the path. *That... might be an issue.* The world beneath was leached of colour, rolling hills and fields and mountains seen through a filter. Grey fuzziness outlined everything. The only solid thing was the book, faintly pulsing with white light. I flipped it open, then focused hard. The shape of a grey path began to appear. A thrill sang through me. *The Vale. Mum.*

I was on the cusp. Putting one foot over the line into the Vale wouldn't do any harm, right? Not with the book blazing in my hands, filling me with boundless power.

My foot rested on the edge of the path as though my thoughts had brought it closer. *Mum's here. I know she is.* But something held me back. Finding Mum wouldn't lead us to the enemy. The traitors, the Vale outcasts, were inside the Court itself. Not the Vale.

River's face appeared before my eyes. Everything went fuzzy, and the next second, I lay on the floor of the mausoleum, my body aching with cold. My limbs felt like dead weights as I tried to lift my hand to check it still worked. The candles flared brighter—he must have activated them to shock my body into waking up.

River's hand was so warm, I yelped when he grabbed me. "Ilsa. God, you're freezing cold."

He pulled me upright, knocking candles aside. I wrapped my arms around him, craving his warmth. "Why'd you do that?" I said through chattering teeth.

"Because your heartbeat slowed to a crawl and scared the shit out of me." He removed his coat and wrapped it around me. "Walk," he said. "It'll help." He was shaking, maybe with fear or anger, maybe because as a Summer faerie, being hugged by an ice block probably wasn't pleasant.

By the time we came within sight of the garden, the sensation had somewhat come back to my limbs. River, however, looked as though he was about to pass out at what I'd told him.

"The Sidhe can *die?*" he said. "I didn't hear what the Winter Gatekeeper said… but it explains how she hoped to dominate them. Any of the Sidhe might be desperate enough to work with humans if it means getting their immortality back."

"Did you hear anything about it in Faerie?"

"Certainly not," he said. "If the Courts spoke of it, then they must have done so behind closed doors. It's not the sort of information they'd want to be spread widely… nor amongst humans."

I drew River's coat tightly around myself, my numb feet skidding in the mud. "Yeah, we're sworn to secrecy. So what are the Sidhe playing at? They must know that human necromancy is even less reliable than this immortality source of theirs. Also, Winter magic can involve raising the dead. Surely that's more logical."

"Not permanently," River murmured. "This… this has the potential to affect the Courts to such a degree, it might even be someone in a position of power behind this. The Erlking is dying."

"Yeah, hence the quest for the missing heir."

He turned on me. "You've known for a while."

"I didn't believe Ivy at first," I said. "Would you? The heir thing turned out to be nonsense, so I hoped this was too. I think the Sidhe could do well to learn some humility, but they're not the type to accept their inevitable fate without trying to drag everyone else down with them."

"Not every Sidhe would want to do that."

"*One* would be enough to destroy this realm," I said heatedly. "Sorry. I'm not blaming you… I know everyone worships the Sidhe, and heaven knows they might even be justified in being a little pissed off, considering how many thousand years they've been immortal. I just wish they'd consider that they're not the centre of the universe."

"I think you're asking for the impossible," River said, but his expression remained dark and grim. "Perhaps… perhaps your mother knew as well."

I stopped walking. "Crap. Maybe the Sidhe sent *her* to find a solution. The Erlking's dying, the Sidhe are desperate, and…" And answers might lie in the Vale? I almost wished I'd gone there after all, but I wouldn't have been able to bring Mum back with me as a ghost. I shook my head, frustration burning below my skin despite the lingering chill, and resumed walking again. "We need more information… but it's a start. I can look around next time I'm on the spirit paths."

"You almost froze to death, Ilsa," River said.

"Then next time wrap me in your coat." It smelled pleasantly of his earthy magic. "This is what I'm supposed to do."

"According to whom?" he enquired. "Not the Sidhe. You don't have to answer to anyone but yourself."

"I can't keep this power and not use it to save Mum," I said. "And stop those outcasts. I wouldn't forgive myself if I let them win."

I might crave the book's power, but I wouldn't be controlled by it. Magic was untameable by nature, but if Ivy could traverse Death, so could I.

"I don't think Morgan can do the same, so don't tell him," I said. "He actually would risk his life hopping up and down the Ley Line. But we need to see Ivy in the flesh for sure. She knows about talismans like mine."

"Does she know who might be behind this scheme?"

I shook my head. "Nope. But it sounds like she brought half the council with her. At this point I'd trust their word more than the Sidhe's."

"The enemy is inside the Summer Court itself." His hands clenched at his sides. "Even if we caught them, I doubt the Sidhe would believe one of their own might be a traitor. But I can't think of any other way the enemy might have reached the Court. Nobody is allowed in who isn't spoken for, and only those with Sidhe magic can cross over at all."

"Then the traitor is Sidhe. It's the only explanation." But who? I hadn't met enough of the Sidhe to form an opinion, and surely if any of them wanted the book, they'd have tried to take it from me there and then. But they of all people knew the consequences of claiming a talisman. Maybe they just… didn't want to be anywhere near Death at all. It wouldn't surprise me.

But what did that make Ivy's talisman? Was mine truly that unique? It was reassuring to meet another human neck-deep in this who wasn't a Lynn. *Though technically she might be, distantly.* The curse hadn't affected her. But maybe we had more in common than shared blood. The way my talisman had tried to reach hers… as though it knew her. I'd learnt so much, yet only had more questions.

The book and the blade. Power beyond necromancy, beyond anything I ever knew. Raw, terrifying power, bound into the fabric of the death realm itself.

Like… a goddess of death.

11

I woke up with my chin resting on my knees, dawn light spilling through the window onto the bookshelves of the library and the bean bag where I'd fallen asleep. I'd sat here for hours at a time as a teenager while Hazel and Mum did their top-secret Gatekeeper training. The textbook fell out of my lap as I stretched, my back aching in protest at the weird position I'd fallen asleep in. I picked it up again, yawning. I'd stayed up until the early hours reading through the book and Great-Aunt Enid's notes, and by now, I knew what magic was in my talisman.

I also knew beyond all shadow of a doubt that I could never allow the enemy to get hold of it.

Hazel knocked on the door, nudging it open. "Have you been in here all night?"

"Wouldn't be the first time." I yawned again. "We're not out of coffee, are we?"

"Not yet," Hazel said. "That must have been some marathon studying session."

"That's one way of putting it." I blinked repeatedly to clear the haze from my eyes.

"Are you sure you're okay?" she asked. "You've been acting… off. I don't know, maybe it's just me. I've felt out of it since my magic got shut down, to be honest." She gave a slight laugh. "Gotta love feeling powerless at the worst possible moment."

"Sorry." I rubbed the back of my neck. "What time is it?"

"Ten in the morning. I sent River off to buy groceries because he's the only one of us with cash."

"I have cash."

"You were dead to the world," Morgan said from behind her. "I had to put my hand in a jar of iron to keep your weird dreams out of my head."

"I don't remember any." Now I remembered why pulling all-nighters was usually a bad idea. I needed at least nine hours' sleep to function, and it probably didn't help that I hadn't eaten a proper meal in what felt like days.

"Probably that weirdness you're reading," Morgan said, scooping up the textbook and Great-Aunt Enid's journal. "Must be a good read if you stayed away from River all night."

I stifled another yawn behind my hand. "I thought you didn't like him."

"He's not my type, but he's decent enough for a faerie."

"Thanks for giving your approval." I rolled my eyes at him.

"He hasn't given her faerie pox yet, so he's one step up from the last guy," Hazel put in.

Why did she have to go there? "Give it a rest," I told her.

"Faerie pox?" said Morgan, tossing the books onto the floor again.

"You missed the epic showdown." Hazel ducked as I threw Great-Aunt Enid's diary at her. "Chill, Ilsa. It was a few months after you left… what was his name, Ernest?"

"No!" I groaned. "If either of you tell Mum or River, I'll kill you."

"I'm not a sneak," said Hazel. "You need to get that tension out of your system. Seriously."

"If you didn't already in the forest," said Morgan, walking over to the desk where I'd scattered all my notes.

"You can't bring up the forest without admitting you both got ensnared by the Sidhe, too," I said. "Did they know they were making out with humans?"

"Probably not," she said. "The magic there sent everyone crazy."

"There you have it," I said. "None of us was in our right mind."

"Keep telling yourself that," said Morgan, picking up the spiral-bound notebook I'd been taking notes in. "Come on, I never got to tease you about this stuff before I left. You didn't crush on a different boy every week like Hazel did."

"Maybe I didn't tell you two for a reason?"

Morgan lowered the notebook. "Holy shit. You mean to tell me the Sidhe can *die* now? Actually die?"

"No, I didn't mean to tell you. You weren't supposed to read that. Give it here."

I made a wild lunge for the desk. My legs were half asleep from sitting on the floor all night so I fell into Morgan and knocked him off balance. He grabbed Hazel's arm to steady himself, and we all fell into a heap.

River walked in, eyebrows raised, holding several bags.

"Hey, River," said Morgan. "Want to join the group hug? Ow, Hazel, you trod on my face."

I disentangled my legs from the others and climbed upright. "Morgan, give me that."

"Nope." He held the notebook triumphantly in the air. "I know the Sidhe can die now."

"So does half the Court," I said. "It's not news. If you go around shouting it, they'll kill you."

"They don't scare me anymore." He grinned. "They can *die*. You know how many thousand years those fuckers have held their immortality over the rest of us?"

"Yes, I do, and that's why you can't tell them," I said. "River, did those two send you running errands?"

"I volunteered," he said. "I figured one of us should check on the village and make sure none of those ghosts came back."

"And you brought us food." Morgan grabbed the bag from River and emptied it onto the desk. It contained several sandwich packets and drinks from the only café in the village. River glided to the desk chair before anyone else claimed it and swivelled around, tossing me a sandwich. Despite the speed, I actually caught it.

"Anything but Everett's baking is good with me," said Hazel, perching on the edge of the desk.

I unwrapped the sandwich and took a bite of tuna mayonnaise. "Thanks, River. What were you three doing while I was in here yesterday, anyway?"

"Plotting a way back to the Court," Morgan said, sitting down on the bean bag next to me. "They didn't like my idea to cross over in spirit form and haunt them."

I decided not to mention I could probably do exactly that. "Nope. Not gonna work."

"You never said if you'd reached any new conclusions from all that studying," Hazel said.

"Except the Sidhe can die now," Morgan added, taking a swig of coke from the bottle.

"All of us knew that except you," Hazel said.

Morgan scowled. "You're joking."

"I did find out some things." I put down my half-eaten sandwich. "Not nice ones."

"Go on," said Morgan. The others watched me as well. "You have that slightly manic look."

"Invocations. Gods. The Ancients." I held up Grandma's journal. "The Ancients. She kept writing that word. The faeries' gods. Anyone know about them?"

"The Sidhe?" said Hazel, around a bite of sandwich. "The ones old enough to remember. Nobody in this realm would know, I wouldn't think."

"According to this, the Grey Vale used to be the gods' own realm," I said. "Until the Sidhe kicked them out, and ripped a piece of their own realm away to do it. That's the Vale."

Hazel and River both looked stunned. Morgan shook his head. "So what? They're devious monsters, we know that. It's no surprise that they killed their gods, considering all they want is to be worshipped on a pedestal."

"It gets worse," I said. "The Vale—it's created as a place with no magic."

"And?" said Morgan.

"No *magic*," I said. "Doesn't that imply the gods *had* magic, just like the Sidhe do?"

"Not necessarily," Hazel said. "I mean, sure, let's go with it. They're still dead. Long gone. It's another strike against the Sidhe, but I really don't see what difference it makes to us."

"Their magic still exists in some form." I held up the talisman, and the glowing symbol on the cover.

Morgan dropped the coke bottle on the floor, where it rolled under the desk. "Are you saying one of *them* is in the book?"

"No." I put the talisman back in my pocket. "But their magic is. Think about it. It's clearly not faerie magic, but it's way beyond necromancy too. Maybe the gods had their own type of magic. I think someone might have bound part of this god's magic to the book the way the Sidhe bind their own magic to talismans. Ivy's talisman is the same. It's not man-made at all, but it's not a Sidhe creation either."

River continued to stare at me. "The gods' magic... it's possible, but I've never heard of such a thing in the faerie realm. Summer and Winter magic are all there is. Life and death. They balance each other. A force beyond death... no wonder this talisman wasn't intended for use in Faerie."

"Whether it's true or not, we still need to get back into the Court and root out their traitor," Hazel said. "And I have a way in."

"How?" I asked. "Holly's gate?"

She shook her head. "Walking into Winter without magic... it's a bad idea. But I know the wild fae near Foxwood, and there are rumours about shortcuts into the borderlands. That would take us directly to the Court."

"The borderlands are easily as dangerous as the Winter Court," River said. "They're lawless at best and deadly at worst."

"Not if you know where you're going," Hazel said confidently. "I know this way in, and it leads straight to Summer."

I picked up what was left of my sandwich and took a bite, though my appetite was gone. There was no safe route back into Faerie without risking our necks, and selfish though it may be, I couldn't get Ivy's talisman out of my head. Going to Edinburgh would bring us allies. But I wouldn't kill the others' hopes of rescuing Mum, however much I suspected that our chances of finding her were low.

"If you know the wild fae, then we'll follow your lead," River said. But he it was plain he thought there was a catch. So did I. I'd never been invited to go along with her and Mum to negotiate with the wild faeries, those who lived apart from the Courts, but there was usually a good reason they'd chosen to leave.

Half an hour later, we left the house, armed and ready for

any kind of trouble. I checked the spirit realm before leaving, but nothing stirred. *Let's hope it stays that way.*

Hazel led us down the hill in the opposite direction to the village, past fields of heather. Snow coated the distant mountaintops, while a harsh breeze reminded me of the oncoming winter. We veered off the path after several minutes, and Hazel stopped walking beside a rabbit hole.

A man appeared from nowhere. Morgan and I both jumped violently. The man was red-skinned and bearded, peering at us with curious eyes. "If it isn't the Gatekeeper's daughter."

"Hey," Hazel said. "We seek passage into the borderlands of the Summer Court."

The man gave a low chuckle. "You truly want to enter the borderlands? You'll never walk out alive."

"We seek passage," Hazel repeated. "What payment will you accept?"

I gave her a warning look—making a deal with any faerie wasn't wise, but on the other hand, Mum had trained her for this.

"Bring me four buttons after your return," said the man.

"Okay..." She glanced at us, her expression bewildered. "Thanks."

He grinned and raised a hand. There was a flash of light, and the hillside vanished.

Tangled forest extended in every direction, larger and more extensive than I'd ever seen. I couldn't even see the sky.

"That was it?" Hazel said. "I thought he was going to ask me to answer an impossible riddle. The first one did."

"Who was he?" asked Morgan.

"Little Person," Hazel said. "They live between realms, or so Mum says. Harmless, but they usually ask for more than that."

"What's the catch?" whispered Morgan. "Everything here wants to kill us?"

"Not if I can help it," Hazel muttered. "This place is divided into territories, some from each Court, and I don't know the boundaries by heart. But if we keep walking this way, we'll reach the main path to the Summer Court."

River looked up at the canopy blocking out the sunlight. "The catch is that he brought us to Lady Hornbeam's territory."

"It was hers or someone else's, and they're all equally bad, to be honest," Hazel said. "This is the closest to the Court."

River swore under his breath. "Be on your guard."

The borderlands stood in total contrast to the open fields and bright sunshine of the main Summer Court. Here, while it was warmer than back home, a canopy of branches blocked out most sunlight, casting everything in eerie shadows. Tangled undergrowth marked out paths winding through the trees. No signposts or landmarks, and while Summer's magic remained in the air, it wasn't as overt here.

It was impossible to watch every tree and shadow at once. I kept thinking I saw people in the branches, hidden from sight. Every rustle and whisper set my teeth on edge. Walking softly and quietly over a bed of branches and brambles was a tall order, too, especially with four of us. River walked quietly and lithely, using his magic to clear particularly tangled bits of undergrowth out of our way, but Morgan kept tripping over tree roots and I wasn't exactly a master of stealth either. Even Hazel nearly face-planted into a pond before Morgan caught her at the last moment. We saw no signs of life around, so I damn near screamed when a faerie warrior appeared soundlessly on the path in front of us. I stopped dead, my heart sinking. He'd moved without so much as stirring the branches, like a ghost.

The man wasn't Sidhe. Half-blood, judging by the fact

that I could look directly at him without my brain seizing up. He was dressed in dark-coloured armoured clothes with a crossbow strapped to his back, and had shoulder-length dark hair and a faint scar on his right cheekbone, the one flaw to his eerily pretty appearance.

"Humans," he said, his voice lightly melodic. "Do you know what Lady Hornbeam does to human trespassers?"

"Shows us nice hospitality?" said Morgan.

The half-Sidhe took one step towards us. Pretty faerie appearance aside, there was something starkly inhuman in the way he moved, and the harsh expression on his face told me that he wouldn't hesitate to shoot all of us down with that crossbow of his.

"If I were someone else, you'd be dead, mortals," he said. "However, one of you carries an object of power. I'm curious about it."

He can sense the book? No—he'd seen it. His gaze roamed over us, as though he could see all our secrets.

"That would be mine," River said, taking a step towards him and holding his blade to the light. "It's claimed."

"Naturally," said the half-Sidhe. "May I see?"

River spun the blade in his hands so it came to a resting position pointing right at the half-Sidhe's throat. "I'm in the employ of the Summer Court, acting as bodyguard to the Summer Gatekeeper through the borderland territories. You can tell Lady Hornbeam that we have permission to be here."

"Including the humans?" Incredulity momentarily crossed his expression, and he didn't seem particularly fazed by the blade inches from his neck. "If you lie, mortal, your lives will be forfeit."

"Mortal?" said River, raising an eyebrow. "You're as mortal as I am, thief."

He let the blade pass within a centimetre of the half-Sidhe's throat before pulling it back, green magic shimmering to the hilt. His eyes glowed with it. But the stranger didn't even flinch, as though having deadly blades pointed at him was a daily occurrence.

"How did you guess I was a thief?" said the stranger.

"I'm a bodyguard. It's my job to make accurate assessments of potential adversaries. Why are you so interested in my talisman? It's not an unusual sight, even in the hands of one of us."

A bitter smile twisted the stranger's lips. "I'm a thief. It's my job to steal anything valuable that passes through her territory, and if any... livestock wanders off, it's my duty to return it to her."

"What is it with you people thinking we're sheep?" Morgan snarled, stepping up to him. "We're not livestock, you stuck-up piece of shit. We're people."

"All right, that's enough," Hazel said. "We're in a hurry. Morgan, get back here. Princeling, go back to your palace and leave us in peace."

"Princeling?" said the faerie, scowling. "You have no respect."

"Neither have you," Hazel said. "I'm Summer Gatekeeper, and for your information, we're on our way to prevent an attack on your Court. So if you'd kindly step aside—unless you'd like to help us?"

"My duty is to my family first, mortal," said the thief. "I can't say it's been a pleasure. If I see you again, I'll be forced to report you to Lady Hornbeam. I rather think she'll be less welcoming than I've been."

There was a flicker of movement, and he was gone, like he'd evaporated into thin air.

"Wow," said Hazel. "They do things differently out here in the borderlands."

"What was all that about claimed talismans?" I asked.

"If it wasn't claimed by me," River said, "he'd have stolen

it. Probably without any of us noticing."

"Does anyone else think we just dodged a bullet?" said Morgan.

"Or an iron arrow," said River. "He was carrying iron. I sensed it."

"They use iron on other faeries out here?" I shuddered. "Okay, that's enough borderland territory for me. Let's move."

Our narrow escape set my nerves on edge, and I walked quicker, thinking of sunny glades and gardens. I'd never expected I'd ever think of Summer magic in a positive light, but I sighed in relief at the sight of blessed sunlight ahead. We reached a clearer path winding into the trees. I glimpsed a meadow at one end, and from the opposite direction, a cool breeze blew.

"Summer," said Hazel, directing her steps towards the meadow. "Crossover territory. This is where the council goes in and out of this realm... it's usually harder to avoid attention here, but that hardly matters."

"Here we go." I spotted two Sidhe on horseback.

One was the female messenger Sidhe who'd spoken to us before, and her expression was pure murder.

12

I went completely still as the two Sidhe spotted us.

"Guilty conscience, mortal?" said Lady Aiten, softly. Her hair spilled over her shoulders like a waterfall, while her eyes were startlingly bright. Her magic whispered over my head, promising thorny pain and sharp vengeance.

"What's going on?" asked Hazel and I more or less at the same time.

"Someone in the Court has died." Magic hummed in her voice with another promise of pain.

Holy crap. "Who died?" I asked. *Please not the Erlking. Or the person who sent Mum into the Vale, for that matter.*

"Nobody you know," said Lady Aiten.

"What are you doing here, mortals?" said the second Sidhe—Lord Raivan. "You would do well to stay away from the Court, considering what happened at Lord Niall's revel."

"There's a traitor *in* the Court," I said. "We're here to warn you. One of your own is working with outcasts."

"They stole our gate," Hazel added. "The Summer Gatekeeper's magic has been compromised. Someone in Faerie stole it. Maybe the same person who committed murder."

Lord Raivan's eyes narrowed. "And what is your own alibi, exactly?"

"Our family is locked into a permanent contract to obey this Court," said Hazel. "All of us. If we murdered anyone, it'd rebound horribly."

"Not him." He cast a sharp look at River, whose body stiffened, his hand dropping to his blade.

"He's been with us the whole time," I snapped. "Ask… damn, who was that thief in the borderlands? He can probably confirm which way we came in. We literally just got here."

"And I am in a contract of my own," River said smoothly. "I'm here to aid the Gatekeeper, and it's my belief that there is a threat to this Court within the Grey Vale."

"Don't think I haven't heard your stories, mortal," said Lord Raivan. "You and Ivy Lane both, spreading rumours of the Vale."

"Ivy was here?" I said in disbelief. "Recently? If she confirmed his story, it must be true. She's *been* there. So has River."

"And if you're not careful, you'll be joining the outcasts yourselves," growled Lord Raivan, directing his horse to approach us.

I refused to give ground. "Lord Raivan, I know why this is happening. I request an audience with the Erlking, or whoever is responsible for locking my family into this contract."

"This realm is not your own, mortal," he said softly. "You're not even Gatekeeper."

"Really? I had no idea."

I saw Hazel wince, and felt bad. But not bad enough to stop. The Sidhe deserved a reckoning, and I'd rather the Gatekeepers were the ones to give it to them than the Vale outcasts.

"Whatever special treatment you think you deserve, mortal, you're not one of us," said Lady Aiten.

"It's not special treatment to show basic respect to someone giving you a warning. If you don't listen, you'll only lose more of your own people. Permanently.'

The grass stirred as magic crept beneath my feet. Every instinct told me to get the hell out, but despite the Sidhe's loathing of mortals, there wasn't actually a rule denying our right to be here, even to ask to speak to the Erlking. The Sidhe just weren't obligated to treat us like people. It was entirely possible the Erlking himself would be the same, but I couldn't resist. I doubted anyone had ever asked the question before.

Lord Raivan actually looked surprised, beneath all the magic, his faerie-bright eyes widening a fraction. 'You should know that even most of the Sidhe haven't set eyes on our king for many years. He takes no visitors."

"Look," I said, throwing caution to the winds. "My magic... it's to do with life and death. He has a life-threatening illness, doesn't he? Maybe I can help. And our family made a treaty with the Erlking himself."

"That is impossible," he said.

"It's fact," said Hazel defiantly. "Why not send a messenger and ask him? There has to be a procedure when the Summer Gatekeeper's life is in danger and the gate is compromised. Otherwise, you'll lose the gate forever. If you don't believe the warnings, I can prove *that* is the truth. I've seen it."

"All messages to the Erlking go through the Seelie Queen," said Lady Aiten.

"So there is a Queen?" I asked, glancing at Hazel.

"There is," Hazel said. "But she doesn't share his power. I don't think she's the one who bound the Gatekeepers, but if it's possible to speak to her, it'd be most welcome."

"Not to her," Lord Raivan said. "She has more important matters to deal with than trivial mortal lives."

Morgan opened his mouth to speak and I elbowed him in the ribs. "If we can speak to her, then it might avert a war. Let us try to convince her."

"I will send a messenger," said Lord Raivan. Nodding to Lady Aiten, he wheeled his horse around and the two of them vanished.

"Seelie Queen?" said Morgan. "Never heard of her."

"They don't talk about her," River said. "Because… it's rumoured that her own power is limited. She carries the title by marriage only, and possesses no powerful talisman of her own."

"Oh." I knew how important magic was to the Sidhe. More than anything else. From what I knew of faerie customs, marriages were almost always for power and nothing more. As immortals, they didn't even technically need an heir, though they'd have to change that soon. Most Sidhe had one or more partners for a few decades, then got bored and moved on. Marriage for love was unheard of. If they did have children, those children then claimed their own territories and intermingled with other families. The Sidhe bloodlines were a tangled mess, which was why I hoped someone else was tasked with finding the actual heir, when it came down to it.

If the Erlking had picked a partner who possessed no powerful magic, maybe he actually loved her. Though I didn't think the Sidhe were capable of love in the human sense. They sure seemed to like making fun of our fragile little human emotions, anyway. But maybe they judged one another in a similar manner.

Lord Raivan appeared again, so suddenly that all of us jumped. "No humans are to enter the Court, by the order of the Seelie Queen herself."

My heart plunged. "Now? It's urgent—I didn't lie. Our gate's already been taken, and our mother—"

"If you were idiotic enough to lose control of your magic, then it's your job to retrieve it."

"Someone in *your* Court took my magic," said Hazel. "It's never happened to any of the past Gatekeepers, so can't you make an exception?"

He cocked a brow. "Really? What is it that makes you children so certain that nobody before you has ever suffered misfortune?"

"That's not what I said," Hazel told him. "And you wouldn't know anything about misfortune, because your magic protects you from getting so much as a paper cut."

"You even fucked up your own realm so nobody would ever have to die," said Morgan. "That's not just unfortunate, it's plain *sad.*"

Anger flashed in the Sidhe's eyes. "If you had the slightest comprehension—"

"Your head's too far up your own arse to see the daylight." Morgan gesticulated at the blazing sun. "Even *that's* probably fake. You're living on borrowed time, and you can call us stupid little mortals all you like. You're doomed."

"Too far, Morgan," Hazel said out of the corner of her mouth. "So, if you don't mind, we're planning on saving your ungrateful necks. Let us speak to the Erlking's representative. If they want to strike us down, that's their prerogative, but I'm not moving from here. And you know what it will cost you if you take my life. Assume the same is the case if you attack my family."

"Lord Raivan, allow me to handle this." A hard-faced silver-haired Sidhe warrior strode up to us, talisman in hand. Like River's, it was carved into the shape of a sword, bright with runes and radiant with power. "I couldn't help overhearing that this little band of mortals would like to speak with the Seelie King."

He turned on us. I froze a little inside. You'd think seeing one Sidhe would neutralise the effects a bit, but if anything, the impact of each Sidhe's appearance was worse. His stare was pure malice, weaponised against us. Thorns twined around the talisman in his hand.

"And you are?" asked Hazel.

"My name is Lord Daival," he said, his gaze travelling across our group. River gripped his own sword so tightly, his knuckles turned white. "As one of you once employed by the Summer Court knows well."

"Actually," River said, "I'm still in the employ of the Summer Court, as it wasn't I who broke the law."

"There is no law against showing mortals their place," said the Sidhe.

An icy pit formed inside me. *He's the one who kept humans prisoner. And River freed them.* The magic surrounding Lord Daival told me that he was more powerful, and had more authority, than any of the Sidhe I'd met so far. When River had said he'd made a calculated risk in freeing the humans, I hadn't quite grasped just how badly it could have gone. Worse, Lord Raivan had disappeared, leaving us alone with him.

"The Court begs to differ," River said. He didn't *sound* terrified, but he must be. Nobody could look at that Sidhe and not feel mortal fear. I did, and I carried the freaking death book in my hands.

"I'm the one who wanted to speak with someone who has access to the Erlking's inner circle," said Hazel. "If not the Seelie Queen, then someone else."

"You dare to ask to speak with the Erlking?" he said.

"Yes, I do. I'm Summer Gatekeeper. Her heir, anyway. It's urgent—"

"As far as I am concerned, you're nothing more than a filthy mortal who doesn't know their place," said Lord Daival softly. "All of you."

"Oh, you're talking about me?" Morgan said. Was I the only person here who felt a normal amount of trepidation towards antagonising the walking nuclear weapon in front of us? Antagonising him was like squirting a water pistol into a troll's eye, or setting a dryad's tree on fire.

Thorns lashed from Lord Daival's weapon, wrapping around Morgan's legs. He swore loudly. "Get off me, you bastard."

"Let go of him," Hazel. The thorns twisted in the air, wrapping around her legs, too. *This isn't how it was meant to go.*

River stepped forward, his talisman gleaming with green light. *No.* He was going to retaliate, and then they'd kill all four of us.

"Let her go!" I shouted at the Sidhe. "Hazel and I are in your service—our family is bound to yours for life. You kill Morgan and Hazel and you violate your own treaty."

"Would you prefer to add to your own criminal record, Lord Daival?" River enquired. "The Sidhe won't forget what you did. Killing the Gatekeeper won't do anything but cause more trouble for you *and* for your Court. It'd be a poor way to repay the Lynn family for their services."

As Lord Daival's attention shifted from me to River, I stuck my hand in my pocket, and grabbed the book.

Power roared through my veins, a wave of cold energy. *I shouldn't feel it so strongly here.* The light brightened, and Lord Daival turned on me, his eyes widening. I didn't have a clue what I looked like to him, but it frightened him, and that was enough. In the realm of light, I shouldn't be able to sense death's touch, but I did. It lay everywhere, beneath the bright magic, beneath it all. It was all fake. I saw the hole of empty darkness where I'd sent those wraiths—

Magic exploded from Hazel's hands, pushing the vines away from her. Her forehead glowed with green light once again. I dropped my hands, and the cold magic faded, even as its ache remained in my chest, insistent, angry.

"You mortals are a disease that must be wiped from existence," said Lord Daival, in a quiet, deadly voice.

"Same old," Hazel said. "Also, you forgot this place gives my magic a boost, too, even now someone's draining it away. You *gave* me this power. If you want to retract your gift, you have to deal with the fact that Winter will have a representative on the human side to protect you from the evil death faeries and you won't."

"We are perfectly capable of protecting ourselves." He wouldn't look directly at me, and hadn't addressed what I'd done. Had I terrified him that much? "Luckily, it's not up to me whether you keep your position or not."

"But it is up to me." A radiant figure with flaxen hair spun with wildflowers appeared from the trees, like a fallen sunbeam given flesh. She smiled, and the world stopped. The last of the thorns faded as her magic whispered through the meadow, a soft caress on my neck. Comforting, and chilling, because now I'd seen that cold emptiness beneath this realm, I knew what shadows lay beneath that beauty and magic.

"May I speak to them?" she enquired. "I rather think I might be of better help for their purpose, Lord Daival."

"Your majesty," he said in a tone suddenly deferential, worshipful.

The Seelie Queen. I should probably curtsy or something, but my legs were frozen, and so was my whole body. The others remained similarly immobile. If the other Sidhe could strike us down, this Sidhe could rend us to pieces without moving an inch.

"That's enough toying with the mortals, Lord Daival," she said, and the spell broke.

"Your majesty," said Hazel. "We didn't want to intervene, but there's something really important we need to tell the Erlking. I'm the Summer—"

"Gatekeeper's heir. Of course you are. I'd know the mark anywhere."

She knows. It might even be her that our family's magic was bound to, because she certainly held a shit-ton of power of her own, talisman or none. I kind of hoped she'd thwack Lord Daival on the head to get him out of the way, but instead, the scene changed subtly, and the five of us stood in an empty field. Lord Daival was nowhere in sight.

"Much better," said the Seelie Queen. "I haven't spoken to a Gatekeeper in a long time."

"So you didn't speak to Mum, then?" asked Hazel. "She… well. She's in a lot of trouble, and so is the Court. There's a traitor, but I guess you already know that. They're working with Vale outcasts."

"There are always traitors," she said. "Always. Where there is power, there's ambition, the desire for more power. Many will violate the laws of the Court to seize it. Many others will put on the appearance of serving while planning to undermine everything we are. We forget our past so easily, caught in an endless present."

I blinked. *She's a little more self-aware than any other Sidhe I've met.* Didn't mean I had a clue what to say to her. She was so terrifying… and when I put my hand in my pocket for the book, it… stuck.

The book didn't want me to show it to her. That meant she couldn't have been the one to bind it, right?

"So you're married to the Erlking?" asked Morgan. "Why not take the throne? He's been half-dead for decades, they say."

Hazel winced, but the Seelie Queen merely smiled. "Ruling isn't what it appears to be. I rather think the whole system needs an overhaul… new blood, as the humans say. If you wish to speak with the Erlking, I do think you'll be disappointed. You're right in thinking he hasn't been coherent for years. But I may be capable of helping you myself."

Hmm. Her words made sense, delivered in her all-too-melodic voice… but the false modesty, the all-too-clear awareness of the flaws in the Sidhe's system… it didn't ring true to me at all. Like a glamour, I saw beneath. She *had* power. She wasn't trapped. She was here on purpose—and nobody else was within sight.

"Guys," I said quietly. "We need to move."

She smiled her pretty smile at me. "Don't you want to talk to the Erlking?"

"You said he can't talk to us," I said. "You have four mortals here in the most secure part of the Court, yet you haven't checked us for weapons. You haven't taken away our iron, and you never even asked what I did to Lord Daival."

"This isn't the Erlking's territory," said River, gripping his sword. "Who are you really?"

"I am exactly who I said I was," she said, her voice soft, her smile pleasant. Cold fear took root inside me.

"What do you want with our family?" asked Hazel.

"Want? Nothing at all. The Gatekeepers are irrelevant, and I'm sure you'd be happier never to set foot in this realm again, wouldn't you?"

Hazel shook her head. "Happier? Sure. A lot of people would also be dead. And if you're really the Seelie Queen, you should know we're tied into a vow with your Court through our very bloodline."

"I hold as little power as any who doesn't rule, and more than most." Magic thrummed in her gaze. "It's time for a change of leadership in Summer. And it's time for you to leave. I hope the Vale is kinder to you than its other inhabitants. You're human, which should work in your favour. Good luck."

The trees faded out, and so did the meadow. The last thing I saw was her brilliant smile before nothing but grey remained.

13

The Grey Vale's paths stretched out endlessly. Coldness permeated the air, not the freezing atmosphere of Death but the absence of life energy and warmth.

Oh, damn.

"Anyone have a map?" asked Morgan.

"I don't believe this," said Hazel. "I can control this place. Right? I should be able to find our mother in here."

"Perhaps," River said. "The Vale doesn't follow a fixed map, and anyone with Sidhe magic can arrange the environment according to their own needs. That includes me, and possibly you as well, Hazel. It's usually just Sidhe, but you probably have enough magic for it to work."

But not me.

Morgan gave me a sideways look as though the same thought had occurred to him. "Great. We'll skip along at random and hope we don't fall in a pond."

"We're in better shape than most outcasts," River said. "They're generally stripped of their talismans before being kicked out."

"Can that thing open a way out?" Morgan asked, eyeing the book's shape in my pocket.

"No," River said. "Ilsa…"

"I'm thinking," I said. "I can only hop over between realms as a ghost, and I probably won't be allowed to take you guys with me." I pulled out the book despite myself, but it didn't light up with helpful information. *The Grey Vale*, I thought clearly, skipping to the back. "Nope. Great. I can travel as a ghost. No clue how to get out otherwise."

"Isn't this a dead end?" said Morgan. Before I could stop him, his body froze. I switched on my spirit sight and saw greyness, but no different to the way the path looked to begin with.

"Yes, it is," I said. "You can't move on here if you die. Those half-bloods were stuck here, that's why they agreed to help out the enemy. Ideally we need to *find* the enemy, and get back into the land of the living. Relatively speaking."

The spirit sight switched off, and the scene didn't change at all.

Morgan shook his head. "I can probably run for miles as a ghost, but it all *looks* the same."

"If I have control, so does Mum," said Hazel. "Right? River, where was she when you last came here?"

"I met her at a house near a lake, but that was weeks ago," he answered.

"What does she think this is, a holiday?" asked Morgan.

"A house near a lake?" said Hazel. "Walk with me. If she was there, it's got to be safe, right?"

"I didn't stay long enough to determine if that was the case," River said. "Wait—this isn't the place to make hasty decisions."

The path ahead flickered, a lake appearing and disappearing again.

"Stop that," Hazel snapped at River. "If we both try to affect the path at once, it'll get confused. Stop—"

She broke off. Cold water flowed over my feet, without warning, and when I took a step, my shoe sank into marshy ground. We'd landed in the marshes at the edge of a vast lake, surrounded by trees. Even the water was the same muted grey colour as the trees.

"Thanks a bunch, River," said Hazel.

River twisted to glare at her. "Magic can't get confused. This was deliberate. Someone else is here."

A chill ran down my back. *Someone else... with magic?* Nobody appeared to be around, but splashes came from the water, and there didn't seem to be a path leading away into the forest. Not without skirting the lake.

"Is that the house?" asked Morgan.

There was indeed a hut on the river, but it sure as hell didn't look like the sort of place Mum would pick to stay in. Ramshackle and tilting at an angle, it looked like one wrong movement would send it plummeting into the lake.

"Mum." Hazel took a step forward. "Damn. I'd normally sense her, but faerie magic doesn't work here—Morgan!"

He swore and pulled his leg free from where it'd sunk into the marsh. "Well done," he said. "Mum isn't here. This is faerieland, everything here wants to eat us—"

Several greyish heads poked up from the water.

"Merrows," said River.

"What in hell is a merrow?" asked Morgan.

"Think mermaids, but less nice," River said.

"Mermaids are dicks," Hazel said. "Great." She took a step backwards. "Get away... why isn't my magic working?"

"I told you," River said. "We're on someone's territory. Their magic is keeping us here."

"Then we'll go back—"

Grey hands grabbed my legs. I swore and kicked out,

seeing the others were similarly ensnared. I grabbed the jar of iron filings from my pocket and threw some of them at the muddy ground, but the iron simply sank into the mud. No use using iron when I couldn't even see my opponents. The hands were buried beneath the mud, pulling me deeper along with them.

River's sword stabbed down into the water. The hands let go of him, but his sword remained wedged in the mud.

"Well done," Morgan said, kicking out. "Ow. Bloody monsters. What's grabbing me?"

"Grindylows," said Hazel. "I can't access my magic here."

Her hands glowed faintly green, but not enough. She'd probably burned herself out fending off those thorns. *Dammit.* All I had was salt and a knife, but the webbed hands latched onto my ankles and refused to let go. The other grey heads drew closer, bobbing in the water. Grey-skinned, human-sized creatures with webbed hands and feet and flat frog-like heads crawled to the surface, grabbing the nearest target—Morgan.

I threw a handful of iron filings at them. So did Morgan. The merrow let go, making furious noises, and oozed towards me instead. The hands holding me dragged me forwards, forcing me to my knees. Sticky mud encased my legs. River swore, throwing an iron knife, but the grindylows' hands rose from the mud to snatch the weapon out of the air. Hisses and yelps came from below—the iron had burned them—but his weapon was gone.

Gritting my teeth, I grabbed the book, slipping out of my body. The slimy mud continued to climb. Morgan was submerged, too, while Hazel clung to a tree branch and River used his buried sword for balance as the swampy mud climbed ever higher.

Better hope necromancy works here.

I floated, pulling the book's power into me, remembering

when I'd been on the cusp of entering this realm. It had power. Not as much as our realm, but so many had died here, I must be able to use necromancy.

The air stirred. Coldness grew, a dark pit forming in the air. *No. Not that.*

The merrows turned around, screaming loudly at the sight of the growing form of darkness above the swamp. As one, they ran back to the deepest water and plunged into its depths. The dark shape continued to grow, cold energy stirring, the surface of the water freezing before my eyes.

With a tremendous cracking noise, River pulled his blade free from the now-iced marsh, while Hazel managed to crawl onto the branch. Morgan freed his leg, swearing loudly. And I continued to float in the air, power burning from my hands as the wraith solidified, drawn to my power. *Go away!*

Magical energy surged from the wraith's hands, only to hit my shield. I jerked back into my body, my feet coming free from the frozen mud. "Guys, run! You can't banish it here."

"You have got to be kidding me, Ilsa," Hazel shouted, clinging to the tree branch.

"I didn't mean to summon it."

I'd meant to get rid of the monsters. I hadn't even spoken the summoning words. But the book's magic attracted the dead.

Hazel's hands splayed and a trickle of Summer magic struck the wraith, to no effect. My heart dropped when River advanced on it, across the ice, blade raised. *Wait... he can do more damage with that here.* The wraith was more solid than usual, so much that I suspected even an ordinary human without the Sight would be able to see it in this realm. Its form was almost human. A Sidhe, a Winter one, who'd died here in the realm of the exiles, filled with so much rage that its magic had survived beyond death.

I swallowed, my mouth dry. Necromantic power still hummed inside me, but I couldn't free this wraith from its prison, not here.

Or can I? It wasn't like I'd ever tried.

I called the book's magic. Power rolled through my veins, pouring from my fingertips, and struck the wraith in an explosion of light. Its shadowy form became more distinct, and I squinted through the grey light, seeing its trapped clawed monstrous true form.

The ground froze underfoot, icy swamp water encasing my boots. Morgan drew something from his pocket—a necromancer's spirit sensor—and hit the button. A jet of concentrated salt slammed into the wraith, knocking it away from me.

"Thanks," I gasped, freeing my leg from the icy prison. I called the book's magic once more, but Death didn't open. My teeth rattled with the torrent of power, but when I spoke the banishing words, nothing happened.

Then I'll have to finish it another way.

Necromantic power filled the air as River attacked it from behind. With his free hand, he raised the sword, green energy shimmering up to the hilt. He threw the blade in an arc, and the wraith screamed as it pierced through its transparent form.

At the same time, I blasted it with necromantic power. The wraith's form cracked all over, pieces flaking away, and it disintegrated.

"It can't reform," River said, treading carefully over the half-frozen ground. I reached the blade first and handed it back to him. "Not enough magic here."

"How'd you find any life energy here in the first place?" Hazel asked.

"There's a little underneath the swamp," River said. "Otherwise, I drew on my own reserves. I won't be able to keep doing that, otherwise my healing ability will switch off."

"I forgot you even had that," Hazel commented. "You're one step ahead of the rest of us."

River shook his head. He looked pale under the swamp water. I'd never seen a Summer faerie use their own life energy to power a spell. It struck me as a highly risky thing to do, but here, it was probably the only option.

"Don't overdo it," I said. "You're the only one here with the ability to cross realms directly if we find a nice Sidhe to help us escape."

"I think we're more likely to find a flying motorbike," said Morgan, swearing as his feet stuck in the melting ice-covered mud. "Can't you or Hazel make this bloody swamp disappear?"

"No," said River. "We need to find an alternate route through the trees." He looked around and pointed to the forest creeping down the lake's side.

"Guys," I said. "I'm sorry. I didn't know using my magic would draw that thing here."

"You did better than me," said Morgan. "I was trying to attack it with my mind. Didn't do a thing."

"We've all probably caught our death of cold, but we're still in one piece," Hazel said shakily. "*How* is Mum coping in this place without magic? The whole realm is set against humans."

"I think it's meant to be set against Sidhe," River said, shaking mud from the end of his blade. "They're banished here with no magic. They'd be dead in a day."

"That wraith wasn't," I pointed out. "It still had magic."

"Then it was an outcast who came here on purpose, I'd guess," River said. "Even those with magic can't survive here. There's no life, and no death either. Not the sort that powers Winter magic."

"This sort, though." I held up the book, the only part of me not covered in swamp water. "It's not powered by being here, but it's not underpowered, either."

Gods' magic. The Ancients. How could you harness that kind of power? Where had it even come from?

The Vale was created when the Sidhe cast out their gods…

My teeth chattered. River drew in closer to me, but he was shivering, too. His eyes had paled, leached of Summer magic. Not a good sign. "Don't do that again," I told him. "Use necromancy if we run into another of those things. I know it probably attracts more of them, but…"

"I'm willing to do whatever's necessary to get us all out in one piece," River said quietly. "To get *you* out of here. I think you should probably put that book away."

We climbed the bank of the lake and walked carefully through silvery undergrowth. There were less wildly growing plants than there were in the borderlands, though the Vale bore a certain similarity to Lady Hornbeam's territory underneath the grey. Of course, nothing actually grew here. The trees looked like ordinary oak and ash, but appeared to be frozen in time, their silvery leaves seasonless and empty of life. Not dead, not alive. I shivered harder, unable to get warm no matter how quickly I walked. The others didn't look much better. Morgan was limping. Hazel's damp hair clung to her face, hiding the Gatekeeper's mark. I doubted anyone out here cared about her status.

"Finally," Hazel said as we reached the path again. "Okay. Take us to Mum, you treacherous dead end of a forest."

The path didn't move. It looked identical to the last one. Hazel sighed heavily and continued to walk. So did I. My legs felt like lead weights, and the swamp water soaking my jeans didn't help. Usually when I used necromancy, I felt more alive and alert. Now I felt more like I'd volunteered my own life energy to River's spell.

The realm couldn't have no beginning or ending. Even Faerie… okay, I didn't know about Faerie. It was usually best not to think too hard about these things when magic was involved.

The book kept glowing. Like it wanted me to use its magic again. *Nope. No more wraiths.* We might not get lucky next time. River was still in the lead, but whenever he looked back to check on us, his face was lined with exhaustion.

"Can't you ask the path to lead us out of this realm?" I asked. "I know there aren't supposed to be exits, but someone's clearly hopping in and out of the Court. There's no harm in checking."

River walked ahead without speaking, no longer moving at swift faerie speed. "No. There isn't one, not open anyway."

The path continued. I groaned. "Okay, let me think. If there's no way out… is there a *person* who can get us out?"

River shook his head. "I wouldn't. That would take us directly to the nearest Sidhe, and just because they *can* leave this realm doesn't mean they'd have any intention of helping us. There are no allies here."

"Dammit." The book glowed brighter, and a shock of energy made me jump into the air. "I think the talisman's trying to tell me something."

"A warning?" said Hazel. "I—" She cut off in a startled shout as tree branches wrapped around her legs, pulling her into the earth.

I ran towards her, and branches grabbed my own feet. "Dammit."

Morgan disappeared beneath the earth. River swore and grabbed his blade, but they'd *gone*. The book glowed brighter. I pulled it out and opened it. The pages shimmered too brightly to read. Necromantic power poured from my fingertips at the branches, but they refused to let go. They weren't alive or dead, so my magic did nothing but rattle the branches without damaging them.

The ground gave way. River shouted my name. I closed my eyes, expecting to be hit by soil, but the earth appeared to be made of nothing but silvery leaves, which fell in slow motion either side of me. I stared, so mesmerised for a second that I forgot about the branches' death grip on my legs.

Then I hit the dirt—or I would have, if more branches hadn't risen to break my fall. We were in a cave, and branches held both Hazel and Morgan captive. Dried blood splattered the ground, and bones lay in crumpled heaps, including human-looking skulls. A foul smell emanated from one corner, where the corpse of a large furred boar-like creature lay on the ground.

"What the hell are you, some kind of carnivorous dryads?" Morgan wanted to know.

Rotting trees, half dead, holding us captive. I swallowed hard. They were the darker Summer magic type, which fed on life energy. If necromancy didn't work, maybe iron would. I grabbed the iron filings container, but I'd lost too many of them in the lake. The iron simply bounced off the branches.

"It'd be nice of River to come and help," Hazel said, struggling against the branches. "Ow. Why'd they take us and not him?"

"Probably because his blade could take them to pieces." I looked up at the high ceiling, grabbing the knife from my bag. Attacking the trees would provoke a reaction, so I needed to move fast.

The knife barely made a dent in the tree's tough branch. I gritted my teeth and sawed harder.

"Doesn't work," Hazel said, hacking away with her own knife.

"Shit." I grabbed the book, skipping for the pages that told us how to get rid of man-eating dryads. There weren't any. *Think, Ilsa.*

"Humans," purred a voice. A humanoid creature with skin like bark entered the cave from the far end. *Ugh. Vale faeries.* I didn't even know what this one was, maybe a cross between a skin-eater and a carnivorous dryad.

"Let us go, you sick fuck," said Hazel.

"It's so rare that my pets get to feast on human flesh..." The creature stepped into the light, which didn't do its bark-like face any favours. Its eyes gleamed like torchlights. "You're a rare gift. So much life..."

Hazel swore, leaning out of reach of the monster's blade-like hand.

The creature laughed. "Your life magic won't work down here... we're all dead."

The spirit realm folded over my vision... and the corpse in the corner rose to its feet. I gagged on the smell. "What the—?"

The human-like bones lying on the floor shifted, then rose upright into the semblance of a person.

"Looks like your prey isn't as dead as you thought," said Morgan.

No way. He didn't.

The furred beast's corpse shambled towards the fae creature. So did the bony human remains. In fact, the whole cave was buried in bones. I tapped into my spirit sight again and reached below the earth. Reanimating bones that old required a surge of life energy, but I didn't need to hold them for long. Just enough to get us out.

Bones reformed into human and fae-like shapes, pulling themselves from the earth. The fae creature backed up, terror suffusing its craggy features. I twitched my leg, drew back and kicked, *hard.* The branch's grip loosened enough for me to cut one leg free and then the other. Hazel had already freed herself, and we went to Morgan. He was almost submerged in branches, his expression glazed as he kept the dead under his control.

The fae creature bolted from the cave. I ran to Morgan and hacked away with the knife, and Hazel joined me. Finally, he broke free from the branches, the silvery light fading from his eyes.

Morgan fell onto Hazel, groaning. "Might've overdone it."

"You're a genius," said Hazel.

"Obviously."

I snorted, then groaned. "River probably thinks we're dead. Can you find him, Hazel?"

"Sure, if I get back to the path." Hazel and I pulled Morgan after us, and we ran towards the only visible exit.

There was no sign of the fae creature in the cave, which had probably run for the hills, and the carnivorous dryads were half buried where the dead had pulled themselves out the earth. But the furred zombie creature kept following us.

"Morgan," I said. "You can't bring a half-rotting corpse home with us."

"Says who?"

I groaned. Hazel shook her head and walked past us through the cave. "I can see daylight up there."

We emerged into undergrowth. Hazel climbed ahead, grabbing tree roots to pull herself up the sharp rise. Morgan and I followed more slowly, having to stop and disentangle ourselves from various bramble thickets and tree roots— thankfully not man-eating ones this time. Eventually, we reached the path. If it was the same path we'd been pulled into the cave from, I couldn't tell. Silver trees, silver leaves, grey light.

"Is River here?" I asked Hazel.

"Don't get so agitated. We won't leave your boyfriend behind."

The path changed before our eyes, revealing River and the fae monster, his sword buried in its neck. Blood splattered his face, but it had the blue tinge of faerie blood, not his own.

His eyes widened. "Ilsa."

Hazel punched the air. "I finally got the bloody path to move where I told it."

River drew closer to me. "Are you hurt?"

"Nope. We escaped cannibal trees by reanimating dead bodies." I glanced at Morgan. "His idea. I wish I'd thought of it."

"I thought I sensed necromancy." River looked me up and down as though scanning me for injuries. "Was this creature the one who trapped you?"

"Yep." I shot Morgan a look. "Call off the zombie boar." I tapped into my spirit sight pointedly, which showed me the energy reanimating its corpse… and I saw the path ahead, swamped in grey light. I hadn't just seen trees like that in the Vale, but in the liminal spaces like the one we'd left the ghost in. Spaces which overlapped so closely with the Vale, it was easy to cross between realms there.

"I have an idea," I said. "I think. Hellhounds can walk in and out of this realm all the time, right?"

"I'm not searching for hellhounds," said Hazel.

"Search for a liminal space, then," I said. "Once we're at a liminal point, I can get us out. This realm *does* overlap with the Ley Line. Its magic—or whatever keeps this realm functioning—is tied to Death, and through that…"

"The mortal realm," River said. "But I always thought the connection was one-way."

"It usually is." I held up the book. "But so is the way into Death. It's worth a try."

I called on the book's cold, unrelenting energy, picturing the liminal space from before.

"This isn't a liminal space," said Hazel, pointing ahead. "It's the forest. Looks the same."

"Some liminal spaces look like that, too. Keep walking. Wait—you're the one who can control the paths, right? You and River, picture a liminal space. I'll try to take us there."

The air went transparent for a second, showing a hillside beneath. Then it turned into woods again.

"This is where we got into the Court," said Hazel. "No way."

"You must have been thinking about it when you changed the path," I said. "Okay. I can use the book to get us out." The grey light grew brighter, and I held up the book, thinking of paths and gates, of ways between worlds.

The path solidified, then turned into the Vale again.

"Nope," I muttered. "Come on." I willed the book's power to keep flooding me, and held up my hands. The air shimmered then went transparent again. With a push, like closing the gates of death, I *shoved* the air, and it parted.

Necromantic energy blasted me off my feet. The gate opened, wide. I pushed carefully, meaningfully—

And a pair of icy blue eyes stared back.

A startled scream caught in my throat, but I didn't move or stop, gripping the book like a lifeline. The gates closed on the terrifying eyes, and I dropped to my knees.

She couldn't have survived. She shouldn't have.

Icy water rose to drench me, and I gasped, spluttering, legs flailing. The cold sky of an autumn day wheeled above me as I heaved myself out of the shallows of a loch. I spat out a mouthful of water. Fresh water.

"Couldn't you have brought us somewhere dry?" said

Morgan, who'd landed in a heap in the shallows. Hazel picked a frog from her hair and stood up.

"Sorry," I said, teeth chattering. The icy water had blasted away my exhaustion. "Did you see that?"

"See what?"

I pressed a hand to my mouth. Holly... did Holly know? Had we unintentionally handed over information to the enemy after all? I wasn't ready for this. Nobody should have the power to bring her back, but the fact that she'd survived at all...

"She's there," I whispered. "The Winter Gatekeeper. She's behind Death's gate. She saw me."

14

Once we'd waded out of the loch—luckily without running into any of the resident kelpies—we began the long walk home.

"We're clean of swamp water now," said Hazel. "Look on the bright side."

"The not-so-bright side is that our nemesis is alive. Or not dead enough," I said.

"It's not possible for her to come back," said River.

"I don't understand either." My vision was splotchy, and my head pounded. "She's there, but not on this side. Yet. I don't know what she's doing, but she still had her power when I banished her."

And she was waiting for me. Whether she was behind what was going on in the Courts or not, I had no idea. But her survival meant things were seriously messed up with the Vale.

Wait—had *I* somehow been responsible for bringing her back, considering all the times I'd used the book? The necromancers were clear about the limits of accessing the realm of the dead, especially on the Ley Line. But I had no choice in the matter. The others would be dead if I hadn't used it, and more would die if I didn't stand between the Winter Gate-keeper and this realm.

Just putting one foot in front of the other was tiring enough. I stumbled forwards, and River put a hand on my shoulder to steady me. His green eyes were concerned. "Ilsa. Are you hurt?"

"No. I think the gate took something out of me." I fell against him, and Hazel caught my arm from behind.

"Don't overdo it. C'mon, we'll get back home."

"I'm fine."

"Now you know how we feel with you mothering us all the time," Morgan said.

"Someone has to," I mumbled. "The Winter Gatekeeper... not just her. How did the Seelie Queen end up being the villain?"

"Of all people, I can't believe it was her," Hazel said. "Don't get me wrong, I've never met her before. But she has power, prestige... there's nothing she can gain from working with the outcasts. We never even found out who died."

"She can gain immortality," I said. "For some, I'd guess anything is worth that. And if they kill their rivals, they don't come back and tell tales. They stay dead."

"It sounds like they've known for a while," River said. "Maybe most of them wouldn't agree with her approach. Some might want their lives to end after so long."

"I think you're being overly optimistic about the Sidhe's attachment to being alive," I said. "Not to mention their magic. Though most of them probably wouldn't ally with outcasts because they'd end up losing their magic if they were caught. That's worse than death for them."

River nodded. "I think you're exactly right."

"But some of them would take the risk," said Hazel. "Nobody's going to question the Seelie Queen's loyalty, are they? It's the perfect setup. She hides behind her status while the others accuse one another."

"But she's not after the book," I added. "Otherwise she'd have tried to take it from me. She'd also have known I could use it against her."

Which made little sense. She couldn't have sent Mum into the Vale, right? The Winter Gatekeeper and the ghost had both had personal grievances with the Gatekeeper and they'd wanted the book for power alone, but the Erlking's wife *had* power.

The Winter Gatekeeper's face flashed before my eyes again. Might she still be influencing people, even though I'd banished her where nobody could survive? Surely she couldn't communicate with the Sidhe, at the very least. But those half-faerie ghosts could move anywhere.

Exhaustion dragged at my limbs, but I forced myself to keep going. Hazel groaned in relief when the house came into view. Only River looked remotely awake. I wished the book had given me healing abilities rather than draining the life out of me, but you couldn't have it all. It'd got us out of the Vale, and that was enough.

Hazel unlocked the door, and we more or less fell into the Lynn house. Getting from the hall to the living room was a blur. I half-lay on the sofa, completely spent. 'Remind me not to drag four people between universes again."

"Remind *me* that all Sidhe are double-crossing bastards," Hazel said, planting herself in the armchair. "For god's sake. What in the world do we do now?"

"Go to Edinburgh and find someone in a position of authority who doesn't want us dead," I said, closing my eyes.

"I meant about the Seelie Queen," Hazel said. "We can't tell them *that.*"

"I can tell Ivy," I said. "She knew the Sidhe weren't immortal before they did, so she knows all about secrecy."

"Might that be why the Seelie Queen's doing this?" asked Hazel. "God—can you imagine accusing her of a crime? If any of us so much as insinuate it in front of any Sidhe, we're dead."

"Precisely," River said. "The best course of action is to do as Ilsa said, and find allies on this side."

"While they plot against us?" Morgan said.

"You saw how quickly the Sidhe will retaliate against you for perceived wrongs," said River. "There is no way to safely pass on that information without putting our own lives at risk. If a fellow Sidhe made the accusation, perhaps, but there were no other witnesses. We need evidence."

"Yeah." He was right, unfortunately. To the Sidhe, power won over anything, even truth. Our word meant nothing at all. Even Hazel's.

"It's not like we found any in the Vale," Hazel said. "Obviously. The Sidhe can walk in and out of that place whenever they like. Any of them might be traitors as well. And the Erlking… isn't exactly keeping an eye on things. She already *is* ruling. Nobody will ever believe us."

———

I woke up on the sofa, cold and aching, but more alert than before. My hair was still damp from the soaking in the loch. I must have passed out mid-conversation.

River sat in the armchair, his eyes closed, exhaustion written into his every feature. No sign of Hazel or Morgan. From the light streaming inside, it was dawn. I'd slept for at least twelve hours. Probably more. My body felt like it'd been… well, thrown into the Grey Vale, dragged through a swamp and then thrown into a loch.

The Vale.

The Seelie Queen.

The Winter Gatekeeper.

Panic clawed up my throat. I took in a breath, slowly, fighting to maintain calm. *Okay. So nobody else has ever faced this before, and nobody will believe us on either side, and I'm pretty sure we've lost most of our allies... but other than that, things are absolutely fine.*

Points in our favour: we'd survived. My family was still alive, if a little battered. I'd tapped into the limits of my power and used it in places even cut off from death. And the Seelie Queen thought we were dead. She wouldn't come after us again... for now.

River's eyes opened. I'd been too exhausted even to tap into the spirit realm, but he'd been watching me all the same.

"Hey," I rasped. "Is it morning?"

"I think so." He still wore his torn, mud-splattered clothes from yesterday. So did I. My jeans were torn from grindylow claws and grasping branches, and the witch spell hiding the mark on my forehead was the only survivor from my weapons stash. Everything else was broken, missing or damaged. Even the container of iron filings.

But not the book. I'd been sleeping with it clasped to my chest, my hands tight around the cover.

"You look awful," he said.

"Thanks."

"I mean it. That book is destroying you, Ilsa."

I shook my head. "There's nothing wrong with me. How else should we have got out of that realm?"

"We never should have been there in the first place," he said. "That talisman's magic is both inside you and inside the book. If you keep pushing it to its limits, you'll break first. The magic is too much to be contained in a human."

"Ivy has faerie magic. Ancient's magic. Whichever."

"I don't know Ivy." Frustration laced his voice. "I know *you*. You know how many times you disconnected from your own body while you were sleeping? We're not even on the Ley Line here. You could have drifted off, and the book would have let you."

My heart jumped. I didn't know he'd been watching over me in more than one sense, let alone that my necromantic powers had been activating while I'd been unconscious. I had no memory of it. Just blurred dreams, some of which River had featured in. I was pretty sure I hadn't floated off into the spirit realm, because in those dreams we'd both been safe and warm and happy, not freezing and tired and scowling at one another.

"I can't control what I do in my dreams, can I?" I said. "I don't know, maybe I got shaken up because the evil spirit I banished appeared and stared at me from behind the gate yesterday. You should worry about her, not me."

"I *am* worried about her," River said. "But I'm more worried about what this magic is doing to you."

"I didn't plan this. It's not like I found the talisman on purpose." I pushed up onto my elbows. "But you know, if I hadn't been there—if I'd ignored the message and stayed in Edinburgh, I'd be living that same life, drifting around like a ghost. I wasn't happy, and the book opened my eyes. More than the Sight ever did. I can't regret that. And I can't imagine things being different. The person I was before—she doesn't exist anymore."

Some events shook up the world. You felt the shift. I'd felt it when I'd opened the window in Edinburgh and Arden had flown in, bringing the scent of magic. I'd felt it when I'd picked up the book and its power had roared through my veins, changing me.

"You have to want this power for you," he said. "Not because you think the book wants you to use it. I might not know that type of talisman, but I know that if you're constantly fighting against it, it's no part of you. It's a separate entity."

A sour taste filled my mouth. "Why can't it be both? Your sword clearly isn't physically attached to you."

He lifted the blade and put it down. Then he stepped away, magic flowing to his hands. The blade didn't glow at all, but the magic dancing over the palms of his hands was undiminished.

"The magic is inside me as well," he said. "I keep the talisman with me in the interests of safety, but it doesn't bother me when I'm not touching it. I control the talisman. Not the other way around." He stepped forwards, lightly tapped the blade's hilt with his foot, and it leapt into his hand.

"You've made your point," I said. "I don't know why my talisman is like this. I can't give it up, though. It's not an option. Do you really trust something so powerful in Morgan's hands instead?"

"It should be sealed away where it can't control anyone."

I gave a bitter laugh. "You *want* me to be a helpless human?"

"You're the opposite of helpless, Ilsa. You were before the book claimed you."

Before the book claimed you. Not before *I'd* claimed the book. Maybe that was my problem, but ditching it wasn't an option. And I wouldn't put up with its side effects to prove a point to River.

I rose to my feet and stepped up to him. His eyes glowed faintly green in the dawn light, and his mouth was curved down at the corners. I wrapped my arms around the back of his head and kissed him. "Chill. I'm not about to take a permanent dive through the gates anytime soon. There are a lot of things I want to do here on earth."

He exhaled and kissed me back, holding onto me like I

was made of glass. "Don't go where I can't come with you," he murmured. "Please."

Oh, River. "I'll try not to."

His hand trailed through my hair, sparking a current of warmth in my blood.

"Hey, Ilsa!" shouted Morgan from the hallway. "You alive?"

"She's fine." Hazel peered around the door. "She wants to be left alone with River."

"No, we need a plan," I said, taking a step back from River as she and Morgan entered the room. "It's time to get to Edinburgh and find Ivy. Unless... I don't suppose you managed to find Holly's house?"

Hazel shook her head. "No. I don't know if the Ley Line moved, or if it's because my magic is fading, but I couldn't find her. I was sure she was on our side this time."

"She might be," I said. "She turned on her mother in the end, you know she did." And she'd given me the books. But how long had the Winter Gatekeeper been lurking out of sight behind the gates?

"Maybe," said Hazel. "Doesn't mean she won't be manipulated."

"I've never met her," said Morgan, leaning on the door frame. "So I'm assuming everyone connected to Death or Faerie is an enemy until further notice."

"Good idea," said Hazel. "At least we have Agnes and Everett on our side."

"And Ivy Lane," I put in. "If she's there, I reckon she can threaten the Seelie Queen. Maybe. Her talisman's on the same level as theirs, and she might have some tips about handling this situation."

Maybe she could explain the dichotomy between what I wanted and what the book wanted me to do. But I wouldn't stop using its power. That wasn't an option.

For the Sidhe, power was enough. But power didn't mean truth, and besides, I couldn't outdo the Sidhe through sheer brute force. They could break me in a thousand ways. But for all their pomp and ceremony, they had the same vices as humans did. They weren't infallible, and they had gaping holes in their knowledge, especially concerning humans.

The person who'd created the book hadn't wanted the Sidhe to know. If the Seelie Queen did, she hadn't said so.

Hazel gave an unsteady laugh. "You know I'm fucked if we all actually make it out of this alive and Mum expects me to interact with the Sidhe as though they deserve respect. They tried to kill us."

"I knew what they were the instant I first saw one," Morgan said. "Maybe that's why the curse skipped me over."

I shook my head. "Well, Mum apparently had an invitation to meet with this council in Edinburgh, but I guess it came after she went to Faerie. Seems a good time to crash their party."

15

Before going to Agnes's place, I stopped at the Lynn family mausoleum and checked the spirit realm to see if Ivy was around. If she hadn't told the council we were coming, we'd have a much harder job explaining ourselves. Then again, there was someone else I could send to pass on a message.

This time, the others all came with me to the mausoleum, where River and I set the candles up again.

"It's fine," I told River. "I stayed too long last time, but I'll only be five minutes this time. If time's up, both you and Morgan have my permission to zap me awake. Deal?"

River nodded. His scowl betrayed his belief that I wasn't taking the danger seriously.

"Come on, I have to warn them we're coming," I told him. "I don't even know what day it is, or if the council is still there." I stepped into the circle. Then I drifted into the spirit world, and looked around the endless grey smoke. "Graves?"

No sign of him. The local necromancers had been quiet since the half-faerie ghosts' attack, probably recovering from the humiliation of not being able to do a thing about them. I rotated on the spot and made for the closest key point. Then the next. The silvery line beneath my feet disappeared in a blur. How much ground had I covered in the mortal realm? Miles, probably. I kept moving, from one point to the next, until the land beneath the line grew familiar. Edinburgh, and the Ley Line, were close by. Maybe I'd find Ivy on the line itself—

I stopped, hovering in the air. Someone else floated close by, an old man in a suit with grey hair.

"Hey, Graves. What are you doing out here?"

The man turned around. "Graves? The name is Lord Sydney, and you must be one of these infamous Lynns."

Oh, crap. Easy mistake to make, considering he and Greaves looked like they might be related. His accent was English, though.

"How do you know my name?" I asked.

He looked at the glowing silver light at my feet as though to confirm I was actually there. "I have an unfortunate partnership of sorts with your distant relation, Ivy Lane."

"Wait, you're Frank the necromancer?"

"The name is *Lord—*"

"Yeah, yeah. Have you seen Ivy? Tell her I'm on my way, and I have epically bad news."

There was the slightest chance Lady Montgomery would lock me in jail again, or the mages would, if I told the entire council about the Seelie Queen being evil. Or worse, I'd be hauled into Faerie and put on trial for lying. There was no way to prove I told the truth, not when the Sidhe were the masters of trickery and glamour. All I had were words—but I of all people knew how powerful words could be.

"Bad news?" said Frank the necromancer. "Is it to do with the downright alarming stories I've heard about you from the necromancers at Edinburgh's guild?"

"Yes, but worse. Is the council still there? I'm coming to

speak to them, now. In person. But I need someone to warn the council that the Summer Gatekeeper needs to talk to them without the Sidhe knowing."

"The Sidhe have no interest in our affairs," said Frank. "And not just anyone is allowed into council meetings."

"Then tell Ivy. Please. I'm not even kidding when I say shit's about to go down across three realms at once."

And all of them might be counting on me.

A flash of light enveloped me, and the next thing I knew, I sat in the circle of candles. Morgan and River stood in front of me, though Hazel had disappeared.

"That wasn't five minutes," I protested.

"Seven, actually," said Morgan. "According to your pedantic boyfriend, anyway."

I glanced at River, who had his arms folded across his chest, one foot resting on the candle.

"All right. If Ivy Lane's necromancer friend tells her and the council we're coming, then we're good." I climbed out of the circle. My skin was a little cold, but not freezing like last time. Travelling along the spirit lines didn't drain me the way crossing realms did.

The mausoleum door opened and Hazel walked back in. "I've asked the necromancers to help the villagers set up defences in case any more ghosts come back while we're gone."

"Good thinking," I said. "I reckon we're the more likely targets... though there's a whole council of magical power-houses gathering in Edinburgh right now."

"And we're joining them," said Hazel.

We walked through the village via Agnes's shop. To my surprise, it was open, and didn't look any worse for wear after the fire. Witch spells could fix anything... except other witch spells. The shelves inside were barer than before, and the faint smell of burning still lingered in the air. Which wasn't that unusual for a witch establishment, really.

"Hey, Agnes," I said, spotting her behind the counter.

"I thought you'd be back sooner," she said.

"Yeah, we got diverted," I said. "We need to get to Edinburgh. Urgently. There's a council meeting there and we need to report someone important from Faerie for treachery before people get killed."

"Come through here." She beckoned through the curtain at the side of the counter, hidden in shadow. Inside was a spacious room that looked like a cross between a sitting room and a laboratory. Everett occupied one corner, surrounded by herbs and ingredients. From the smell, he was making replacement illusion spells for the ones lost in the fire.

I watched for a moment as the small outline of a dragon materialised over the chalk circle he'd etched on the floor, flew in a circle, then disappeared into the illusion charm lying in the centre. Everett caught my eye and grinned. He didn't have his wife's overwhelming personality and it was easy to forget that most of the dangerous and useful spells we used were hand-crafted by him.

"You all look terrible," Agnes commented. "How long did the faeries keep you for?"

"Believe it or not, it was only a day." I climbed over boxes of ingredients to the seating area, and told her a summary of our recent events. I didn't know what shocked her more, the Seelie Queen's treachery or the Winter Gatekeeper sticking around after death. Mostly because she didn't react to either of those revelations with anything other than her usual calm detachment. I wished I *could* bring her to Faerie. Her aura of absolute calm and confidence would be a blessed contrast to the Sidhe's ridiculous dramatics.

"I can't find Graves," I said. "He wouldn't be able to stop the Winter Gatekeeper even if he was still alive, and if she could get through the gates, she would have already. She's just hanging there."

Agnes nodded. "You're right. It'd take a vast amount of power to bring her back."

"I don't get this," I said. "Is the Seelie Queen working with her? I guess they could theoretically communicate through the Grey Vale, and the Queen can walk into *this* realm if she wanted to. But I don't see why she'd want to. Undermining her own Court isn't wise."

"Mum doesn't have anything on her," added Hazel. "Tons of speculation on the Erlking, not so much on his wife. Pretty sure she isn't even his first wife. No idea whether they have children... apparently they don't do family trees there. Guess because nobody dies, they don't see the need to keep a record of who's related to whom. But it's a pain, because we have nothing to go by. If we could speak to the Erlking himself... but none of this explains how our family wound up tied to them. It's not her who's in control of the curse."

"The Erlking?" I asked. "No... all the stories say Thomas Lynn met a faerie *queen*, right?"

"You know stories," said Hazel. "If even our family doesn't know the full truth, nobody else will."

Agnes turned to me. "You said you'd come to a conclusion about that book?"

"Yeah, you might say that. Its magic isn't Sidhe, but from one of their exiled gods. The Ancients. I don't suppose you've heard of them? Even Mum didn't mention them."

Agnes went very still. "Who told you this? The Ancients' magic shouldn't exist in its original form."

"You met one?" said Morgan.

"I'm not *that* old, you ingrate," she said to Morgan. "There are stories of Ancients visiting this realm at least as old as the Sidhe, if not older. I'd be more inclined to think of the Ancients as the Sidhe's powerful predecessors rather than gods in the omnipotent sense."

"Obviously they're not all-powerful if they got kicked out and exiled," said Hazel. "Why did Mum not tell me this? For that matter, how do *you* know?"

"Over the years, I've met a great many people whose magical talents fall outside of the usual boundaries," said Agnes. "This village was one of many places of safety for supernaturals in the old world, but some were intended as places to hide from each other as much as from humans. They say the gods were shapeshifters with immense power, including an unconventional relationship with the divides between realms."

My mouth dropped open. "Does that mean they might still be out there somewhere?"

In the Vale? Or—between the Vale and earth, or the liminal spaces? Anything was possible.

"You're saying our family dealt directly with one of these gods?" Hazel asked.

Agnes shook her head. "By all accounts, the gods are dead. But their magic lives on."

"Because the Sidhe didn't just kill their gods," I said. "They stole their power."

"Precisely."

Chills raced down my back. Maybe that wasn't all they'd stolen. Ivy's voice replayed in my head: *a cauldron full of blood.* Whose blood? Perhaps the Sidhe had manufactured their own immortality, and they'd stolen from the gods to do so. And the power of one of those gods rested in *my* hands.

"So—I'm supposed to use the book against the enemy? Banishing the Winter Gatekeeper didn't work the first time.

And I don't know if I can even use it on the Sidhe. But I can use it in their realm, even in the Vale."

"It nearly killed her," River said to Agnes. "The book's power… is there any way for Ilsa to protect herself? It's more powerful than a human."

"Most of us with power struggle to find that balance," she said. "I could erase all the memories of every person in this room, at a great cost. I've lost friends over it… people who claimed to want their memories erased but didn't understand what they were really asking for. It's a personal choice, and unfortunately not one I can help with."

I thought not.

"Why tell her?" said Morgan, jerking his head at Agnes. "She might be an enemy, right?"

"No, she isn't," I said. "Also, unlike someone, she won't stride into Faerie and get into a fight."

"I'm tempted to," Agnes muttered. "Of all the skills I could have had, I was always glad to have one which did not drag me into a position of diplomatic conflict. My sister got involved in supernatural disputes and paid dearly for it. But staying here hasn't done me any favours. The village, however, needs protection in any form I can give it. If you want to reach Edinburgh before the meeting, I'd suggest leaving now."

"Leaving where?" said Morgan, looking around the room.

"Here." Everett indicated a mirror of clear glass, which didn't bear so much as a scorch mark from the fire. If anything it looked brighter than most mirrors did, as though sunlight was trapped inside it.

"What's that?" I asked, getting to my feet.

"A very rare transportation device," Agnes said. "There are two. The second is in Edinburgh, in the mages' headquarters. I must ask you to tell nobody else about this mirror. I'm looking after it for a friend of mine, and she won't be happy if anything happens to it."

I walked up to the mirror, examining its shimmering surface. My own reflection stared back, my forehead still glowing. Damn. Lucky I hadn't seen anyone else on the way here.

Morgan looked sceptically at the mirror. "So we just dive through?"

"If you want to land on your face, yes," said Agnes. "Most of our spells were damaged in the fire, but you might find these helpful." She held out a handful of bracelets, and a familiar pendant.

"Illusion," I said. "Er, why not tell me my forehead was glowing?"

"Honestly?" said Agnes, looking me in the eyes. "You're more yourself with that mark, if it makes sense."

I guessed it did. Kind of. "Thanks," I said, taking the spells and passing them to the others. "And for all your help. Good allies are in short supply lately."

"That they are. Best of luck to all of you."

Everett beckoned to the mirror, and Morgan put one foot through, wobbled, then disappeared into the shiny surface.

"Whoa," Hazel said. "You're full of no end of surprises, Agnes."

She jumped through after him, leaving River and me behind.

"Thanks," I said to Agnes and Everett. "So... I don't know if we'll be coming back this way, but if you need our help, let us know."

The mirror's surface shimmered. River and I stepped through, emerging in a long corridor. A gargoyle statue sat at the far end. Otherwise, nobody was around. The corridor was panelled in dark wood with deep blue carpets, but unlike the necromancers' place, it seemed to at least have central heating.

There was a coughing noise from behind us. Had the gargoyle statue moved? It seemed to be pointing down a corridor on our left, which led to a staircase.

Nodding to River, I went to meet the Council of Twelve.

16

"Wish I'd dressed up for the occasion," Hazel whispered as we walked downstairs. "If I could scrape together enough magic to make the four of us not look like we wandered in here by accident…"

"You have the circlet," I said. "I have the glowing forehead. River and Morgan…"

"We're not supposed to be here," Morgan said. "Lucky I don't give a crap, and River walks around like he owns the place anyway."

River blinked. "I don't."

"Yeah, you do," said Hazel. "Might work in our favour now."

"I was kind of hoping to go to the necromancer guild first," I said. "Since they actually know us."

"I'm expecting Lady Montgomery to be invited to the meeting," said River. "If it involves all the local head supernaturals, they'd invite her. This is the mages' headquarters."

That'd explain the elaborately carved banisters and expensive-looking carpets. We descended the stairs into a spacious entrance hall dominated by a large crystal chandelier.

"Fancy," said Morgan. "Where's this meeting?"

"This way," whispered a voice.

I jumped. A young woman with black hair cut fairly short and a lip piercing that I was surprised passed the necromancers' regulations winked at me. "Thought I'd catch you sneaking in."

"Technically I'm invited," I said.

"And your family?" asked Jas, necromancer apprentice and one of the people I'd first met after signing up at the guild.

"Touché. What are you doing lurking outside?" She wore her necromancer cloak, which technically fitted a formal event like this, but I wouldn't have thought a novice would be permitted entry to a top secret council meeting, even Lady Montgomery's assistant.

"I'm not allowed in, but Lady Montgomery asked me to come along and translate her meeting notes into legible English when it's over. Fun." Her words sounded plausible, but they way she lurked out of sight of the door made me suspect there was something she wasn't telling me. Still, the door at the hall's side, half-open, revealed a large meeting room filled with chairs. Voices drifted from within, and I moved closer. I spotted several ghosts, one of whom I recognised as Frank 'Lord Sydney' the necromancer, in conversation with a younger but equally dead man I didn't know.

In the chairs, groups of witches, shifters and mages sat in distinct groups. There didn't seem to be a seating plan or dress code. The mages were dressed like they were attending a fancy societal function, the witches wore bright outfits more suited to an outdoor party, while the shifters wore torn, muddy clothes as though they'd come from a brawl. Some of them were bleeding. At least we didn't look that unusual in our slightly battered clothing, though River attracted several stares as we walked in. Maybe they thought we were the faerie division, since I hadn't seen any half-faeries yet.

A tall man in a dark suit stood apart from the others, looking over everyone who entered the room. He had striking grey eyes and neatly combed dark hair. Human, but something dangerous shimmered in his eyes and stirred the air when we got close to him, like a brewing thunderstorm. *Mage Lord, definitely.*

"I don't believe we've met," he said to Hazel. He spoke in an upper-class English accent, his gaze travelling from Morgan's scuffed shoes to River's talisman sword.

"I'm Hazel Lynn. Summer Gatekeeper's heir."

"I was told to expect you," said the mage. "Mage Lord Colton. I've tried on a number of occasions to get hold of your mother."

"She's usually busy in Faerie," said Hazel. "You're the founder of the council, right?"

"Yes, I am. Ivy told me about you." His gaze slid to me. "You're Ilsa Lynn, correct?"

Now the mages all knew who I was? "Yeah, I'm Ilsa." What had Ivy actually said about me? The book wouldn't have allowed her to tell anyone about my magic, which would make explaining how we'd met kind of tricky. "This is Morgan, our brother," I added. I was pretty sure bringing random relatives along to an important meeting wasn't traditional, but the Mage Lord nodded to both of us as though we hadn't barged in on the council's gathering without an invitation. Had Ivy told him we'd all be coming?

The Mage Lord's attention focused on River. "And you are?"

"My name is River," he said. "River Montgomery. I'm a

senior member of Edinburgh's necromancer guild. My mother runs the necromancer council."

The door opened behind us, and Ivy walked in. She wore ripped jeans and a leather jacket, and her talisman was sheathed out of sight. Despite her clear human appearance, whispers followed her, a ripple of alertness travelling through the seated supernaturals. I envied her easy confidence walking amongst a group of people with enough power to break a hole in the universe, but anyone would be confident if they had as much magic hidden away as she did.

The Mage Lord's expression softened a little as he looked at her. "These are the people I was told to expect?"

"Yeah, that's Ilsa," said Ivy. "You know nobody can get in here without passing those wards they got from the necromancer guild."

Oh. He must be the fiancé who wasn't pleased with Ivy's hobby of travelling around the Ley Line as a ghost. Maybe I should send him and River off to talk about the metaphysical risks of necromancy.

"Yes, but it wouldn't surprise me if someone decided to target the meeting," said Lord Colton. The hint of a threat in his voice suggested whoever did so would be very unwise.

"Just don't break up any more shifter brawls," Ivy said, her hand brushing against his as she walked past.

"Is that why they're all covered in mud?" asked Hazel, moving after her towards the seats.

"They refused our generous offer of cleansing spells," said Ivy, taking a seat in the back row. "They've been on edge ever since we got here. Suppose they're justified in being a little pissed off considering Drake nearly drove them into the sea on the long drive up from England..." She shook her head. "I don't need to bore you talking about what a week it's been. Sounds like you've had a tough one of your own."

"Yeah, you could say that," I said, pulling out the seat next to her.

River leaned closer to me. "Ilsa, you talk to her. I'm going to speak with Lady Montgomery and the mage council, to bring them up to speed on recent events. Not all of it. Just the…"

"Public story?" I said wryly. I still didn't know if I planned to tell everyone about the Seelie Queen's treachery, or if it was a better idea to keep that information quiet until we knew for sure what to do about it. The last thing I wanted to do was wreck the council's hard-won peace with Faerie.

He moved swiftly away, while the rest of us took seats at the back. Ivy cast a look across the others. "I didn't know you were bringing… your family?"

"I'm Hazel Lynn," said Hazel. "The Summer Gatekeeper's heir. That's our brother, Morgan."

"I'm very important," Morgan said. "I'm a necromancer and psychic sensitive."

"Cool," Ivy said. "I'm your distant relation, apparently. All of you."

"Really?" said Morgan. "Don't you get the Lynn curse?"

"Curse?" Ivy blinked. "I'm not bound to serve Faerie, if that's what you mean. Frankly I think they want to get rid of me, since I pretty much forced them to join the council."

"You did?" asked Hazel.

"Yes. I'm *trying* to do this differently to the mages' traditional approach of asking the most influential people rather than the people who are actually best suited for the job, but they're set in their ways. Shifters pick their representatives by right of combat. Mages try to assassinate one another, while it's difficult to get necromancers to volunteer anyone who's actually alive. The witches are the only supernaturals who actually stick to the original rulebook and vote on a leader in a way that doesn't usually involve anyone dying.

But you can see how it gets dicey when you bring the Sidhe into it. They've been stuck in limbo for a thousand years or more, and they don't want to be ordered around by humans."

"So were the Gatekeepers ever involved?" I asked.

"I think they were, with the original council," Ivy said. "According to Frank, anyway. But the council disbanded after most of them died in the invasion and most of the records were scattered. I don't know how long your mother's been Gatekeeper, but it might have been before her time."

"Then Grandma's ghost could have told us." A pang went through me. I hadn't had chance to properly think about what her no longer being around meant. I hadn't spoken to her for years before I'd returned to the Lynn house, but I missed her all the same. "Is there a record somewhere of past members?"

Ivy frowned. "I thought there wasn't, but perhaps there is here. Vance—Lord Colton—will know. I'll ask him after the meeting."

"Is it even starting today?" asked Morgan. "Or are we waiting for the Sidhe?"

My heart lurched. "They're not coming here?"

"No," said Ivy. "You have no idea... actually, I think you can probably guess how hard it is to get them to commit to a meeting place and time."

Hazel snorted. "We spent ages trying to convince them there was a traitor in their own Court, but they ended up getting us thrown out instead. And now we know who the traitor is, but telling them will get us all killed."

"Who is it?" asked Ivy.

"The Seelie Queen," I whispered.

"There isn't a Seelie Queen," said Ivy. "Unless... actually, I've heard someone mention his father was assistant to the Queen... holy shit."

"Assistant?" said Hazel. "Not—Lord Daival?"

"Never met him, but I've heard the name," Ivy said, frowning. "Damn. What did the Seelie Queen do?"

"Told us she's planning a coup and threw us into the Vale," I said. "I got us out, but… I reckon it's to do with the immortality thing. The Sidhe were already pissed off because someone got murdered in the Summer Court."

Ivy's eyes widened. "Thought that might happen. They used to kill one another to gain power all the time, apparently. All that happened was that the person they killed came back, told on them to the Court, and cue exile."

"Charming," I muttered. "Yeah, they flat-out refused to speak to us. I don't suppose you know what s wrong with the Erlking?"

She shook her head. "They'd never tell me. So you're saying the Seelie Queen is working… with the Vale outcasts?"

"And possibly the Winter Gatekeeper's ghost," I added.

Ivy swore. "You've got to be joking."

"The Sidhe are in charge," Morgan said. "I don't know why this is a surprise to anyone."

"It's not a surprise," said Ivy. "It's just fucking inconvenient. I can't help with the Gatekeeper… I'm about as far from a necromancer as you can get. That I can walk between realms as a ghost is a side effect of my magic."

"So the original owner couldn't do that?" I said, keeping my voice so quiet, Ivy had to lean closer to hear.

Her eye twitched. "No. The Sidhe… I doubt it would have occurred to them."

"Not the Sidhe." My hand reached out of its own accord to the hilt of her blade. Power brushed my hand, alien yet familiar. Intelligent. Alive.

Ivy's whole body went deadly still, like a coiled viper ready to spring. "I really wouldn't do that. I don't think it recognises you as a threat, but—"

Morgan moved his chair back so quickly he nearly fell off it. "Can you not throw your weird magic around in here?"

I dropped my hand. "Sorry. I wish I knew where the book came from, that's all. The Sidhe won't believe any of us. All we have left to use against them is knowledge. They try to bury their own past because it terrifies them. I reckon that's where the answers are."

"Never mind the past," said Morgan. "It's just us now, isn't it? We need to fix it."

"You can do both," Hazel said in a low voice. "Ivy... Ilsa said you have a talisman like hers. Does that kind of thing run in the family, too?"

"This?" Ivy tapped the blade hilt. "No, I won it from a Sidhe by accident. I'm new blood. The connection with your family is distant, if at all." She leaned back, her eyes narrowing in suspicion when River took the last empty seat in the row. "You were with them, too?"

"Yes, I was. My father is Lord Torin... I believe he has some connection with your council."

"Oh. Quentin's other family," said Ivy. "So you're in on this."

"I was initially hired to protect the Gatekeeper with my life," River said. "Afterwards, we worked as colleagues at Edinburgh's necromancer guild."

Her expression remained distrusting, and the look in her eyes told me quite clearly that she was assessing whether or not he was a threat. Like when I'd put my hand on her talisman. It was a challenge. Most people, faced with Ivy, would run for the hills. River's eyes narrowed. I *liked* Ivy, but I had to squash the urge to tell her to stop glaring at him.

Power crackled overhead, drawing my attention to the front of the hall. Everyone fell silent. Several mages gathered on the stage, with Mage Lord Colton taking up central position. Immediately, all eyes went to him, and it was easy to tell why. His presence was like lightning contained in a bottle, radiating enough power to bring the whole building crumpling down like it was nothing.

"We're gathered here to discuss the future of the council, particularly in light of recent events in the faerie realm and in this one," he said. "No word of this meeting will leave this room without my permission." He paused as though to let the message sink in. "You may have noticed we have a few guests. Lady Montgomery of Edinburgh's necromancer guild has joined us, in addition to the city's mage council... and the heir to the title of Summer Gatekeeper."

His attention went to Hazel. She sat up straighter.

"The Gatekeepers are peacekeepers bound to work between the faerie realms and this world," Lord Colton went on. "Their title refers to the gates between this realm and Faerie, which are under their watch."

There were a few mutters of dissent, along the lines of *they did a great job keeping the peace, didn't they?* The whisperer probably meant the invasion. Indignation spiked on Hazel's and Mum's part, though I held my tongue.

"We keep the peace with the Courts, not the Vale," Hazel said, rising to her feet. "The Gatekeepers and the Council of Twelve worked in secret to maintain the peace even in the face of evil, even when it almost destroyed us. And let's just say it's not a voluntary position. My mother is the current Gatekeeper for the Summer Court. She's on Faerie on a mission, which means there's a faerie vow controlling her every move. You know what happens when you disobey a faerie vow?" she asked. "You die. One of her children could get killed and she still wouldn't be allowed to return home."

"You're requesting, what, an escort into Faerie?" said one of the mages.

"No, we're asking that you don't talk shit about us behind our backs," Morgan said from behind her.

He was right, but this wasn't how I'd imagined the meeting would go.

"The Gatekeepers have something to say about recent events," said Lord Colton. "Let her say her piece."

I hoped Hazel knew what she was doing. She stood tall, in the same commanding way Mum did. Her circlet blazed. She must have doctored it with a spell to cover for her magic fading.

"The recent activity on the Ley Line was due to one of our own betraying us in an effort to cheat death and attack the Sidhe," said Hazel. "Ilsa stopped her. But it created a knock-on effect. Wraiths, faerie ghosts most people can't even see, are escaping into this realm. Half-faerie ghosts are attacking people, and again, most people can't see them until it's too late. And we think they're working with a group of outcasts in the Vale, through Death. Oh, and someone's trying to bring down the Summer Court, too, and they won't listen to us," she added. "That's it."

"We cannot negotiate with the Summer Court if they don't send representatives to us," said Lord Colton. "Unfortunately, they prefer to talk on their own territory, on their terms. If there is indeed another Vale threat, then they would require proof at the very least."

I figured. The council had been a long shot, and even the people in this room would be hard-pressed to outdo the Sidhe. Besides, I didn't *want* to kick off a war. I just wanted them to believe the truth, without putting anyone at risk of ending up in the crossfire. Since their enemies were also Sidhe, potentially with godlike powers, it was no wonder they hadn't managed to kill all of their outcasts. The same immortality that kept them existing indefinitely had kept their enemies alive as well.

"Most of us aren't able to walk into the Vale on our own power," said Hazel. "Since we don't know the nature of the threat we face, we're asking for the cooperation of the necro-mancer guild and the council. That's all we ask. For access to the necessary information to deal with this threat."

She sat down again. Only Morgan and I could see her hands shaking. And possibly Ivy, too, but she was tensed, her attention on the shifters. None of them was paying any attention. Two were even asleep. *Really.*

"Does anyone else have any points to address?" said Lord Colton.

As one of the other mages began talking, Ivy leaned back in her seat. "Did you say wraiths?" she whispered to Hazel.

"Yes," River said quietly. "They've been escaping into this realm for some time. Even within Faerie itself. It was the first sign of the conspiracy in the Vale, but the Siche won't believe they're a threat."

Ivy gave him an assessing look. "That doesn't surprise me. So you can destroy them?"

"Most human necromancers can't," I said. "And my talisman is the only thing I know that can kill the worst type."

Ivy nodded. "Then I'll help you find the records. If we end this conspiracy, we end the wraith problem along with it."

"There's just the slight issue of one of the most powerful people in the Seelie Court being involved," I said. "Don't tell anyone the full story until we have proof."

17

To my surprise, Lady Montgomery waited for us outside the meeting room when the gathering drew to a close. A stern-looking woman with her grey hair pulled back in a bun, she looked us over with an expression close to relief, particularly River. At her side stood Jas, who looked almost as out of place as we did.

"I'm glad to see you made it back," said Lady Montgomery. "I wasn't aware all four of you had security clearance at the council's meetings, however."

Ah. "Er, the Gatekeeper's family has authorisation," I improvised. "While our mother is occupied in Faerie. And River's our companion."

Jas's eyes bugged out, and I could tell she wanted to ask a bunch of questions. I assumed she'd been given some level of security clearance to be here at all, even if her only job was to translate the boss's notes into legible English. We really should have rehearsed a cover story beforehand, but I hadn't realised the guild's top ranked members would be here.

Lady Montgomery waved a hand. "Never mind the reasons. River told me you were in your family's home, but he didn't mention you'd be coming here this soon. I assumed you had family business to take care of first."

"We sort of do," Morgan said. "It wasn't meant to take this long, but Faerie took two weeks from us."

"I understand how Faerie works," she said. "What I don't understand is why none of you asked me about the Gate-keepers' involvement with the council sooner. I might have been able to help you find the information."

"There was no time," I responded. I decided not to add, *and you thought we were villains at the time.* "All along, I assumed one of my ancestors worked for the necromancer guild. Then that ghost showed up. What she said implied the Gatekeeper at the time when she was alive was just passing through. But when I was looking for records at the guild, I should have been checking the mages' records instead. Most Gatekeepers weren't necromancers."

Lady Montgomery nodded. "Lord Colton was right to say that many records of the original council were lost in the invasion, but they had a working partnership and shared resources, which is a position we'd like to return to." She beckoned us into the room behind her, a dusty library filled with tall shelves. "Jas can help you find what you're looking for. The first council worked on a large number of missions concerning the supernatural community, many of which also involved the necromancer guild."

"I thought so," said Hazel. "Honestly, we'd like to know if there were any Lynns connected who *weren't* Summer or Winter Gatekeeper. We're trying to find out which genera-tion first started using the book."

Perhaps it didn't matter. What we faced was on a scale beyond anything we were equipped to deal with, and even the necromancers' records likely wouldn't tell me where the book had originally come from. Considering none of my ancestors had been thoughtful enough to leave instructions behind, I doubted anyone else would have admitted to making a deal with the gods. If they'd even lived to tell the tale.

Lady Montgomery took a stack of papers and passed them to me. "These are the names of previous council associates, as a starting point. I looked them up when Ivy told me you were coming."

So even she was on speaking terms with Ivy Lane.

I took the papers in hand. Names, names… *Lynn.*

"Great-Grandma," said Hazel, reading over my shoulder. "She died before we were born, when Morgan was a baby."

"I don't remember her," Morgan said. "I do remember Grandma, but she wasn't Gatekeeper like Ilsa."

"And the generation before was the one who trapped the ghost, right?" I said. "So there have been at least four generations who wielded the book. Do you know all the past Lynns on Winter's side, too?" I asked Hazel.

I'd once had the family tree memorised, but memories faded with time, and I'd always harboured a sense of resentment towards them for banishing the non-Gatekeepers from the records.

"Not Winter," she said. "Not a Gatekeeper. But maybe she *was* from Winter. The sister of the current Winter Gatekeeper. Dammit, I wish someone had an actual family tree…"

I thought back to the names on the walls of the mausoleum. I'd walked through there enough times, seen the names engraved deep into the stone.

"The book passed from Winter to Summer," I said. "They wielded it first. Maybe one of them was first to claim it. No wonder none of our history books mention it."

And no wonder Holly had felt entitled to its power.

I looked down to see Jas watching me across the table. "You weren't kidding about that power you have, were you?"

"No." She also wasn't supposed to know about it, but I

was pretty sure everyone at the necromancer guild knew my magic was an unconventional type by now. "I didn't know you knew the council."

"I don't. Lady Montgomery requested I search the archives on your behalf, since I'm already here and I'm familiar with how the necromancers' archives work."

Hmm. Before, the idea of letting yet more people in on our family's secrets worried me, but at this rate, it'd all go public soon enough.

"Okay," I said. "I guess I can read this, but knowing Aunt Candice, she dragged her top-secret family information right into the afterlife with her."

Jas paled. "What?"

There was a tremendous screeching noise from outside, and Ivy ran into the room, her talisman gleaming blue. "That was the emergency alarm. Someone breached the security."

Lady Montgomery moved swiftly out the door, pausing in the entrance hall as the rest of us hurried out of the library behind her.

"Jas," she said, "take a warning to the council."

Jas's eyes widened. "But—"

"Go. Someone has to."

She took off, while I tapped into the spirit realm. There was an odd shimmer when Jas ran past that caught my eye for a moment—before my attention was drawn to the greyish light up ahead.

"It's in the spirit realm," I warned. "The Ley Line. Something's coming through."

As we ran through the open doors of the guild, the air split apart in blue light. Solid-looking ghostly shapes blotted out the sky, and I stopped running. "There's too many."

Too many wraiths to count, and they all hovered directly above the crowded tourist district. *Oh no.*

Lady Montgomery ran to the guild's exterior walls. The

air above them shimmered with light as protective glyphs activated, and a grey filter indicated a powerful iron spell on the gates in addition to the iron built into the building itself. Behind the shields, we were safe. Outside the walls, the first screams rent through the air along with the smell of undead and burning.

I dug a hand in my pocket, pulled out a knife, and checked the spells Agnes had given me were within easy reach. Panicked people ran down the street, away from a group of undead lumbering along, some glowing with the taint of those possessed by wraiths.

Ivy ran out to meet them, her talisman flashing bright blue. Apparently her faerie magic came with grace and speed to go with it. River ran alongside her. Within seconds, all the undead lay in rotten pieces, the wraiths' lights extinguished.

"Guys, River and I will lure down the ones in the sky," I said to Morgan and Hazel, passing by the wards. Lady Montgomery took off in the opposite direction to Ivy, a blade in her hand and determination etched on her face.

"I can help." Morgan pulled the iron band off his wrist and ran past the wards. He halted, his gaze turned to the sky. *He's using his psychic abilities.*

"Any luck?" said Hazel, moving in behind him with a witch spell gleaming in her hand. "I'm going after the undead."

Morgan shook his head. "No. I can't reach those bastards. But I can get the ones on earth."

Three more undead ran around the corner. Hazel threw the witch spell at the nearest, and its head exploded. *Nice one, Agnes.* Before they could reach the crowded streets, the other two collapsed, screaming, the wraiths torn from the physical bodies. Morgan must have blasted them with a psychic shock. River moved in to cut their bodies to pieces.

I stood on tip-toe to check the best route to reach the

wraiths—and a sudden roaring noise rent the air. "What in hell is that—hellhounds?"

"Shit," said Ivy. "Attacks on the Ley Line have negative effects on shifters, too. It forces them to transform and lose all reason."

"You've got to be bloody kidding me. We can't deal with both."

"We're too far from them." River took a step back, necromantic energy lighting his hands. "And there aren't enough necromancers."

The meaning was clear. I pulled the book from my pocket. Power hummed to my fingertips almost instantly, and the world turned transparent.

The first wraith descended from the sky, yowling, my spirit sight showing me its miserable trapped form caged in death. I shouted the banishing words, as loudly as possible, but it didn't slow. Winter magic shot from its hands, aimed at both of us. I lunged in front of River, and its magic bounced off my shield, disappearing into the clouds.

"You'd think they'd have told one another that doesn't work by now," I gasped, conjuring another necromantic attack. The air shimmered as my attack joined with River's, passing straight through the wraith without so much as stirring the air. Worse, the rooftops trembled, not designed to repel magic, and several tiles came loose, swept into the breeze. Horror took hold of me. The last time I'd seen a wraith create a tornado, it'd nearly caused terrible damage on a much smaller scale. "There are people in the streets who might get hurt. Is there a mage with a shielding ability or something?"

"On it," said Ivy, one-handedly sticking her phone into her pocket while wielding her blade with the other. "Vance is a displacer who can move the air around to make a shield, but he doesn't usually deal with things that volatile—"

A second current of air smacked into us, damn near sending me pitching sideways. Lord Colton had appeared from thin air.

He can teleport? Holy crap.

"Can you do it?" Ivy asked.

"Possibly," he said. "But you'll need to finish them fast."

"Yeah, slight problem," I said. "There are less than five people in this city with the ability to banish *one* wraith, let alone fifteen. Ivy and I are two of them."

Lord Colton swore under his breath. "Then I'll give you all the time you need." He nodded to Ivy, then disappeared again, reappearing on the rooftop directly beneath the swirling mass of roof tiles. My heart dropped as they fell onto him—and rose again, repelled by the air current from his hands. *Whoa.* The whole storm continued to swirl around, but harmlessly held out of reach. He must have a high control level to be able to do that.

More undead lumbered around the corner, wrists gleaming. *Shit.* "They're wearing strength enhancer charms!" I shouted to the others, running in to help. River lunged with inhuman speed, his blade rending the undead to pieces. Hazel ran past, urging terrified onlookers to move to safety. Morgan blasted his spirit sensor into the crowding undead, but there were too many for anything other than a faerie talisman to fight.

Ivy, however, backed away from the battle, her eyes on the wraiths in the sky and the Mage Lord below. Several other mages were ascending the buildings to join him. "Air mages," Ivy said. "Not great. They have the potential to make it *more* volatile. We need to get up close. You can banish them, right?"

"Yes, but I can't kill them. Only the book is powerful enough to banish them all, and if I open it down here, innocent people might get caught."

"Got it." Ivy headed down a side road. "We have to get away from the fight if we're going into the spirit realm. Get up close."

I spotted Lord Colton and the mages beneath the wraiths, hands splayed, power pushing the torrent of fallen roof tiles into the sky. As I watched, every piece of debris vanished into the air. Lord Colton's arms dropped to his sides.

"Did he displace them?" I caught up with Ivy next to the wall at the alley's end. Here, the wraiths couldn't see our physical bodies, and with any luck, we'd be able to bring them down before the enemy realised where we'd run to.

"He can't do that indefinitely," said Ivy. "Ready to go in?"

"Yeah." I gripped the book in my hand, and stepped out of my body. All around the sky, wraiths flew around, throwing handfuls of magic at the panicking crowds below. I aimed for the nearest, keeping both eyes on its shimmering magic-infused form. Throughout the spirit realm, other necromancers did battle, too. They must be projecting from within their own spirit boundaries, but even the top-ranked ones would stand no chance against faerie magic.

"All right, Ilsa?" Jas waved at me, ducking a magical attack from one of the wraiths, her hands glowing. I guess I'd been wrong to think necromancers couldn't face up to faerie magic.

The book gleamed in my hands, but the wraiths remained distant, refusing to get up close and personal. They wanted me to come to them. The magic flying around Death blurred the fog to a darker grey, but the air around Jas's shimmering spirit form flickered oddly for a moment, and a brief shiver of inexplicable fear traced down my spine. The feeling vanished an instant later as Jas blasted the wrath with kinetic power, and the wraith's attention turned towards me.

"Get over here!" I yelled. Damn. The closer I drew, the further away the wraiths appeared. They were miles above the city, and we were too close to the Ley Line to open the gate.

"They're trying to trick me into breaking the veil," I said aloud into the fog. "Guess I'll have to take them down the other way."

I held onto the book's power and shouted the banishing words at the top of my lungs. My voice echoed in the empty space, with no result. Worse, the wraith which had conjured up the tornado turned to me, flinging debris in its wake. Blue light exploded over the rooftops, smothering the houses in icy rain beneath the fog of the spirit realm. Winter magic. Threads of light connected the wraiths, wreathing the sky like vibrant blue tinsel. By the way they were all glowing, there ought to be a dozen tornadoes up in the air, but there was still only one of them. *Huh. Wait a moment.*

"Ilsa!" River shouted, seeing me floating above him with the book in my hands.

Another whirling tornado shot past him—at the alley where my body was hidden. *Oh hell.*

I checked back into my body as the building crumbled on its side. Screaming came from inside. I ducked, arms over my head to shield myself. Ivy shouted a warning, and the tiles slid out of reach, disappearing before they hit us.

"Damn," she said, on her feet, her fists clenched. "I don't suppose you have faerie healing powers?"

I clambered to my feet, hoping that the other necromancers had been projecting into the spirit realm from a safe distance. "No. Do you?"

She nodded, moving down the alley away from the half-collapsed building. "Vance saved our necks—but his shield's down."

The building the Mage Lord had been standing on had been hit. He must have teleported out of the way, and dropped the shield in the process. Debris flew wildly, breaking windows, growing in strength. A monstrous tornado, ripping into anything it touched.

A whirl of air struck outside the building, and Lord Colton appeared from thin air.

"Thank god," Ivy breathed.

"There seems to be one wraith controlling the others," said the Mage Lord.

"Because there's only one wraith," I said. It was more obvious from the ground, where the tornado's path remained below the wraith which had attacked me. "The others are an illusion. Its magic must have been able to create illusions when it was still alive. I need to get to the spirit realm again—"

Alarming creaking noises came from the collapsing building next to us. Bricks crumbled inches away, and everything vanished in a whirl of air. The next second, Ivy and I had appeared where the zombies had been. Apparently the Mage Lord could displace other people, too.

River ran in front of me, bits of undead dropping from his sword. "There you are," he said breathlessly.

"I need to get to the wraiths," I said. "They're clones—fakes. There's only one genuine wraith, and its magic is controlling the others. Kill it and they all die."

The spirit realm would take me back to the target—but tapping out of the battle would put me at the mercy of the murderous wraiths.

"I'll check," River said. His body stilled, and I swore, moving in front of him. "River, don't—"

The wraith turned on me. I both saw it in the sky and felt it in the spirit world. Icy power gathered in its hands, forming spear-sharp icy blades.

I threw myself over River's body, and the magic hit my shield with the force of a car collision. A current of air flung me off River, throwing us apart, smashing the glass in the nearby windows. I climbed to my knees. My teeth rattled with power, and I called on everything the book had. My body left the ground as an uncontrollable rush of energy alighted the book in my hands. The wraith flew back, roaring in anger. I didn't know I'd drifted into the spirit realm until its magical blast shoved me back, into my body. I half lay across the cobbled pavement. And River…

He lay on his back, hands shielding his face. Blood soaked his side, and between strips of torn clothing, a deep wound lacerated his ribs.

"River. *River.*"

Healing abilities didn't work on death, and near-fatal injuries needed more time to heal. Time we didn't have.

The debris rose again, crashing on us like thunder.

18

I closed my eyes and called the book's power to my hands. Cold light burned my palms, striking the debris with the sound like rippling thunder. Before the tornado could sweep it up again, Lord Colton appeared, hands spread wide, pushing back against the wraith's tornado-like assault. *Holy crap.*

River's eyes opened. He groaned. "The wraith... it's the central one. The only one using magic..." He coughed, blood wetting his mouth.

"Shit." I looked desperately at the Mage Lord, but all his attention was on keeping the tornado from hitting us.

"River!" Lady Montgomery ran to us. "The mages' headquarters is shielded—get him off the battlefield."

River's eyes half-opened and he managed to climb to his feet, but pain glazed his eyes, and blood dripped onto the cobblestones.

"Watch my back!" I shouted to Lady Montgomery, letting River lean on me. The blood alarmed me, but he was six feet of solid muscle and there was no way either of us could single-handedly carry him while fighting off the dead. When an undead got too close, Lady Montgomery made liberal use of her curved knife, which she'd soaked in salt. Hazel, Ivy and Morgan had disappeared. Worry twisted in my gut. *River...* I couldn't let him die.

Once behind the safety of the wards, Lady Montgomery crouched down beside her son, hands gentle as they examined the wound. Her face was pale, her mouth pinched. "This wound will take several minutes to heal even with his powers. Can you watch him until then?"

"I know which is the real wraith—I have to go into Death to kill it," I said.

"Then use everything you have," she said.

I nodded, blinking back tears, and scanned the sky for the wraith. River was right—it appeared more solid than the others, and if I looked closer in the spirit realm, threads of blue Winter magic extended to connect the wraith with the others. One wraith was behind all the magic—and it could only use it in one place at a time. Right now all its attention was on the whirling tornado pushing against the Mage Lord.

I slipped out of my body and rose into the sky, higher, higher. Magic bounced off my shield. Two of the false wraiths closed in and I raised the book, calling on a little of its power, but not too much. Cold light pulsed from my hands, pushing the wraiths back. I focused on my target, and slammed it with all the power I had.

One of the clones disappeared. I kept up the assault, second by second. Every sound below was muted, every emotion locked out, and nothing existed but me and the magic, and the talisman. We didn't fight one another. There was no struggle. I needed its power and it would bend to my will.

Two more wraith clones disappeared.

My hands trembled on the book. My whole body ached as though I'd pulled more than my spirit here into death. But I wouldn't break. The book wouldn't break, and if I wanted to access its full power, I'd be its equal.

One by one, all the clones vanished as the wraith's magic was pulled back into its body. Readied to attack. I gritted my teeth and braced myself for the impact.

The wraith kept on pulling power, its body glowing blue, the colour of Winter magic and blood. Now, deep in the realm of death, the wraith had solid form. Like a person. No… a Sidhe. My heart climbed into my throat. In his hands appeared the likeness of a blade. A talisman.

No. It can't have survived beyond death. It had so much magic that it'd managed to manufacture a weapon, while I had nothing but the book.

The wraith moved in a blur, and the blade went through my ghostly form. Magic pulsed from its edges, and I laughed, more in relief than anything. "You can't hit me with magic even now, wraith. We're at a stalemate."

"No, we aren't," shouted Ivy. She ran—or floated—wielding her own sword, and stabbed the wraith through the chest. The edges of her blade lit up blue, drawing on power from somewhere close by. The wraith writhed and screamed, its body pulsing with magic, and aimed at Ivy.

Not before I got in the way. I took the hit side-on, the magic dissipating into the air. Ivy's eyes widened, and the wraith struck again. She stabbed it through the chest, her own blade vibrating with power. Even in the spirit realm, it clearly cost her a great effort to hold onto it. I gathered necromantic power, took careful aim, and struck the creature from behind.

"It's too solid," Ivy shouted, her blade wedged in its chest. "And not enough. It's—stuck."

"Not for long." I raised the book, and shouted the banishing words. Pinned by Ivy's blade, the wraith couldn't flee.

A wrenching scream tore from its throat. A last explosion of blue magic struck my shield, dissipating as the wraith's body crumbled to ashes.

Ivy lowered her blade. "You're immune to faerie magic?"

"I swear I told you that," I said breathlessly. "Thanks. I have to go. River... he got seriously hurt."

"I'm sorry." Her mouth turned down at the corners. "One creature did so much damage..."

"I know. Who in hell summoned it? I'd almost say it was a diversion, but they didn't hit any of the main supernatural hubs."

Ivy turned around on the spot. The spirit realm was too blurred to see the world beneath—and the air shimmered, showing a familiar path. The Vale.

"The Ley Line's unstable," she said. "Really unstable."

"The summoner!" I said. "Someone did the summoning... it came from above the rooftops."

"I saw it," Ivy said. "In the real world, anyway. It was on the building behind where the Mage Lord was. But we're in the dead part of Faerie."

I stared at my feet. A transparent silvery line lay beneath, the only light in the grey haze.

"What—the Death Kingdom?" I'd read about the part of Winter territory where the goddess of death resided, but it didn't sound the same as the void I'd pushed the wraith into.

"Not here," Ivy said. "This is the path of the dead. It used to lead from the Death Kingdom to the Sidhe's source of immortality, but now there's nothing here. It's close to the place the Vale used to be, before the Sidhe ripped it away."

I stared along the silvery line. "Seriously? Is this where the gods...?" Had my book come from here? Worry for River beat in my chest, but the silver line shone with a familiar alluring light.

"The gods never walked here," Ivy said. "Or hell, maybe

they did. Do you know how a faerie talisman is usually created?"

"Forged from the heart of a tree and infused with magic," I said. "Faerie magic, or… gods' magic. How?"

"The Sidhe ripped the gods' power out when they were still alive," Ivy said, a distasteful expression on her face. "Using a ritual and an Invocation. However that book got into your family, no human could have done it."

"But it's not the faeries'. It can't be."

No Sidhe had wielded this book. I knew it as surely as though the book itself had told me.

"Maybe there *is* someone with answers," she said. "Does the book have a name?"

"A *name?* What, like a summoning?" A suspicion took root inside me. "You *met* one of the gods? I thought they died."

"What's left of it," she said. "They're not alive. They died. The talismans are all that's left of their power, and while it's kind of conscious, it's not the same as the real thing, trust me. It can be controlled. I found the one whose magic is in my sword by speaking its name."

I took the book carefully out. "Can you read this?"

"The symbol?" She frowned at the cover. A syllable left her lips, cold and sharp.

Silence answered. Silence, and a chill breeze.

"Worth a try," said Ivy. "Don't say the name in the Courts. The Sidhe have this weird superstition about speaking the names aloud."

"Like necromancy." I put the book away in my pocket. How my clothes still existed here, I had no idea. "To summon a person, you have to add their name to the summoning spell. Same with dark magic, Vale magic…"

"Dark magic?" echoed Ivy. "You didn't. Did you? Tell me you didn't summon worse than a hellhound."

"No. Why, is there *worse* than hellhounds?"

"Yes, but I think you need a different spell for the really nasty sort. Not just the Vale. There are whole dimensions with no life in them… I shouldn't be giving you ideas."

"I'm not the sort of person who summons monsters without a plan, don't worry. Things have a tendency to spin out of control wherever the book's involved."

Her mouth quirked. "I can tell I'm going to have my work cut out helping you."

"Did you just volunteer to train me?" My voice rose in surprise. Not that I didn't want to work with Ivy, but I'd assumed by default that I was way out of her league as far as possible mentees went.

"Sure," Ivy said. "There was no one around to explain this shit to me, and I spent ten years running from it. You should get back to River. He seems to really care about you."

"Yeah, he does." Wow. Ten years? That'd teach me to make assumptions.

She smiled. "Treasure it. Trust me, there are some things better than all this power."

The realm of death faded around us, bearing us back to the land of the living.

19

I blinked awake. I was cold again, but not unbearably so.
I lay on my back, on a fold-out bed. The room
appeared to be an infirmary, and the bustling noises
around me and strangers hurrying in and out told me the
injured from the battle were being brought in. Not the
necromancer guild, but the mages' headquarters, judging by
the wood panelling on the walls. Beside my bed lay the rucksack I'd brought with me containing my spare clothes, which
Morgan or Hazel must have fetched from the library. I didn't
see either of them in here.

A loud commotion drew my attention to the corner.
Bloodied and injured shifters were restrained and strapped
to the hospital beds. *Ah. They're still out of control.* Most were
wolf or fox shifters, but some were larger, unfamiliar furred
animals. Others were partially shifted with their hands or
feet wrapped in claws or paws. Anger simmered in the air,
almost a kind of magic itself.

I managed to sit upright, my body aching like I'd run a
marathon.

"Nice to see you in the land of the living," said Jas. She

and Lloyd sat at another of the fold-out beds—or rather, she half-lay on one of them, while he applied a healing spell to her injured leg.

"You too. I thought you were probably too close to that wraith." I grabbed the water glass someone had thoughtfully left on my bedside table and downed it.

"No fatal injuries this time, eh, Jas?" Lloyd said.

Jas swatted him in the arm. "Cut it out. People are hurt."

"Including you," I said. "How did you fight that wraith? What was the…?" I didn't know how to explain what I'd seen. The weird shimmering around her spirit that seemed oddly different from the other necromancers.

"The what?" she asked. Her tone, however, suggested the subject was closed—and more to the point, there was no sign of River.

"Nothing. Where's—?"

'There." She pointed feebly over Lloyd's shoulder at another bed, where River lay unconscious.

Lady Montgomery stood beside him, her gaze catching mine as she realised I was awake. "You killed it?" she asked.

I hurried to her side, the best I could with my legs still shaky. "Banished it. Ivy helped. Is River okay?"

"He's still healing. The person who summoned the wraith was found dead at the site of the summoning," Lady Montgomery said. "It seems he was used as a sacrifice in the summoning."

"Blood magic," I said, before remembering I'd never actually told her about the times I'd used it in crisis. "Half-faerie?"

A moment passed, in which she gave me an assessing look. "Yes. Your brother has been helping to track potential suspects."

"Are he and Hazel okay, then?"

"Yes. She's helping him with the tracking."

I breathed out. Everyone was safe. Nobody had died. Yet

why did I feel like this was a prelude to something worse? If only I knew what was going on in Faerie.

I sat down on the bed again, reaching to squeeze River's hand. No response. I slipped into the spirit realm. There, I could see the glowing outline of his spirit.

"River?" I reached out and my hand passed right through him. "You scared me."

"Don't worry about me." The glow died down so I could focus on his face. Death's light made his golden hair look like a halo.

"I couldn't not worry about you. Why are you here? You can't be…" I couldn't say *dying*.

"I'm checking this realm while my body is resting."

"How do you do that?" I waved a hand at the spirit realm in general. "You're sound asleep in the waking world. When I do the same, I start floating off."

"You haven't had as much practise," he said. "I don't mean skill, I mean spending days or nights wandering this place. You learn how and when to disconnect. But I think the problem with that book is that it pushes you to the brink every time you use it. You burn out."

"Maybe you're right." I reached for his hand, slipping my fingers through his. I concentrated on the sensation, and he felt more solid by the second. At the same time, I became conscious of the book's presence glowing in my pocket.

The spirit realm changed, showing forested paths, transparent and empty.

He hissed out a breath. "The Vale."

"The place itself isn't scary," I said. "It's kind of sad. Empty. They made it this way on purpose. Maybe there's a way to undo the damage. If they can make themselves immortal, they can fix their own realm, right?"

"I don't think so," said River. "They have no desire to face their own shameful actions."

I blinked, then thought back. "Lord Daival?"

"He's one of the most respected members of the Court. He captured and tortured humans openly and suffered no punishment for it. This is what we're up against. If we expose the Seelie Queen... I'm not sure even her guilt will be enough."

"Then I'll show them this." I held up the book. "The talisman scared them. It's all we've got. They only understand power." I quickly told him what Ivy and I had discussed. "Its power isn't Sidhe—it might not be superior, considering the Sidhe killed and kicked out their gods, but it's terrifying to them, and that's enough."

"The Sidhe kill what scares them. Even death." His eyes flickered with emotion. "I have faith in you, Ilsa, but the Sidhe—when I was first invited into the Court to claim the talisman my father wished to offer me, I was eighteen, and my head was full of ideas and impressions of the Summer Court and what I could offer it. The Court shattered those illusions within minutes of my arrival." He took in a breath. "They have no need to desire change, only fear it, and the best we can do is protect ourselves and those we care about from the aftershocks of their selfish decisions."

"We can do more." I remembered Ivy's words, and imagined a shattering cauldron of blood. "They're not the only ones with magic. And they'll never be able to do this." I gripped his half-transparent hand tighter. "You wanted to give them the truth, right? Prove how powerful the Vale is? This is how we do it. Get straight to the Seelie King by any means possible."

He looked down at our interlocked hands. "We'll discuss it later. I think I've worried my mother enough."

"You worried me, too."

"I never thanked you for saving us," he murmured, his

free hand trailing down my arm. I felt the flicker of his touch before it faded, and so did we.

A moment later, I blinked awake in my own body. The shifters' yowling had quietened down, at least, but there were far too many people around for my liking. River sat up and walked to Lady Montgomery, where I took a moment to reorient myself in the land of the living. By now half the hospital beds were empty, witch healing spells having taken care of the worst injuries. The raging shifters had mostly left, too. I got to my feet, looking down at my clothes. Muddy, stained with River's blood, but I'd suffered no injuries of my own. River's clothes were in a worse state, shredded and streaked with blood. He looked like he'd been wrestling with the shifters, and had won.

"Is your wound okay?" I asked, as he turned away from Lady Montgomery and walked to me.

"Yes, of course it is. I keep spare clothes at the guild, but my place is closer."

"Your flat?" I hadn't seen it, because we'd never even had a proper date. "Can't you just glamour it off?"

He gave me a tired smile. "Honestly, I'm all out of glamour for a while. Come with me? My shower has warm water."

"Warm water. Tempting."

So was he. Without Death clouding my vision, I could see him, clearly as he saw me. Battered, tired, and so damn tempting. Death had come too close to cutting him off from me forever.

I grabbed my rucksack and hurried after him out the doors.

Outside, you wouldn't have thought a wraith had tried to lay waste to the city. Most of the debris had already gone, while the damaged buildings were surrounded by cloaked figures I thought were necromancers until I got close enough to see them levitating the damaged bricks. Telekinetic mages. Must be a useful power. There wasn't much River or I could do to help with the clean-up, so we made our way from the mages' guild to River's ground-floor flat.

"I still haven't told my housemates where I've been for the last few weeks," I said, following him inside. The single-room flat was a little small but otherwise cosy. A bookshelf stacked with paperbacks also housed several withered plants, while dust covered everything in a faint layer.

"You can shower first," River said.

"Thanks." As much as my head had been filled with different ideas about what we might do in there, there was nothing remotely sexy about mud, blood, and bits of zombie.

Clothes discarded, I stepped into the shower. Not quite as intense as the house's one, but I'd take what I could get. I let the warm water soak into me and exhaled in a sigh.

"Should I be joining you in there?" River's voice came from outside. "I'd like to know what you're doing that makes you feel that good."

I tipped my head back and moaned. "Nothing makes me feel as good as a warm shower."

"Is that a challenge?"

Grinning, I finished rinsing my hair and switched the water off. "Maybe. Want me to clean your wounds?"

"There aren't any. There's a lot of blood."

I grabbed a towel. Flirting was one thing, but the shower was barely big enough to stand in. "Sorry, River, but anyone who's had sex in here must be a contortionist."

"Who said anything about sex?" He arched a brow as I walked out wrapped in a towel. "I was thinking more along the lines of me touching you. Massaging the pain away. Making your toes curl with pleasure. That type of thing."

"You mean, what you did in the forest, but with fewer

clothes and no interruptions." I strode all the way to the bed. "Then you'd better hurry up and wash that blood off."

He groaned, but ducked into the bathroom. I shamelessly admired the view from the back, inhaling the earthy scent of his magic. The formerly decaying house plants had come to life again, sprouting flowers I didn't know. Summer magic— pretty but deadly sharp. And so much more.

I moved my blood-soaked clothes to my rucksack, and the talisman fell out. Water dripped onto the book from my wet hair and disappeared as though sucked into nothingness. I'd gained more control over it in the last fight, but not enough. I closed my eyes and tried to push the thoughts away. I was here for River. The damned book didn't matter a bit.

River reappeared in the blink of an eye. His hair was wet and tousled, falling over his pointed ears. Not so much as a blemish touched his lightly tanned skin, which was fairly noticeable because he was wearing only a towel. My mouth went dry and I folded my arms across my chest, suddenly overcome with self-consciousness.

He reached out, grabbed the book, and tossed it onto the bedside table.

"River, that thing contains the power of an ancient god."

"It's getting in the way of the view." He ran his hand lightly through my hair and kissed me on the mouth. *Oh.* "As I said..." His hand slid down my spine, under the towel. "Touching you." Both hands dug into my shoulders, kneading the cramped muscles. "Massaging the pain away..."

"Can we skip straight to the pleasure?" I let the towel fall and wrapped my arms around his back, pressing my damp skin against his. It was his turn to moan, kissing me back, fiercely, deeply. His hands explored my skin, not pausing, stroking the fire inside me. He nudged my legs apart, working his way up my inner thighs. I tried to hang on, but he was relentless, each stroke bringing me closer to the brink, each soft tease threatening to destroy my grip on sanity. Slowly, mercilessly, until my bones turned to water and I writhed beneath him, gasping for breath. As his fingers delved into me, pleasure exploded up my spine and I cried his name into the pillow.

Then I saw the towel had fallen away, revealing every inch of him. I reached for his erection and he groaned. "Ilsa."

"Condoms?"

"Top drawer." He spoke through clenched teeth.

"You knew you'd have me here eventually, huh." I one-handedly opened the drawer and removed a condom, momentarily letting go in order to slide it onto him.

"I was counting on it," he breathed, positioning himself above me.

"Then I'd better make it worth your while." My fists clenched on the bedsheets as he thrust into me.

We found our rhythm, and time disappeared, leaving only pleasure, a warm hot tingling sensation running from head to toe.

We lay tangled together, and he kissed the top of my head. "I wish we could stay here a week."

"I don't see why not." I stretched out on the bed, wrapping my legs around his. "There. You can't move."

He twitched, then effortlessly slid one leg free, gliding on top of me.

"Cheater," I murmured against his mouth. "I'll make you scream this time."

There was a buzzing noise. He leaned and picked up his phone from the table. "My mother is rather perturbed by my sudden absence."

"Crap. I bet Hazel and Morgan are, too. They've been playing their part at making this city safe while we've been..."

"Taking care of important business." He rolled off me. "Unfortunately, the Mage Lords seem to have decided we're to accompany them to dinner with the council tonight."

"Yeah, it's not a date if there are a dozen terrifying mages around," I said. "Might be a good time to announce our relationship to your mother…"

"She knows," he said. "I told her."

I tilted my head. "Before you told me?"

"You told me yourself, not in so many words." He kissed me on the mouth once again and walked to the closet in the corner. "We can't get out of this one. Sorry."

"And then we're coming back here?"

He grinned. "I'm frankly intrigued to find out what I can do to you in that shower."

2O

I didn't manage to corner Hazel and Morgan until the following morning. The council had called another meeting, more exclusive this time, so the four of us weren't invited. We met at the witch-run Cassandra's Cafe instead, where I picked the table in the far corner so nobody would overhear us.

"I can't believe they didn't invite us to the meeting after all we did in the battle yesterday," Hazel said, her mouth full of pancake. "Dicks."

"Actually, I think that might work in our favour." I poked at my food, my appetite noticeably absent. "The council... I'd say they'd work great as a backup force if this goes wrong, but none of them can actually set foot in Faerie without being at a huge disadvantage. Except Ivy. But I think the Erlking will only speak to Hazel or me alone."

I'd thought it over. One Sidhe had authority over all the others—and was also in a position to send the Summer Gate-keeper off to the Vale without anyone else knowing about it. He might be hidden behind layers of security, but there *must* be a backup measure put into place in case anything happened to the gate. How the enemy had stolen it in the first place was still a mystery to me.

"He won't speak to—" River began.

"Any of us," I said. "We've been through this. Trust me. Ivy will come and help us after the meeting."

I hadn't told them my plan yet, mostly because I wasn't sure it'd work myself. Just getting into the faerie realm itself seemed a tall order. And I wasn't the only one who'd been scheming.

"Necromancy," said Morgan.

"No," said Hazel. "Don't be ridiculous."

"It's a good plan."

"No, it's reckless and suicidal."

I rolled my eyes at them. They'd been arguing over the same points since after the battle yesterday. Morgan had decided that since he'd raised the dead in the Grey Vale, the Courts could use a shock of their own.

"I didn't mean zombies this time," Morgan said. "Someone died there, right? Can't we bring them back to testify?"

"You think the Sidhe would stop screaming at the sight of a ghost long enough to listen?" said Hazel. "That's if they don't turn you into a hummingbird."

"Actually…" I began.

"Don't encourage him." Hazel swiped the remainder of my pancake from my plate. "Hey—Ivy's here. Must have been a quick meeting."

I climbed to my feet, spotting Ivy weaving her way through the café. She turned heads even in here, probably because she hadn't bothered to disguise the fact that she was heavily armed.

"Hey," she said. "Good choice of venue. Damn, I wish I could get some of those pancakes…"

"Anything new come up in the meeting?" I asked.

"Same old." She rolled her eyes. "We're expecting another attack at any moment, but nobody knows where it'll come from or what form it'll take. Also, the Sidhe still haven't shown up. Something about a murder."

"That's what we were talking about," I said. "Morgan thinks raising the guy who died so he can testify to the Court might help, but I guess they wouldn't much like that."

"No, they wouldn't," said Ivy. "Even if it *was* possible. I never thought you could use necromancy in Faerie at all. But I've been thinking about what you said… and I think you might be right."

"What did you say?" Hazel said, looking suspiciously at me.

"I have an idea." I glanced at River. "I was waiting for Ivy to show up to share it. All our other plans risk us getting arrested. What we need is a direct way to get to the person who put the vow on us. There's one type of magic that's direct in that way."

"What, vows?" said Hazel dubiously. "Vows *are* direct, but only if you know the wording."

"We know one word." I pointed at her forehead, then at mine. "The Gatekeeper's binding mark… it's not just a mark. It means something."

"An Invocation," River said, in a low voice. "Neither of you can read it?"

"Can you?" said Hazel defensively.

He shook his head. "No. I only know a few words. I assumed since it was your family's, it was restricted to Gatekeepers only."

"I'm not Gatekeeper yet," Hazel said. "I know the final stages of my training probably involve learning all the Sidhe's secrets… and Mum definitely had some other way of getting directly into the Court. I always assumed it was down to the gate. But our symbol is carved into it."

"Exactly," I said. "It's a long shot, but... Ivy can read the language. Every word."

Hazel's mouth fell open. "But... how?"

"Instinct," she said. "Honestly, I've no idea. It's a side effect of my magic. Only people with Sidhe magic can actually speak the words aloud without consequences. I'd say you probably can, since you have the Gatekeeper's magic."

"Damn." Hazel shook her head. "This is way off the rulebook."

"I didn't think that mattered," I said. "Apparently the words are so specific that if they belong to a person, it takes you straight to them. So if we get into Faerie and speak that word, it'd take us to the gate, or to the person who put the spell on our family in the first place."

"Since it's a binding spell, I suppose it would take you to the caster," said River. I thought he'd approve of my plan. The book might terrify the Sidhe, but vows were a type of magic they'd created themselves, and respected. Unless they'd stolen that magic from the gods as well, but the point still stood. We had few other options.

"Oh." Hazel's expression cleared. "I get it. You can't use magic to get into Faerie if you aren't one of them, but if we work *with* their magic... the vow, if I used it in a literal sense, it'd act as though I'd have to *immediately* go and obey the one who put it on me, I'd be dragged straight to the Erlking and nobody would be able to stop me."

"The only downside is that you might not be able to take anyone with you," said Ivy.

"It's the bloodline," I said. "That's what the vow binds. It doesn't bind to a specific person until they take the position as Gatekeeper. If both of us speak, we'll both be taken there."

"How did you know?" said Hazel, surprise flashing across her face.

"I worked it out. Don't you remember?"

Our gazes connected. She remembered as well as I did the months leading up to her magic manifesting. Morgan had already passed the age where his magic might have shown up. But with the two of us, it might have been either of us who took the position. We hadn't known.

We'd sworn to break the curse.

Our plans never amounted to anything. Hazel seemed committed to her position at first, and whenever it became too much for her and she wanted to run away, she found me, and we pulled out all our old notes. All our guesses from what Mum had said, about the nature of the curse, and the possible wording of the vow. And how it might be undone. The entire family was bound to the one who spoke the Invocation. That *should* mean that since Hazel wasn't actually Gatekeeper yet, I should be able to go with her.

I was counting on it.

"So you want to go alone?" said Ivy. "The two of you?"

"The more people who go into Faerie, the more chances they have to hurt us," I said. "I need to tell the Erlking—if he really is the original caster—what I am. And that his wife's plotting against the Court."

"I can tell you how to pronounce the word here," Ivy said. "But we'd need to go into Faerie to actually get into the Seelie Court. Speaking those words draws on all the faerie magic in the area. There isn't much in this realm normally, and the two of you aren't used to handling the magic. It's... destructive. Powerful."

River rose to his feet, his face paling. "If it's that dangerous—"

"I'm just telling you what I know," said Ivy. "I used an Invocation to banish someone powerful when there was hardly any magic left in this realm at all. It's do-able. But I have to warn you of the risks."

"I'm lost," Morgan said. "How would speaking this magic word help at all?"

"Vows aren't set in stone," Hazel said, her eyes gleaming. "If someone swears *I will obey you,* the person it's cast on might decide it means *once.* So they obey, then they stop. If their will is stronger than the person who put the spell on them, they can't be compelled to obey them again. Of course it usually ends in a stalemate because the Sidhe are equally powerful. But the Erlking is indisposed. He's weak. If I figure out what exactly the vow said, I can outdo him. Or if it turns out the family's mark *is* the vow, or means *Gatekeeper,* it carries its *own* magic."

"Guess I'm sitting this one out," said Morgan.

"We need someone to keep an eye on things here," I said. "One problem… I guess we need to either find the Ley Line or a liminal space. Somewhere close to Faerie."

"I can find the Line," Ivy said. "We should leave before the council tries to stop us."

River was silent as we left the cafe and walked down the road, following Ivy's lead. Even my spirit sense didn't tell me the Ley Line's general direction, nor the book. But if Ivy could speak the gods' language aloud, then surely I could as well. I'd speak to the Erlking, and demand he get back our gate, and Mum along with it, or die trying.

There was no other way to end this.

The book's magic hummed in my veins. We drew to a halt, looking up at the peak of Arthur's Seat.

"We seriously have to climb the hill?" I said.

Ivy tilted her head up. "I can see a shit-ton of faerie magic up there. Must be a liminal space."

"Or the local half-faeries throwing a party," I said.

We began the steep climb. River could easily have taken the lead but hung back to walk at my side, occasionally looking at me as though to check I was still there. Finally, I grabbed his shoulders and kissed him in full view of the others, and probably half the tourists, too. He stared at me, his eyes stunned.

"If the Erlking doesn't let me come back, I'll tear a hole between the worlds with my own hands," I said to him.

"And if you're not back in a day, I'll do the same from this side," he said defiantly.

"Save your proclamations of love for after we've finished saving the world," Morgan said. He didn't look unenthusiastic about missing out on another trip into Faerie. On any other occasion, I'd have been happier sitting it out. But this was different.

Ivy glanced at me as the line drew closer. I saw it now, shivering with magic, tinted green. "That guy... River. He's a registered necromancer, right?"

"Yes," I said, unsure what she was getting at.

Ivy said, "We've been trying to get half-faerie representatives on the council for a year now, but they don't like having conflicting loyalties, and they always pick the Court. They're not keen on the idea of cross-supernatural cooperation. Neither are the shifters, but they can be bribed. We can give the shifters access to resources. Half-faeries don't want or need them." She shrugged. "But he seems to know both worlds, so he's a prime candidate. If he wants to. Just making a suggestion."

"He does," I said. "Lady Montgomery trusts him, too. Assuming we survive this, I'm not letting the council make any decisions about Faerie without consulting the Gatekeepers. Hazel isn't, either."

"I thought not," Ivy said. "Right... here's how you pronounce the word." She spoke it quietly, but the air hummed with magic.

I turned to Hazel. "Let's hope it's enough. If it's the god's language, and I have the gods' magic, it should work for me as well."

"Actually," Ivy said, "the Erlking once had—and created— a similar artefact himself. Lost, now. But he knew the gods. Maybe he's complicit."

I blinked. "You're telling me this now?"

"I don't know him," she said. "But... you be careful who you tell about the book."

"I will." *But it's my choice.* I'd get the Seelie Queen arrested no matter what.

Hazel and I stepped directly into the spot on the Ley Line. A place of potent magic. It tugged at my spirit, the Grey Vale calling for me. I paid it no attention, and looked at Hazel instead. Her face was a mirror of my own—stern resolution with a hint of fear.

We spoke the word aloud. And the forest moved. *Forest? Holy crap.*

Between one breath and the next, the Ley Line had shifted, the hill had vanished, and only forest remained. Summer territory.

21

Trees surrounded us, thick evergreens. The Seelie Court. The vow had brought us to the right place… but I'd hoped it would take us directly to the caster. The Erlking. Nobody appeared to be around, though the sounds of vibrant life surrounded us. Earthy smells, moss and berries and summer flowers. Birdsong. Sunlight.

Hazel's breath caught.

The forest flickered… and the glamour faded. The trees shrank to cadaverous shadows, hunched and dead. Rotting flowers wilted beneath, and the smell of decay caught in my nostrils. A throne appeared, made of the dead roots of a tree trunk.

For an instant, I was certain we'd accidentally wandered into Winter's Court, not Summer's. But the man on the throne wore the green and gold markers of Summer. His golden crown was edged in thorns, and his eyes were alight with Summer magic. He rose to his feet, one hand resting on a carved staff. Power hummed from it, and to my alarm, the book shifted in my pocket. My vision tinted, and I knew the mark on my forehead had begun to glow of its own accord.

"This is what happens when you bind with a talisman of the gods." He was beautiful, as all the Sidhe were. But everything around him was dead.

"How?" Hazel asked, her voice choked. "This... is this where the decay started?"

"No." He laughed, a rich laugh. "This part of Faerie has always been rotten to the core. His hand wrapped around the staff's hilt. It glowed faintly, but most of the glow, the only light here, came from him.

His talisman... he must have absorbed the magic into himself, and it was the type of Summer magic that drained life away. He couldn't touch anything without killing it.

Including us.

Holy crap. He's not sick. Everyone else is allergic to him.

"Why would you claim something like that?" I asked.

His gaze travelled to me. *Don't look directly in his eyes...* but I could, and they didn't dazzle me. I was too stunned to look away.

"I could ask you the same question."

He knew. He recognised the same magic in me. And while his eyes glowed with Summer power, the talisman he wielded was not of this world.

Did he *kill the gods?* Why was he king, if his magic could destroy every one of his subjects?

"What did you wish to ask me, mortal?" he enquired.

"You... bound our family." I forced the words out. "You must have spoken to our ancestors. The other Gatekeepers. The ones you enslaved."

"Enslaved?" he echoed. "No... no, your ancestors chose to bind themselves in service to our Court."

Bullshit. "Nobody would choose to hand over their own children."

"We don't die," he said. "The vow works in whatever way is necessary. There is always a Gatekeeper."

"There's apparently always an Erlking, too, but you're in serious danger," I told him. "Your wife is a traitor. The Court is dying."

He looked at me through vivid green eyes, his lip curling into a smile. "This part of the Court is always dying."

"Not here." I waved a hand vaguely. "How are you still the king? You... you don't even need to command obedience."

He could take a life with a touch... yet he didn't scare me. Maybe because anyone here could take our lives with no effort. He held no power over me—no more than the other Sidhe did, anyway.

"You misunderstand, mortal," said the Erlking. "I assumed, since you found your way to me... but I suppose nobody speaks of the gods anymore."

"You killed them."

His eyes caught mine. "No, mortal. I took in this power because nobody else would."

"I was told you created things... artefacts that could destroy worlds."

"Is this to do with whoever destroyed the gods' ring?" he asked.

"The what?" said Hazel blankly.

"We've no idea what you're talking about," I said, though a suspicion took hold of me. Ivy had mentioned a talisman... and she'd destroyed at least one, if the source of immortality could be called such a thing. No wonder the Sidhe didn't like her.

"Pity," he said. "I wanted to thank them. I spent years trying to rid myself of that monstrosity, but it was stolen from me. Of course, I cannot leave this grove without damaging the rest of this realm, so I was unable to retrieve it. Others from my time created those artefacts. The Courts were created to defend ourselves against them."

"I thought... it was to do with bloodlines," I said. "The heir..."

"Anyone can claim a throne," he said. "But I will not relinquish my power as long as this talisman exists. I don't need to spell out the damage it would do in the wrong hands."

No. He didn't. And ridiculously, I'd forgotten he was Sidhe, and couldn't lie. Every word he'd said had been the truth.

"You tied your life force to the talisman," I said. Almost like... necromancy, in a way. For the Sidhe.

"Most of us weren't alive in the time when the gods walked amongst us," said the Erlking. "The Ancients, the Powers... they were known by many names, and were by all accounts merciless and terrifying."

"They say the same about you."

The Erlking smiled. "I suppose they're right. But there are horrors that would put the darkest Unseelie faerie to shame. There are reasons our realm needs immortality to thrive... and I suspect you have guessed that's what I sent your mother to find."

"In the Vale," I said. "The gods' magic—what's left of it—ended up there, right? Unless you have more talismans lying around..."

"There may be others," he said. "I sent her for knowledge, nothing more. But you should know... I have been unable to call her back. Whatever force holds her is stronger than our vow."

My breath caught. "Stronger?"

Hazel gasped. "So... something has her captive?"

He shook his head, a frown darkening his face. "I cannot pinpoint the nature of what holds her. She lives, and she is still within our realm. Yes, I count the Vale as part of this realm, though most do not. You must find her yourselves, if at all."

Then we will. We have to.

"That's not all we came to ask you about," I said. "Your wife…"

"I know she plots against the Court, the fool," he said. "None of her schemes have ever amounted to anything. She knows what will happen if she defies me."

"She murdered someone. Permanently. I'm sure of it. And she tried to kill both of us. I think she's behind whatever took Mum."

The only thing stronger than the Erlking was… another god. But Ivy had said they'd died out. All of them.

"Again," he said. "I'm unable to leave this grove to check up on my scheming spouse."

"Then what are we supposed to do?" I asked. "You know she'll kill us if we accuse her publicly. And you must know we're not strong enough to kill her, and even if we were, we'd face execution for murdering a Sidhe whether she is guilty or not."

"Then you must choose. It's not up to me… but I can help. Your mother is in the enemy's hands. So is the gate. The one thing they don't have is that talisman. Don't let them get their hands on it."

"They don't want it," I said. "She could have taken it from me… how do you even know about it?"

"Because I knew it in another form," said the Erlking. "I cannot say for certain how it gained the shape that it did, but a piece is missing."

A piece is missing? "I don't understand."

"There is much even the Sidhe don't know. But I will say that my wife believes that if she finds the source of immortality first, she will be strong enough to wield a talisman of her own. And while I would like to be reborn again, there will be war if one person controls the source."

"Just what *is* the source of immortality?" said Hazel.

A cauldron of blood. A chill raced down my spine as he looked us over.

"Your own magic forbids you from claiming it," he said. "But you will be unable to speak a word of this to anyone else. The lifeblood of the Ancients carries the essence of immortality. They were endless until we forced them not to be. I claimed this throne because I feared the powers the other Sidhe, especially Winter, would claim without being kept in check. In the end, I was too late. Every god was killed or exiled, reduced to a shadow. And their lifeblood kept our shameful secret alive." He paused. Not a sound echoed through the clearing, and hardly a breath disturbed the silence.

"I watched Sidhe fall, entranced by those talismans, or driven to madness," the Erlking continued. "They were exiled, where they formed their own kingdoms to threaten us, over and over again. Immortality has taken more lives than it has saved, and I rather think your realm has paid most dearly for it. But many disagree. They see it as the natural way of things."

"What can *we* do against the gods?" I asked. "How are we supposed to find our mother?"

I already knew the answer.

"The book," he said. "The missing piece. I haven't seen it for a while. It used to visit here... maybe it speaks to another now."

"It's alive?" said Hazel dubiously. "It can speak? I thought you said the gods weren't alive anymore."

"Not as they were."

That's no answer. Now I was even more confused. Was he toying with me on purpose?

"You should leave," he said. "It was dangerous, what you did. I wish I could offer more help."

"You could help by telling us the name of the god inside this book," I said. "Speaking it aloud didn't do anything."

But we'd been in Death at the time. Maybe its owner was here, in Faerie.

"Not here," he said sharply. "You'll alert other things if you speak that name. Go. Before you're discovered here."

"Wait—"

But the forest faded, turning to hillside once again. The city unfurled below, wreathed in sunshine. As though nothing had happened.

As though the foundations of the universe hadn't shifted.

"What in hell was that about?" Hazel said, her hair blowing about in the breeze coming off the coast. "He said the gods weren't alive. And they aren't. But one of them has Mum and one of them's flown off with part of your book's power."

Flown off.

"Hazel," I said quietly.

Her brow furrowed. "What? You have this weird look in your eye."

"I think…"

"Ilsa!" River shouted. He and Morgan climbed up from below. They must have been waiting down the hillside.

"Knew they'd make it out," said Morgan. "So, what did the Erlking have to say?"

"I'll tell you on the way down," I said. "One quick question, Hazel—in all your research on the family history, did you find out how long Arden has been in our family?"

Hazel frowned. "No. Where's Ivy?"

"She teleported off with that mage of hers," said Morgan. "Something about the council… I dunno. Where is that little bastard of a bird, anyway?"

"Probably with Holly," said Hazel. "It's not like *he* could have got us to the Erlking, anyway."

"Maybe he could have," I said. "He's tied up in the vow as well. Who did that?"

"The Erlking did?" said Morgan.

Hazel shook her head, still frowning. "He didn't mention it, but he must have. Who else? Arden's a shapeshifter faerie… he was probably sent as a spy. I mean, Arden works for both sides. Maybe Winter sent him instead. Which proves he was a traitor either way."

"What else came from Winter?" I asked.

Hazel looked at me. Then at my pocket, which was still glowing faintly from the close proximity of the Ley Line. "You can't be implying what I think you are."

"I'm lost," said Morgan. "River is, too, but he won't admit it. Or he's too busy messaging someone."

River's attention was on his phone instead. "I'm listening," he said. "But he's right—I don't know enough of your family history to make a judgement call on the bird, only that he can't be trusted and works for both Courts."

"As a neutral force, he said. I remember," I said. "Which part of the Court is neutral?"

"The borderlands?" said Morgan. "Or the Vale?"

"Right…" I shook my head. "This is a long shot. I might have wildly misinterpreted what the Erlking said, but he said the book had a piece missing. Someone bound up its magic, and it must have been a Sidhe… a Winter one. But its power originally came…"

"From the gods, I know," said River. "You think you know which god it was?"

"Oh, for crying out loud," snapped Hazel. "Ilsa thinks Arden is a god." She snorted. "Sorry, Ilsa. But you know, that's a wild mental leap to make. The gods are supposed to be more powerful than the Sidhe."

"Not with their magic removed," I said. "They're mostly dead. Or exiled. To the Vale… I'm not saying I have the slightest clue how its magic got in here, but who dragged me back to the Lynn house in the first place?"

"Wait," said Morgan. "There were ravens flying around when I went back to Edinburgh. My memory's kinda hazy, but I remember following one…"

We looked at one another. Hazel looked sceptical. So did River. But I couldn't explain how I knew.

"The book has a really annoying personality," I said. "It's demanding and bossy and refuses to give clear answers. Makes sense that it has part of that damned raven inside it."

"Doesn't that mean you should be able to call him?" said Hazel. "He's… Ilsa, I'm not being mean, but that raven has never listened to you in his life."

"He has the last few times," I said. "He got us into Summer… but he's only allowed to obey the Gatekeepers. There's definitely a vow on him to that effect. And vows probably work just as well on the gods as the Sidhe. The Sidhe borrowed the rest of their magic from them."

"Arden," Hazel called. I shushed her, but she ignored me. "Arden, Ilsa thinks you're a god." She laughed. "I wish it were true. It'd help us now for sure. But he's been *no* help in times of crisis."

"Like I said." I pulled the book from my pocket. "He's vow-bound. I don't think we should summon him here. It's not like the Erlking… we know he's a god."

"I know Faerie's magic has gone to your head," said Hazel.

I didn't even have the energy to be annoyed at her for not believing me. "Then let me try summoning him. If he's a Vale creature and in this realm, I can use necromancy. Worst case scenario is we know one theory is out. Deal?"

22

The mages must still be in a meeting, because nobody was in the lobby of their headquarters. I'd have picked the necromancers' guild as a safer place to try to summon Arden, but the iron bindings would likely stop us. It wasn't like I actually knew which realm he was in. We'd try necromancy, then if that failed, blood magic. Not that I'd mentioned the latter part yet. Maybe I didn't need to. If Arden was really bound to our family, then that alone should make him answer our call.

River brought the candles with him, laying them out on the floor of a spare room.

"Can you summon someone who's not a ghost?" asked Morgan.

"If he's in the Vale or the Ley Line, since he's originally from the Vale himself," I said. "This is as controlled a setting as we can get, and if he's pissed at us for figuring out what he is, then we need all the protection there is."

Not that a dozen candles and an iron and salt barrier felt like much against the gods, but the magic users of times past must have found a way around it. The gods had been involved with this realm for at least as long as the Sidhe had.

I also wielded his power. Part of it. For what it was worth.

I faced the circle. Spoke the words. And ended with the Gatekeeper's name.

There was a whirl of smoke within the circle. And then… the winged form of the raven appeared.

It actually was him.

Hazel's jaw dropped. Morgan backed slowly away. And River drew his blade so fast, it blurred.

"You," I said to Arden. "Nice of you to show up to help. Have you been helping the Winter Gatekeeper instead?"

"Actually, I've been giving her terrible advice for weeks," he said blandly. "I wondered when you'd work it out."

"You might have told me sooner," I said heatedly.

"To prove what, exactly?"

"That you're on our side, and not out to kill us." The book nearly *had* killed me several times. "You think this is fun? You *want* us to die?"

"No. I would prefer to avoid a war. The enemy wants war and your own path will lead to the same. Therefore, I work for nobody."

"But you're still working for her," I said through clenched teeth.

"No. I serve the other Winter Gatekeeper."

"Holly," I said. "You're still… an Ancient. Your magic…"

The raven cackled. "If I had powerful magic independent of that book, I would have used it to break this spell."

Hazel mouthed, *Holy shit.*

I arched a brow back at her so as to say, *I told you so.* Not that I felt particularly triumphant now it hit me that the only way to access the full extent of my book's power was to wrangle obedience out of the most unreliable raven in any realm.

"You nearly got us killed before," I said to him. "You're not trustworthy at all. How do we know you're not the one behind the whole scheme? You must have been as powerful as the Sidhe are. Before whatever got you trapped in that form."

His eyes flashed furiously. The book glowed in my pocket.

"Yes, I suppose you could say I was. The first Winter Gatekeeper thought it amusing to keep me chained," he said dismissively. "I served her every whim for many years, unable to leave their home. Then one day, the dead came through the gate. They attacked the house when the Gatekeeper was absent. Their daughter was left behind." He paused. "The girl was somewhat accomplished at necromancy, as the line ran in both sides of the family. But it wasn't enough. Something evil was coming through the gates. Chained as I was, I couldn't fight it. So I handed my powers over to her. The power was volatile and nearly killed her. After she succeeded in banishing the dead, she sought the help of the council and they offered to bind the power to the book. Such was its power that every one of them was sucked beyond the gates, forgotten, leaving only the book."

I rocked back on my heels, wishing I'd brought a chair to fall into. "You woke the book for me so I could wield it against a similar enemy. But you hid most of the right information from me until it was too late. Why?"

"Your idea of the 'right information' would have wrought destruction if used at the wrong time."

"And you'd know? You weren't even there."

The raven flapped his wings, hovering within the circle. "The book's original owner knew the dangers it posed. She knew the gates wouldn't be closed forever. The oblivion beyond the gates waited, and others waited to claim it. So she kept the book and left no record of how to use it."

"If she'd left a record, I wouldn't have been running around clueless while people got hurt," I said, folding my arms across my chest.

"Or you might have died yourself. You should know what the book does when its power isn't contained. You are not the same as one of us. You're mortal."

"No shit," I said. "I know I'm mortal. The book has been tearing me apart every time I use it. But there's no other option. Is the whole point in it that I turn into a martyr or let the worlds fall apart? It's not like the Sidhe are exactly careful with their magic either."

"Of course they aren't," said the raven, his beady eyes gleaming.

"Can you at least tell me where Mum is? She's in the Vale. Along with the gate. And whatever is holding her is stronger than the Erlking. What are we supposed to do?"

"Kill it. Everyone can die, even the gods," the raven spat.

The summoning circle trembled. Then the ceiling opened, and plaster dust rained down. Shouts came from outside, but sounded oddly muted.

I've seen this before. "Did you do it?" I demanded. "You're breaking the house."

"Not me," he said. "Caw. Run. *Run.*"

A tremendous blast of icy air rushed into the room, and Holly ran in through the open door. She looked at the summoning circle, then at me.

It wasn't her eyes looking at me, but the Winter Gatekeeper's.

"Finally," she growled. "If only I'd known there was one of the gods beside me all this time…"

My spirit sight flickered, showing me *two* spirits where there should only be one. The Winter Gatekeeper must have crossed over from the gate, long enough to latch onto Holly's body and temporarily possess her. And her magic had come along for the ride.

Arden screeched. His body shifted forms, to a larger bird with sharp talons, and he lunged out of the circle at Holly. Before he struck her, he collided with an invisible barrier. Dust continued to rain down, and creaking noises came from overhead.

The Winter Gatekeeper's laughter came from Holly's mouth. "The curse still binds you even in that form. You cannot harm the current Gatekeeper... and now that's me once again."

But I can. The book's power hummed in my fingertips, and the binding words left my lips—

Not before she screamed a word. My body left the ground, slamming into the wall. River shouted my name, and a rain of plaster dust drowned out everything else. I pushed away from the wall, my vision swimming.

The window shattered in an explosion of glass and Ivy Lane jumped in, pointing her blade at Holly. "I have no idea who you are, but you look like someone I have to kill."

"Ilsa." River ran to me. I groaned. The book's power... Where was it?

An Invocation. She spoke an Invocation. The words of the gods—she'd done something to my magic. And the house. The rain of plaster dust had stopped, and though creaking noises came from overhead, the building had stopped collapsing.

All eyes locked onto Arden, who kept shapeshifting. Morgan spoke the banishing words, but Arden didn't vanish from the circle.

The Winter Gatekeeper laughed lightly. "You can't so easily banish a god when you summon one, you foolish children."

"Go back to hell," I growled. I didn't want to hurt Holly,

but I'd restrain the evil spirit by any means necessary. *Come on, book.* She couldn't have indefinitely blocked its power.

River's hands lit up, and he ran at Holly, blasting her in the direction of the circle. He wasn't bound by the spell not to harm her, but Holly barely stumbled. A knife appeared in her hands. *No.*

Ivy got there first, but Holly shouted an Invocation again. Everyone in the room fell to the ground, pushed by a relentless force. I could barely raise my head to watch as Holly grabbed Arden's struggling body and stabbed him in the throat. Blood poured over her hands.

"Lifeblood," I whispered. "Shit."

"Tell me that bird isn't what I think it is," Ivy muttered.

"I can't do that. Sorry." The powerful force continued to press on me. "She's trying to recreate the cauldron of blood. That god... his power's in the book."

Holly gasped, falling to her knees, as the Winter Gatekeeper's spirit let go of her, dissolving into the bloody mass on the floor.

The blood rose like a living force, encasing the Winter Gatekeeper's spirit like she was solid. Her outline gleamed, no longer remotely like a ghost. The god's blood filled in the gaps, binding her to the land of the living once more.

"I am the first to be reborn," she said, with a smile.

Holly stared at her in horror, at the *thing* that had once possessed her, given life once again. The Winter Gatekeeper's raven-black hair was glossier than it'd been before. Her face was angular and her ears pointed. Black armour encased her body, now taller and sleeker than a human's. She'd always been striking, but now she was breath-taking—and raw Winter magic shone in her glowing blue eyes.

"I'll let the Sidhe queue up to beg to be next," she added, then spoke a word. The blood on the floor disappeared in a whirl of light, which passed into her hands. In the blink of an eye, she held a book covered in leather the colour of blood. "I thought this was an appropriate host for power. Ancient tomes hold magic, don't they, Ilsa?"

I couldn't respond or move. My throat was dry, my mind fighting the instinctive fear of setting eyes on one of the Sidhe. She might still superficially resemble the mortal she'd been before, but my mind screamed *wrong* at the very idea of one of *them* standing in this realm.

"How the hell did you know that language?" said Ivy. "All records in this realm were destroyed."

"Knowledge can be relearned and recovered," she said. "But I think you know I have allies in dangerous places. And now the source of immortality rests with me alone."

She was truly immortal now. Had even the Sidhe started out the way they were? Or were their own bodies artificial creations of the blood of their predecessors?

Think, Ilsa. I twitched my hand, remembering I still held the book. The symbol on the cover had gone, and from what I could see of the edges of the pages, they were entirely blank.

The Winter Gatekeeper's Sidhe form raised a hand, deflecting Ivy's sword.

"You don't think you're the first posturing immortal I've had to kill, do you?" Ivy said. "You're nothing."

The Winter Gatekeeper's hands glowed, forming a blazing current of Winter magic, and threw it at Ivy. Ice shattered the walls, striking the falling debris, burying Ivy beneath it. Hazel and Morgan shouted in alarm, and River grabbed my arm. I moved my body to shield him, and the magic ricocheted off the Lynn shield—but not Ivy.

She lay limply on the floor, blood pooling around her. I gasped and moved forwards, but she lifted her head a little.

"The faerie killer is down," said the Winter Gatekeeper, turning on me. "And the Gatekeeper's power is bound."

And we can't banish her. Because she no longer had a soul in the sense that humans did. She'd entirely merged with her new Sidhe body. The only way to kill her was to take away the source of her immortality. But there was one type of magic she wasn't immune to.

Necromantic magic swirled from my hands, merging with Morgan's and River's, and slammed into her. She hit the remaining piece of wall, which collapsed. Icy shards rose from the ruins, but bounced harmlessly off our shield.

Her mouth twisted with hate. "I'm no longer bound by the agreement not to harm you."

Her magic... her magic had been reset. That's all a vow truly was—a binding of magic more than words. She could harm us. We could do likewise. But our magic-proof shield would hold. It had to—

A sword flew through the air. River fell back, bleeding, but his aim was true, piercing Candice Lynn through the chest. She screamed in fury, blood spilling down the front of her newly glamoured clothes.

"How's that for lifeblood?" shouted Morgan. "You're weakened by iron now, too. Bet you never thought of that."

Ice spread from her hands, flowing across the floor and up my legs. Hazel and Morgan, too, and River. Like the transforming spell in the faerie realm, there were some kinds of magic that could bypass our shields, and this was one of them. My legs locked together, instincts screaming at me to run before whatever had stopped the guild from collapsing wore off. It was too quiet outside. What in hell had happened to the council?

Ivy rose shakily to her feet. A spear of ice sent her down again. *She has healing powers...* but they must have a limit. And a newly reborn Sidhe had enough power to bring down an army.

The Winter Gatekeeper advanced on me. "I must ask you to hand over that book, Ilsa," she said.

"You know I couldn't do that even if I wanted to," I said. Not that it mattered, in theory. Arden's death had left it blank. I'd never be able to read it now.

"Your allies won't come to help you," said the Winter Gatekeeper. "You're alone. If you give me the book, I'll spare this city. I've no intention of starting a war. Our role is for peace, after all."

"You've got to be fucking joking," said Hazel. "You tried to incite a war with the Sidhe when you were a ghost. Now you're one of them. Do you think they'll welcome you to their Court with open arms?"

"I spent my life studying the Sidhe. Some have already agreed to join me. We really do need new blood in the Courts. So many half-faeries and fallen Sidhe are waiting for their new bodies..."

No. It can't end like this.

The book began to glow again. Her words couldn't bind it indefinitely. She might be Sidhe, might have killed Arden, but the book's magic would always outrank hers.

She raised a hand, and the house's ceiling fractured. Water slid over the ceiling at impossible angles, hardening to sharp ice. There was nowhere to run. If she brought it crashing down on us, we'd be crushed under several floors of debris. Not even Ivy or River could heal from that.

Panic gripped my chest. My gaze fell on Arden's lifeless body lying beside the still-glowing candles, an empty summoning circle.

The ceiling cracked. A piece of ice came down, landing inches from my foot. The Winter Gatekeeper held out a hand.

"Give me the book."

I pushed the last of my magic at the candles. They flew

outwards, striking the corners of the room, and I shouted the words of binding.

River caught on and joined me, Morgan chiming in a second later. She hadn't bound us not to use necromancy, and we'd turned the room into a magic-proofed circle. The building wouldn't collapse on us… but we'd also trapped the Winter Gatekeeper inside the circle with us.

Fury suffused her features. "You dare resort to human tricks?"

"Human tricks?" I said. "You're talking like a Sidhe already."

My hands glowed, and I hit her with necromantic power, pushing her against the circle's edge. If I got her outside, she'd be crushed by her own magic.

"I command you to open the book," she said. One word came from her mouth, and the book ignited.

She'd read the word from the cover, activating its power. The book's magic filled the circle, and the shape of the gates appeared, ready to drag us all in. Death tugged at my body, and at the others, too. Everyone except her. Mortal death held no threat to her. She stood calmly, while the others, even Ivy, began to drift towards the gates…

No. Please no.

My body glowed all over. I felt the gate close in, and knew it would pull me in, not her. Because she was immune. And if she took the book, if she won that power over… she'd be the Gatekeeper *and* Sidhe. I couldn't let her do it.

"Sorry," I said. "I can't let you do that. You won't get your wish."

I stepped out of my body, concentrating all my will on the book, on pulling it with me into Death the way Ivy carried her sword through the void.

Her eyes widened in disbelief as my body fell to its knees, the book no longer in its hands.

I lunged at her hand, and grabbed the book of lifeblood.

It came with me into death, an item made of both living and dead realms. The momentum sent me flying to the very edge of the gates. The place where if I went beyond, there would be no returning.

I focused on the book, at pulling the gates closed, but my spirit was already being pulled into the void. The Winter Gatekeeper screamed in fury as the gate swallowed me up.

I floated away. The book of lifeblood came with me. A newly forged talisman. Already, the gods' blood seeped through the pages, rotting away. It wasn't meant to be contained in an object like this. The cauldron had apparently been an exception.

She'd never meant to pass on the power. Only hoard it for herself.

I let the book go, and it floated into the empty void.

Without the lifeblood, she wouldn't be reborn if one of the others killed her. I had to hope they'd have the chance before the circle ran out of power. I'd taken away her shot at immortality, and she'd be out to take as many people down with her as possible.

River's pained expression floated before my eyes. Silent, dry tears fell down my cheeks. The world beyond the gate didn't look like much of anything at all. But I'd gone too far now. My body would be dead, but like a necromancer Guardian, I'd endure. The book... the book would do what it needed to, and that was it.

Hazel and Morgan.

Mum.

River.

Oh, god. I'm sorry.

At least Ivy would be able to visit me…

"What's supposed to be here?" I asked of thin air. "This is Beyond?"

"Not even Guardians get to see that," said a voice. Frank the necromancer appeared from the gloom. I felt stupidly relieved considering I didn't even know the guy. It was just nice to see a familiar face for a second.

"What a let-down." I scrubbed my eyes, but no traces of tears remained. "You knew I was Guardian material when you saw me, right?"

"I assumed you'd have longer in the realm of the living before you moved on," he said.

Pain gripped my heart. "So I'm dead. For real."

"Most would be. As for that book of yours… it remains to be seen."

"Yeah, but now you have to tell me all your secrets. You know the Vale. You knew… did you know about the Gatekeeper's curse?"

He floated on the spot against a backdrop of nothingness. "Only superficially. My predecessor knew more than I do."

"Wait, there's a Guardian older than you are?"

"He chose to move on."

I blinked. "I didn't know there was a term limit."

"Do you really want to spend an eternity existing here? Would you answer the question the same way in ten years?"

"I've been dead five minutes. Give me some time to get used to it before asking me difficult existential questions," I said. "Can I get into Faerie from here?"

"Not directly."

"The Vale," I said. "The enemy is in the Vale. One of them."

I'd left the others to face the Winter Gatekeeper alone.

She was outnumbered, but she was also pure Sidhe.

She's vulnerable to iron, and she's not used to being one of them. The others would think of a plan. Someone had to. Because my job was only to hold the book.

The book, whose owner was dead.

Wait.

"Can you find an individual person?" I asked him.

"No. Not here. Most move on…"

Right. Of course. For a god who'd endured for generations, it had probably been a relief in some ways. The book remained blank when I looked at it. Arden was gone.

I hoped I hadn't died for nothing. If the Winter Gatekeeper broke the circle and declared herself Queen of the mortal realm…

I'll warn the Sidhe first. It was all up to me.

I floated back towards the gates. Almost immediately, the ground turned into the path to the Vale. The Ley Line… The territory blurred, and I found myself near the borderlands. There was a path here which led to Winter, and I floated through. Nobody accosted me. Probably, they couldn't even see me. But I could see them. And I could see dozens of half-faerie ghosts, floating on the brink.

"She's not coming," I told them. "Whoever told you that you would get to live again, they lied. You're stuck here forever. With me."

"You're supposed to die," said one of them. "We're supposed to sacrifice ourselves to kill you."

"And you think you'll be reborn after that?" I said. "They lied. You can see it. You must be able to."

Life and death were two sides of the same coin. Their magic might look different, but it was as much a glamour as this entire realm. Beneath, the empty darkness waited, called by my book's power.

The ghosts were crying, holding onto one another,

looking around desperately. Summer and Winter alike, united in death.

"Those wraiths," I said to the half-faerie ghosts. "That's what'll happen to you if you die here. But I can get you out. Wait for me. I have a couple of things to take care of."

I cast my gaze around, looking for the path into the Summer Court—and spotted another ghost floating apart from the others. Not speaking. And unlike the other ghosts, he was Sidhe.

"You died," I said to him. Less time had passed in this realm than I'd thought.

"You're... human." He stared at me. "How are you here... like this?"

"Good question," I said. "You need to tell them who killed you. It was the Seelie Queen, right?"

"How did you—?"

"She tried to do the same to me. Look, as a ghost, you can make yourself visible to them. Like a glamour. I can't explain how to do it. I... haven't been dead long, and I'm not Sidhe." I glanced over his shoulder. Other, living Sidhe gathered in the meadow at the end of the path, entirely oblivious to us. "Watch."

I floated to the Sidhe. The book's power hummed through my veins.

"Wisp," said one of the Sidhe. "Which of you is spinning a glamour?"

"I'm not a glamour," I told him. "I'm the Gatekeeper. And I'm here to warn you that one of your own is planning a coup. You need to gather an army to come to the Vale, or the Death Kingdom, right away. They took Summer's gate."

"What magic is this?" demanded the Sidhe. Oh, Lord Raivan. What a surprise.

"Hey," I said, waving at him. "I'm dead. And so is this guy. The Seelie Queen killed him."

All eyes turned to the Sidhe ghost, who'd apparently figured out how to turn himself visible after all.

"Lord Voren," said one of the Sidhe. "What have you done?"

"He's dead," I said. "Permanently. This is what you'll become when you die, and that'll be all of you if you don't come and help me. The Seelie Queen is conspiring with Vale outcasts."

"She speaks the truth," said the ghost.

"You're a glamour," snarled the Sidhe. "A trick."

Oh, for god's sake. The problem with living in a realm where nothing was 'real' in the normal sense was that even truth wasn't absolute. For all I knew, Sidhe ghosts could lie. And according to everything the Sidhe understood, ghosts didn't exist.

"I'm here to warn you," I shouted. "The Seelie Queen is a traitor, and her people are forming an army in the Vale. If you search for the gate—the Summer Gatekeeper's gate—you'll find someone has moved it from the Ley Line into the Vale."

I hadn't thought such a thing was possible. It was fixed to the Ley Line. Hell, maybe it was still there, but hidden. It wasn't like I'd checked the entire Ley Line. And Ivy had told me it led through the path of the dead…

"Just trust me," I said to the dumbfounded Sidhe. "The fallout of this will hit the Courts whether you want to help me or not. Also, there's a new Sidhe on earth who stole a temporary source of immortality and made herself Sidhe, so she'll probably come back to make trouble as well."

There was a flash of white light, and several people appeared in front of the stupefied-looking Sidhe. Quentin the brownie stood there. Behind him were Ivy, Hazel, Morgan and River.

"There she is," Morgan said, pointing at me. "Knew she'd

be doing something risky."

"What the hell are you doing?" I hissed at them.

"Helping you," said Hazel.

"You're not supposed to be here."

The Sidhe stood frozen, staring at us. Lord Raivan scowled. "You again?" he said to Hazel.

"You can't keep me away," Hazel said. "We're looking for a criminal who ran into the borderlands."

"The Winter Gatekeeper ran away?" I asked, trying to catch someone's gaze. River's eyes were on the body in his arms. *Oh shit.* He'd brought me—brought my dead body here with him. What in hell was he thinking?

"She broke the circle," Ivy said to me. "She's wounded, and pissed off, but she managed to cross into Faerie. She figured that ability out fast."

"We got her," Hazel said. "When she was distracted taunting you, I set up an iron spell. She walked right into it."

"Her skin turned grey and started falling off," added Morgan.

"Nice," I said. "But—did she run into Faerie, or the Vale?"

"It shouldn't be hard for them to find her if she's here," Hazel said. "They can sense iron from a mile away, and she has a whole stake embedded in her spine."

I stared at them, the Sidhe entirely forgotten. "How did I miss that?"

"Because you were too busy trying to sacrifice yourself," said Hazel.

"If she'd taken that book, we'd all be six feet under. Where in the world are the Mage Lords and the necromancers?"

"Dealing with the undead plague she raised with her last piece of necromancy," said Hazel. "Holly ran to help. I think she feels bad."

"She ought to," said Morgan. "She killed you."

"She's not dead," River snapped at him, apparently oblivious to the Sidhe witnessing the whole thing.

"Can we debate whether I'm dead or not after we find our runaway gate?" I said. "And the Winter Gatekeeper."

Lord Raivan stepped forwards. "Get off our territory," he snarled. "*All* of you."

"Ask the Erlking," I said desperately. "For god's sake." I'd wanted the Sidhe at my back. Not my friends to risk their lives again. But time was running out. Mum was trapped, and if one of the gods was really responsible, even the Sidhe might not have a chance.

Quentin stepped forward to talk to them, but their faces said it all. He was only a brownie, the others were mortals, and they still didn't believe I was real. Let alone the other ghost. We were running out of time.

Ivy caught my gaze. "I hope you have a plan."

"Get the Sidhe to follow me and confront the Seelie Queen. Didn't quite work out that way. Their dead buddy is there and they don't even think he's real."

"Figures." Ivy rolled her eyes. She was still covered in blood, but her injuries had entirely healed. Faerie magic—or gods' magic—really was something. "You're looking for your mother?"

"The gate," I said. "Or both. I think one of the gods has her. But the gate can't move from the Ley Line. I reckon it might still be there."

Her eyes widened in understanding. "I think I know where it is." She glanced back at Quentin, who was still talking to the Sidhe. "We're on our own, though."

"Fine," I said. "How do we get there from here?" Bringing four living people with me hadn't been on my plan.

"Where are you two sneaking off to?" asked Morgan.

"To find Mum, and the gate," I told him. "I'm dead. There's literally nothing they can do to hurt me. Except hurt *you,* which is exactly why I came here alone."

"Tough shit," said Morgan. "We're your family. We're here whether you like it or not."

The fool. All of them. My eyes burned. They'd totally thrown off my game.

"Fine," I said. "I don't *know* what we'll find at the end of this. Ivy, where's the quickest route? Through borderland territory?"

"This path leads there, eventually," she said, indicating the way I'd come in. The path bent at improbable angles and wove away into shadows. "I can probably find it."

"Probably?" said Hazel.

The Sidhe ghost floated to my side, his eyes wide and staring. He probably didn't know what to make of my bizarre mismatched family.

"Sorry they didn't believe you," I said.

"Something is calling me," he said. "Something beyond…"

Ivy nodded to me. "Go after him. He'll lead us in the right direction."

The path changed as the Sidhe's ghost moved forward, floating upwards. Uphill. River and Ivy turned in the ghost's direction, while Morgan gaped at the spot where the meadow had been seconds before. It'd gone, to be replaced by a steep hill covered in half-dead trees. The smell of death drifted on the breeze, and a cold sensation spread through me. Something close by called to my spirit, and it wasn't friendly.

Ivy hissed out a breath. "Death Kingdom… he'll pass through this way, but we need to find the *old* path of the dead."

"How do you know all this?" asked Hazel. "You've been here a lot?"

"No," said Ivy. "A couple of times. It all looks familiar, and when you have their magic, you get attuned to it."

The hill levelled off. The ghost kept floating onwards, into mist, but Ivy paused. "We need to find a path…"

"I'm starting to think you don't know the way," Morgan said.

River didn't say anything. He still carried my body over his shoulder, his blade in his free hand.

"You shouldn't have come," I told him. "Not with me. I'm not alive."

"Ilsa, you're still breathing," he said, his jaw set. "I won't give up on you."

"This way," Ivy called. "The path of the dead is a liminal space, so it overlaps with the Ley Line." She took off again, weaving through the trees, her body outlined in shimmering Winter magic. A path began to appear between the trees, squashed flat, as though trampled by a million hooves. As the trees thinned out, it became more distinct.

"Don't walk off the line," she said over her shoulder.

I'd never have been able to keep up with her if I wasn't a ghost. Hazel and Morgan ran behind River, downhill, as the path widened and the trees turned grey until the path almost resembled the Vale. It led in a straight line into nothingness in either direction.

"This was faster when riding on a hellhound from the Vale." Ivy looked up and down the path. "This way. Just keep moving in a straight line."

"I'm sorry, did I hear you say you *rode* on a hellhound?" I asked.

"Long story. Keep close behind me. Anything might have moved in since I was last here."

"Wonderful," said Morgan. "And I thought being a *human* necromancer was weird."

Eventually, the path widened into an empty clearing with dead grass and little else. In the middle of the patch of the grass lay the family's gate. Summer's gate.

Mum was tied to it with thick ropes, her eyes closed. Aside from a thin gash on her cheek, she looked unharmed. Alive.

My heart seized. *The first thing she's going to see is my dead body.* I looked desperately at River, but Mum didn't stir. And nobody else was around.

"Well?" I asked of the echoing silence. "Who's behind this? Not the Winter Gatekeeper... isn't anyone going to own up to this?"

Mum's hand twitched, but she remained unconscious.

"Come on," I said. "I thought the Sidhe liked to show off. Or are you saving it until after you expose your new immortality source to the realms?"

"I'll get her down," said Morgan. He walked towards the ropes that held our mother, and a blast of magic knocked into him. He flew back several feet. Hazel caught him before he fell.

"It's... magic." His whole body was shaking.

My heart climbed into my throat as I looked closer at the gate. The Gatekeeper's symbol on the top gleamed, while between its bars, eerie light shone. Not magic... not the type I knew, anyway. Or maybe I did. There was something seriously powerful beyond that gate.

"I thought the gods were dead," I said quietly. "Except Arden."

"They *were* all dead," Ivy said. "The last one *told* me, before he died. But... maybe not. If Arden survived, it makes sense others did too."

Ivy clearly had more to tell me... but whatever was beyond that gate was more than Summer or Winter magic. Magic fed on life or death, and from the state Mum was in, the realm beyond the gate was feeding on the Summer Gatekeeper's life force, and on the family's magic.

I know what they did. The Sidhe—the Summer Queen—

had opened a way into the hellish dimension beyond the Vale itself to capture one of them, to use it to give themselves immortality once more. The gate was unbreakable. There was probably no stable way to open such a rift within their own realm without risking total destruction. But here—the mortal realm was right on the other side of the line.

Think, Ilsa. I might wield the gods' magic myself, but mine was a whole different beast. And so was Arden. I was only guardian of one gate, not this one.

"Hazel, can you feel the Summer gate's magic at all?" I asked.

"Only the Summer Gatekeeper is tuned into the gate to that degree." She stepped up to Mum. "I should be able to get her down…"

"I wouldn't waste your life, child," said the Seelie Queen, stepping into view. She looked at us appraisingly—especially at me. "You look a little less substantial than before, mortal."

"That's your problem," I said. "I was always mortal, and I never saw it as anything other than an asset. I have no reason to fear what comes after. I've seen it. People like you, though… what is it about death that scares you so much? The fear of losing your power, or the fear of coming face to face with those you wronged and exiled in person?"

Her mouth twisted. "Do you know what happened here, mortal?" She indicated the dead grass, the empty space around the edges of the liminal space.

Ivy shifted on the spot, her hand on her blade's hilt. *Go on. Kill her.* Of all of us, she was the only one who'd actually killed a Sidhe.

"This is the space where the realm of death meets the mortal realm," the Summer Queen said. "Nobody from the Courts or in either realm can find us unless they know the path's location. It's forgotten… lost." Magic streamed from her hand, above the gates, to the sky. The air rippled, and the ripple passed through me, through the gates I could barely feel here. This place was the fabric holding the worlds together. "This is the end of the line as far as your realm is concerned... in more than one way."

The implication was clear. As though conjured up from the depths of my memory, I saw a sky afire with magic, dark winged shapes wheeling above, dead turning to life to death again as the ripples shook the world.

The invasion... they started it here.

This was where the horsemen who'd invaded the earth had ripped the realms apart. But if that gate opened, worse than the invaders would escape. Maybe some of the gods had been exiled for a very good reason.

"Don't open the gate," I warned.

The Seelie Queen stood beside the gate, one hand on its edge. Too close. None of the others could move to strike her without risking the gate opening and swallowing Mum whole.

"Why do you need her?" Hazel burst out. "The Summer Gatekeeper's power is the same as any of the Sidhe's. Any one of them would do."

"Incorrect. What type of magic is stronger?"

"A vow," I said. "You can't be serious. The Sidhe tie themselves in knots with vows every other week. I'm pretty sure enslaving my family isn't the most powerful or important thing they've done."

"No," she said. "But it *is* a vow that links directly to the Erlking himself—and to a gate which might easily be manipulated for another purpose."

"For what? You want to bring back the monsters you exiled in the first place? Do you think they'll obey without a fuss, or was stealing their magic once not enough?"

"I never had the chance to steal their magic," she said. "He kept that from me. Kept it all from me. *Lost* his magical talismans. He took the throne to take away my power."

I laughed, mostly in disbelief. "You can't kill what's already dead. *I* can, but you're not like me. You're weak."

Mum lifted her head. Shook it. "No. Ilsa…"

"The mortal wakes," said the Seelie Queen. "You have no idea what it cost me to win over one of his playthings. In the end, I had to hijack his servant for my own, but this human woman kept outmanoeuvring my plans."

"She's a Lynn. It's what we do," I said. "If you're waiting for me to use the book to break open the gates of death, you'll be waiting a while. You can't control me or compel me like this. And if you open that gate, there's an army of Sidhe behind us, waiting to arrest or shoot you on sight."

"Then I suppose it's time to finish this." She eyed the gate. "That's enough of the Gatekeeper's power."

A knife appeared in her hand. She lunged, and everyone moved at once.

Hazel slammed into her before her knife hit Mum, knocking both of them out of the way, while a ghost rose from the fog, directly behind them. Ghosts appeared everywhere, half-faeries, angry and staring. Necromantic power hummed through the air, and Morgan's eyes glowed white. He'd brought them here, or they'd followed me, to see me keep my word.

"You never planned to help us," they said to the Seelie Queen. "You lied."

"You pissed off a bunch of people," I said. "Look and see."

Her mouth twisted in a snarl. "You pathetic mortals."

Ivy lunged, her blade spearing the Seelie Queen in the chest. She gasped, her body collapsing, but behind her, the gate rattled.

It was too late. Too much power had gone into it, and the god would break free.

Mum positioned herself in front of it. I knew that look. I'd probably worn it myself when I'd surrendered to the gate.

"You can't give your life, fool," snarled the Seelie Queen. "It's too late. If you don't let me go, it'll break out and destroy the line and everything on it."

"What the fuck did you think would happen?" I shouted.

The Seelie Queen collapsed onto her side. Blood spilled out of her wound, but she probably had healing magic. She wasn't the biggest threat. A huge indistinct shape beyond the gate hummed with power. It was a living, breathing talisman, amplified to max. Too dangerous to be allowed into this dimension. The gate would break apart.

Mum's eyes closed and she spoke a single word, a word of power. Everything stilled, even the gate.

"Hazel," she said. "Are you ready to take on the position as Gatekeeper?"

"Don't you dare!" she screamed.

"The only way to close the gate is to surrender its magic to the next Gatekeeper." Her face was set. "It's the only way to end this."

The gate… it belonged to our family. When it passed on, it'd be reset. The link to the god's world would be gone.

The Seelie Queen lunged at her—and smacked right into the Erlking's staff. He'd caused no damage here, because everything was already dead.

The gate stopped trembling. Mum dropped to her knees, the Gatekeeper's symbol gone from her forehead.

The Erlking whirled on her. "You—what have you done?" he demanded.

"You come to cast judgement on me now?" said Mum. "It's too late. You could have stopped her."

"She's the one thing I cannot destroy."

I stared at him. He was touching the Seelie Queen, and

she was wilting, but she didn't die. She must have super-charged healing powers. *Holy crap.*

"There must be a Gatekeeper." His eyes brimmed with power. "If nobody steps up to take this power, the gate will be the enemy's to take."

"I'll take it!" Hazel shouted. "I'm the next in line. I accept the position."

Her forehead lit up, and the circlet glowed with renewed life.

"You fools," snarled a familiar voice. The Winter Gatekeeper appeared on the path. She looked awful. Her skin was literally falling off, showing the bones beneath. She really hadn't considered the possible downsides to being Sidhe. The more powerful the magic, the worse effect iron had. An iron knife stuck out of her spine, yet she kept walking.

The Seelie Queen pushed against the Erlking, who held her back with both hands. If he let go, she'd lunge for the gates again. Hazel was unprotected. But nobody could take their eyes off the Winter Gatekeeper's walking, Sidhe-like corpse.

A word flew from her lips, and everyone fell to their knees. Even the Erlking.

Everyone except me.

I smiled at her. "You just can't keep me down."

"Give me that book," she growled.

"Let me think about that. No."

At my words, the gates opened behind me, a whirling curtain of darkness. The half-faerie ghosts began to drift through. Morgan grabbed Hazel, while River tightened his grip on my body.

"You should be dead," snarled the Gatekeeper, her eyes burning pits of electric blue light.

"Here I'm as alive as you are," I told her. "Or you're as dead as I am. Take your pick."

"That book is my family's by right," she roared.

"You forfeited that right when you tried to kill my mother."

When the truce had been put into place after their major argument. I'd been too young to really think about what'd happened, but given what the Winter Gatekeeper had done since, it was plain to see Mum had come up with that story to hide the fact that the other side of our family wanted us all dead.

"Then your friends will pay the price," she said softly.

Her hands glowed blue, and undead swarmed the path behind her. Reanimated faeries of all types, ranging from redcaps to trolls—all revived, under her control. She might no longer be a necromancer, but she used the corrupt version of Winter magic, which came close to necromancy and blood magic.

My own body climbed down from River's arms, glowing with the same light. He exclaimed in alarm.

"Don't you dare," I growled at the Winter Gatekeeper. Death's gate remained open, a torrent of roaring darkness beckoning, but even the call of death wasn't enough for the Winter Gatekeeper this time around. The rising dead glowed with Winter power, even my reanimated body.

River faced not-Ilsa, his whole body trembling. A single tear fell from his eye, tracing down his cheek. His blade glowed bright green, and I knew he was giving his own life force to fuel its power. "Get the *fuck* away from her or I'll make you regret you ever came back into this world."

"River!" I shouted. "Behind you!"

The undead swarmed. Ivy leapt into action, talisman slashing off limbs and slicing throats, a whirl of faerie magic and light. Morgan ducked his head and several undead collapsed, the wraiths that possessed them screaming from the psychic assault.

Summer's gate stood forgotten. The Erlking's hands remained locked around his wife's throat, but she wouldn't die, and he couldn't help us. Being able to break everything you touched made no difference when everything was already broken.

The Winter Gatekeeper beckoned to me. "Give me the book and I'll stop this. Lives fuel life, deaths fuel death," she said. My reanimated body turned towards River.

Dammit. I am *still alive in there.*

I drifted downward, pulling all the book's power into me. The dead faltered, and the banishing words rose to my tongue. I spoke them aloud into the echoing silence, finishing with a single word. The name. Arden's true name.

The space beyond the gate of Death turned to blackness. The Winter Gatekeeper screamed in fury, magic springing to her hands—pure Winter magic, Sidhe-strong and deadly.

No. I concentrated on my body as hard as possible, imagining the hands moving under my own control. The Winter Gatekeeper's spell locked around my body in a vice grip. Ice shot from her hands, only to crash into Hazel's shield. With a hoarse yell, Hazel lunged and threw a handful of iron filings into her face. Aunt Candice screamed, holes appearing in her skin as the iron burned through to the bone.

I raised my ghostly hands, and pulled the book's power back into myself again, this time reaching not for the gates, but for the kinetic power I'd rarely used. I aimed at the iron shards, and *pushed.*

The Winter Gatekeeper choked, falling to her knees, as the iron shards left the container in Hazel's hands, piercing her neck, her hands, her legs. With a final burst of power, I found my waiting body and called the book's power to fuse me back into mortal skin.

My human hands moved, taking the iron dagger from my pocket and stabbing her in the chest.

The Winter Gatekeeper fell, blood pooling onto the ground. The glow in her eyes dimmed, and the undead faltered as her magic lost its grip on them. River lowered his blade, catching my gaze, relief etched on his face.

Holly ran up the path behind her, holding a pair of iron handcuffs. She stared around at us, at her mother's limp body at my feet. The Winter Gatekeeper shuddered, bleeding rapidly, her skin decaying.

"I'm sorry," Holly said, her voice breaking on the words. She dropped to the ground beside her mother, grabbing her hand as though feeling for a pulse.

Half-faerie ghosts hovered above her, accompanied by the Sidhe I'd thought had already passed into the realm of death. They grabbed onto the Winter Gatekeeper's spirit as she floated out of her body, staring in confusion.

"Did you really think you couldn't die in that form?" I said to her.

She let out a scream of rage, but the dead grabbed her, swarming her, dragging her along the path and out of sight. Leaving the living behind.

The Erlking held his wife in a death grip, a grim expression on his face. The gate... wait a second. Summer's gate had gone. I bloody hoped it was back at the Lynn house where it belonged.

Mum had her arm around Hazel. Morgan stood staring at the fallen dead. And River's arms came around me in a crushing hug, his tear-streaked face brushing my cheek.

Nobody moved for an instant. Then Ivy shook droplets of blood from her sword. "I don't know about you guys, but I reckon we need to get *her*—" She jerked her head at the Seelie Queen—"into jail before someone else starts breaking things. Deal?"

I couldn't have agreed more.

24

The Erlking took us all back to his territory in a flash of light, still holding onto his struggling wife. Everyone except the Winter Gatekeeper, who he left dead on the path. Ivy stared at the throne and the dead trees with an expression of interest—I hadn't had time to explain the Erlking's talisman to her before my impromptu trip into Death, but she'd surely drawn her own conclusions. As for River, he was more interested in keeping as close a grip on me as possible. I had the impression he'd have happily carried me out of there on his own, except someone had to give the explanation to the Sidhe. Mum and Hazel stood close together, while both Morgan and Holly hung back as though expecting someone to throw them out.

Another flash of light heralded the arrival of two Sidhe on horseback. As luck would have it, one of them was Lord Daival.

"Take her," the Erlking growled at them. "She is to be put on trial for treason."

"Speaking of treason," I said, eying Lord Daival. "He conspired with her. Lord Daival did."

River finally released me with one hand and said, "She's right. Lord Daival is a traitor to the Seelie Court."

Lord Daival looked at him with narrowed eyes. "Mistreating mortals does not make one a criminal."

"But conspiring against the Courts does," River said, his voice clear. "Question him. He can't lie."

Lord Daival turned on both of us, thorns springing from his hands. "You accuse me of treason?"

"Actually," Ivy said. "I've seen that before. Where did that magic come from?"

Lord Daival scowled. "What—"

"Heard of the princess of thorns?" Ivy asked. "How about the Lady of the Tree? Both were Vale outcasts, and stole that magic. You couldn't have got it any other way. Lord Daival is a traitor."

The others moved in a blur, surrounding both Lord Daival and the Seelie Queen. I was too tired to take in their shouted arguments, while the Erlking yelled his version of the story from the opposite side of the clearing. Nobody seemed to want to go near him. Hazel and Mum conversed in whispers, probably trading Gatekeeper secrets. For once, I didn't mind that I couldn't hear them. Feeling River's warm hand on my back was enough.

"I think we're done here," said Mum. She sounded tired, but there was that Gatekeeper steel in her tone all the same. Her eyes were on the Erlking. "I would like to return home with my family. I trust the Summer gate has been returned to its rightful place?"

The Erlking looked at her. I'd forgotten until now that she still hadn't technically upheld her end of the bargain and found whatever he'd sent her to find in the Vale—but with her title gone, that vow no longer existed.

"Yes," the Erlking said. "I sent the gate back to where it

belongs. Take care of your family. I will call for the heir when the time is right."

A shiver ran down my back. Hazel would be Gatekeeper next. She'd go through the Summer Gatekeeper's trials… and I didn't know what came next. Mum hadn't told us, because her vow forbade it. Only the current Gatekeeper knew all their secrets. Hazel would have a hell of a lot to learn. But after all this, she was ready for it.

I couldn't get used to seeing Mum as *human*. Her forehead was smooth skin not marked by magic. Still young-looking for her age, but more vulnerable than I'd ever seen her. She and Hazel looked so much alike now. Complicated feelings rose when I looked at her, so I turned to River instead.

"I hope Hazel's ready for it," I muttered. "We never did *break* the curse."

"Doesn't mean we can't," said a voice I didn't expect… Holly. She stood apart from the others, the circlet on her forehead glowing faintly. "What's wrong with his magic?" She jerked her head at the Erlking.

"If I told you, he'd probably have to kill you," I said. Holly being here was blatantly against the rules of the Court, but nobody appeared to have noticed her.

"I think you should have left her alive," said Ivy. "The Winter Gatekeeper. She deserved to see the inside of a Sidhe's jail."

"Guess that'd be fitting for someone who wanted to live forever," I admitted. "But you can't take your eyes off these people without them causing more mischief."

"Can't argue with you there," Ivy said.

White light flared around us, and in the next instant, we stood at the end of Summer's garden. The Lynn house sat at the end, flowers back in bloom, and magic hummed in the air as though it'd never left.

Except with one difference.

Mum finally turned away from Hazel to look at me. Then Morgan.

Holly cleared her throat. "I should go home and make sure the Winter Gatekeeper didn't wreck anything else. I—thank you. All of you."

She hurried off. All of us watched her leave to avoid looking at one another. Morgan shifted to the right like he was trying to hide behind River, who still held onto me as though afraid I'd keel over.

Ivy spoke next. "Is there a way back to Edinburgh from here? Because I should update the council. And the Mage Lord. Before he sends his messenger into Faerie and pisses them all off again."

"Sure, the Path should still be there," Hazel said. "I'll show you."

"Traitor," Morgan said under his breath.

River released me and made to follow Ivy and Hazel, but I grabbed his arm.

"Don't you even think about it," I said. "You kept me alive on her orders. Also, I've met *your* family. Mum, this is my boyfriend, River."

Surprise flashed in her eyes. "We've met."

"I know," I said, "but I wanted to make it official that I don't hold it against him for keeping secrets on your orders."

Oops. Apparently I still held some pent-up anger after all, even though Mum had doubtless not wanted to worry us into following her into the Vale.

River pulled his arm free. "I should go with them. The council requires a report, and they'll want to hear from a witness from this side."

"Yeah. You should know, Ivy wanted to talk to you about joining the council as well."

He blinked. "The council? On earth?"

"They need half-faerie representatives, apparently."

He ran a hand through his hair, as though suddenly conscious of his dishevelled appearance. I probably looked worse, but I'd *died*. Technically.

Mum's attention was on Morgan. *Oh no.* Maybe it was for the best that River didn't witness the fallout.

"I'll see you soon, Ilsa," River said. "You can come back to Edinburgh from here, right?"

"Yeah, I can." Kissing him in front of Mum would be too weird, so I briefly hugged him. "Soon, I hope."

Because I think at least one of us is about to get disowned.

River walked swiftly to catch up with Hazel, while I looked at Mum.

"I could have died," I said, drawing her attention from Morgan. "You and that damned book nearly got me killed a thousand times."

She didn't say anything. Tears fell down her face. I hadn't seen her cry since Morgan had run away from home.

"I didn't mean…" The words stuck in my throat. "I get that it wasn't all your fault. Faerie vows. But really? This?" I lifted the book, my hands shaking.

I didn't expect her to break down. I didn't know how to handle it. She never had, not in my lifetime. The moment she'd taken on the mantle of Gatekeeper, nothing else mattered.

"You knew," I said to Mum. "You knew exactly what you were handing over to me, didn't you? Or was it all Arden?"

"I shouldn't have run away," said Morgan.

Mum looked like she didn't know where to turn.

Hazel walked back towards us, eyebrows raised. "Nobody's screaming. Is it good news?"

Mum hugged her, somehow pulling Morgan and me in as well. Nothing in our family was simple or easy. Words weren't adequate. They couldn't encompass years lost or promises broken, or impossible vows, or ancient gods. Under everything, we were human. Whatever the Sidhe did to us, whichever talismans we claimed, it's what we'd always be. Human. Mortal. Not lesser. Not better. Just… us.

"Tell me what happened," Mum said, her voice hoarse, wiping her eyes with the back of her hand.

It took some time to get the story out. Or parts of it. I still didn't know everything about the years Morgan had been gone, nor while I'd been away. Nor how long Mum had wandered through the Vale alone, looking for something that might not even exist.

"I didn't want you to have to do this so early," she said to Hazel, when we'd moved from the garden into the living room.

"You didn't have to give up your circlet." Hazel shrugged one shoulder, leaning back on the sofa. "We Lynns have the self-sacrificing thing down, right? Ilsa's still the expert at that. She freaking *died.*"

"I know," she said, her eyes glittering with unshed tears. "I didn't know about the book. I only knew it existed because of the bird… where is he, anyway?"

"Dead," I said. "It was his magic in this book."

By the time I got to the part about the gods, she looked about ready to faint. Morgan continued to lurk near the living room door like he planned to make a quick exit.

"I knew of the Ancients," Mum said softly. "I didn't know the Sidhe took their power."

"Pretty sure there isn't anything the Sidhe *haven't* tried to take," said Morgan.

"They're not so keen on mortality," I commented. "Pity. The world behind the gates of death… it's really not that scary."

"Change is what they fear the most," Mum said. "That much is obvious."

I thought of the Erlking in his empty clearing, the

destructive magic inside him kept under control. He could destroy so much with that power, yet chose not to. I could live a thousand years and never understand the Sidhe. As for their gods… maybe I understood a little of why they'd been exiled.

"If you don't want to take on the position, we can try to find a way around it," Mum said.

"Are you kidding?" said Hazel. "Who else in all the realms is qualified for this? Until we can get the Sidhe to stop killing everything they see, I'm sticking with the position. It'd be nice if it was a voluntary thing, though. Just saying."

"I spent most of my childhood trying to find a way around the vow," she said. "I'm sure most Gatekeepers before me did. In the end, peace comes with a cost. When that peace disappeared, in the invasion… it might be that something different is needed."

"The council wanted to speak to you," I said. "They're in Edinburgh. I guess you've been missing their messages because you've been in Faerie. Anyway, a bunch of them came up from England…"

"And they're probably breaking everything," she said. "The English mages have no concept of subtlety."

"Have you ever met Lady Montgomery of the necromancer guild in Edinburgh?" I asked.

"No," she said. "I've heard of her."

"River's mother," said Hazel. "Ilsa's hoping you'll get along with his family. Seems a safer bet than his faerie side… his father isn't terrible for a Sidhe, though."

Mum shook her head. "When did my children grow up?"

"Aren't you throwing me out?" Morgan blurted. "I could tell you all the terrible things I've done."

"It doesn't matter." Mum shook her head. "Life is too short to waste at odds with those we love. Now the Sidhe's magic no longer binds me, I intend to get to know my children a little better."

"You might be here a while," said Morgan. "We're very complicated."

"We're also living in Edinburgh at the moment," I added. "Well, two of us are."

Surprise suffused her features. "You joined the guild?"

"Yeah," I said. "Since the book's power mimics necromancy. Why didn't you tell us we had necromancer ancestry?"

Mum exhaled in a sigh. "It didn't seem pertinent. Neither of you had manifested any signs of magical talent, and... I didn't want to get your hopes up."

No kidding. It was a selfish choice, but who was I to criticise? Morgan and I had both left home. Hazel had flaunted the rules on a consistent basis. And look how much trouble we'd managed to cause in her absence.

"Did the Erlking send you to the Vale in person?" I asked.

Mum nodded. "He did. I believe he was unaware of his wife's intention of usurping the gate until long after he'd sent me away. But then Arden came to see me. He told me about my Aunt Enid's magic and that the Winters were searching for its source, and he offered to guide the book to someone who would use it to protect our family and prevent Candice from using it against us. I had no idea its powers were so overwhelming and that it would put you in so much danger." Her sad gaze passed over all of us. "When River came back to me with news that the book—the Ancient—had picked you as the host for its magic... I was horrified. I knew that the book would not relinquish its hold on you, but as long as the vow bound me, I couldn't leave the Vale. Nor did I know that Arden remained connected to the Winter Gatekeeper even beyond death."

"But she didn't know what he was, not at first," I said. Not until we'd summoned him.

Arden had saved us, in the end. The book had begun to glow in my pocket again, as though trying to get my attention. I gave it a brief glance, then turned back to my family. The talisman could wait.

———

Hazel had left the Path to Edinburgh open, so the following morning, we walked out of the house onto the country lane. The illusion had reappeared as though it had never left, including the darker shape of the Winter Lynns' forest behind the house. Holly hadn't come to speak to us yet, but who knew, maybe she and Hazel would become friends when Hazel started the Gatekeeper trials for real.

The country lane vanished as Hazel led us down the Path, onto Edinburgh's cobbled street. I twisted to give her a look. "I knew Arden was messing with me by opening Paths halfway up Arthur's Seat."

Hazel snorted. "Last time you climbed it willingly."

And now I had to relive the whole experience in front of the council. Frankly, I had no idea what to tell them. Parts of the story made little sense without mentioning the gods, the Erlking, or the real source of my magic. But the council had been put together to deal with threats exactly like the ones I'd faced. The former council, and countless Gatekeepers, had given their lives to protect secrets that weren't theirs. Maybe I'd be the first to bring those secrets open into the light.

The council room was more packed than last time, or maybe it was my nerves. Even Agnes and Everett were there. My chest tightened. Words had never come easily to me, like Hazel. Next to me, Ivy gave me an encouraging nod. Hazel stood on my other side. I wasn't alone. I turned from the Mage Lords' expectant faces to the crowd, and began my story.

I didn't tell them everything in the end. Truth was a necessity, but the Erlking's talisman was a secret he kept to preserve his own Court, and wasn't my secret to share. Summer's gate, too, I glossed over, not wanting any necromancers to get ideas about summoning things from those dark dimensions. But I was fairly sure the most intelligent amongst the crowd could work out from the context that whatever had tried to get out of the gate was no faerie or Sidhe. As for the Winter Gatekeeper, Holly clearly hadn't had an invitation. It'd take a while for the council to trust her side of the family again, but I made it clear that it wasn't Holly's fault that her mother had schemed with the outcasts.

Ivy told some parts of the story. So did River. We'd barely got a moment alone, and when the council finally allowed us to sit down, I was tempted to grab him and pull him out of the room. Neither of us were official council members yet— if that ever happened. My head buzzed with residual nerves from putting myself out there, but speaking the truth was liberating in a way. The book decided to say its piece by glowing brightly in my pocket all through the meeting. Perhaps that was Arden's contribution to the story. I kept the raven out of my account, partly out of respect for the dead, partly because I wanted to look into the past a little more before I made it public. I made out that the Winter Gatekeeper had returned using conventional necromancy and the outcasts' help, leaving out the fact that she'd turned herself into a Sidhe. Her brief immortality attempt was overshadowed by what the Seelie Queen had done.

When the meeting broke apart, Lady Montgomery came to thank me in person. Then the mages did. I was dizzy with remembering names and titles, let alone being scrutinised by a bunch of complete strangers. Hazel handled the whole thing better, but she'd been trained for it. And Mum, who took over the story when words failed me, and told of the final battle from her own perspective.

So now the entire mage council, plus a bunch of assorted high-ranking supernaturals, knew about the book. They knew what I could do. And they seemed to respect me for it.

"Need a moment?" asked a voice from the side. Jas stood there, a high stack of note pages nearly masking her face. "I could fake a ghost attack to get you out of here for five minutes."

"It's appreciated, but no thanks. Aren't you allowed in?" I moved to the door, away from the crowd.

"Nope. Not high-ranked enough. I wanted to hear your speech, but they soundproofed the doors."

"You got to skip the boring parts at least," I said. "Where's Lloyd?"

"Saving my spot at the coffee shop the instant I get out of here."

"I like the way you think." I didn't know if the two of them were an item or not, but I had every intention of getting River somewhere alone the first chance I got. "Before I forget—what did you do in the battle? When you fought the wraiths? I've never seen you use necromancy like that before." I'd been racking my brains trying to figure out where I'd seen the shimmering halo around her spirit form before, and seeing the Winter Gatekeeper's army of the dead had reminded me that I'd barely scratched the surface when it came to true necromancy.

When Jas blinked at me, a hint of wariness in her expression, I reached into my pocket, withdrawing the talisman for a moment. "I know all about unconventional magic, believe me. Just curious."

She smiled. "I bet you do. I know who to ask if I need

help." Her gaze went towards the crowds of other supernaturals—specifically, the witches, who crowded around in groups—and then the council.

Ivy stepped in. "There you are," she said. "Hiding from the crowd?"

"Yep." I glanced to the side, where Jas had performed an impressive disappearing act. "Anyway, I wanted to ask you something… can you read this?" I held up the book, revealing the new section which had appeared in the back. It contained a few words I couldn't read, but I figured Ivy might be able to.

"Yeah," she said. "It says… *watch your step, amateur.*"

"Seriously? Dammit, Arden."

I couldn't hate Arden, despite his keeping the truth from us up until the last possible moment. I could only imagine navigating the wave of vows and promises to keep our family safe. And he had done so, really.

As Ivy turned to speak to the Mage Lords, Hazel dragged Morgan towards me. "He's being… Morgan."

"I only dozed off for two seconds," Morgan protested.

"You left your body and kept wandering around as a ghost," Hazel said.

"I didn't see," I said honestly. "Since when did you have the spirit sight?"

Hazel shook her head. "No clue. I only saw Morgan, anyway. It's not fair that two of you get to be honorary necromancers and not me."

"Hey, you get to start actual Summer Gatekeeper training soon," Morgan said.

"Soon. There are still a few things I need to talk to the council about, but I think Mum's trying to make up for lost time." She gestured across the room, where Mum was in conversation with several mages. And Lady Montgomery.

"Oh." Crap. Despite what I'd told Mum yesterday, I wasn't *quite* ready for this.

"Relax," River said from behind me. "She's not saying anything bad. Singing your praises, actually."

"Has Lady Montgomery told her the part where Morgan and I broke you out of jail to stop the apocalypse?"

He grinned. "No. But you're still in one piece after telling her the rest of it, so I assume there's no danger of any of us being turned into trees."

"Not unless the Sidhe turn up," Hazel said. Her forehead gleamed with Summer power. "Actually, *I* can do that now. Hmm."

Morgan scowled at her. "Don't you even think about it."

I glanced around at the crowd. "I didn't expect this big an audience."

"The whole necromancer council showed up," said River. "To hear you speak."

I blinked. "What? Have they forgotten how I nearly got them killed?"

"I think they have the full story by now." His hand slid into mine. "It's fine. You have an open membership at the guild for as long as you need it."

Morgan frowned. "You're not staying?"

I shrugged. "For now? Sure. What about you?"

He nodded. "Yeah, I'm staying at the guild."

"But you'll come and see me," said Hazel. "Both of you. I'll need a distraction from the Sidhe's gruelling trials."

"Of course we will." I looked at River, who'd squeezed my hand meaningfully. "Be back in a minute."

I walked after River, out of the room. The moment we were alone, he wrapped his arms tight around me. "Ilsa."

I sealed my mouth over his. "Thanks for not giving up on me."

"It was out of the question." He stroked my hair with one

hand, the other wrapped around my hips. For a moment we just held onto one another. I felt him exhale. "You didn't give a definite answer to your brother's question."

"About whether I'm staying here?" I pulled back from him a little. "That depends on whether you decide to take up the council's offer or not."

He frowned. "Why?"

"Because obviously, my choice will involve the easiest and quickest way to be right next to you whenever I feel like it. In person, not in the spirit realm."

"Then you're not going with Ivy? I thought—she told me she intended to help train you."

"I don't need to go with her," I said. "I can use the spirit line… stop looking at me like that. I'm not going to die, and besides, I don't need to open the book whenever I have a problem to solve. I'm in control of this. Everything I did was intentional." I kissed him on the mouth, and the spirit realm briefly unfolded around us, muting the world to grey. Another second, and the waking world came back. "See?"

I jumped as his lips traced down my neck. "What if I gave you an incentive to stick around?"

"You don't need to. I've always felt more at home here than anywhere else. I assume you're not leaving."

He shook his head. "No. Considering the state of things in the Summer Court, I'm intending to tell them I won't be taking on any more assignments."

"Wasn't I worth it?" I winked at him.

"Of course." He trailed a hand through my hair, tucking a loose strand behind my ear. "I only want to bodyguard one person now."

"I thought you were going to try to compete with Ivy on who gets to finish my necromancer training."

His mouth quirked. "At this point, I think we'd be hard-pressed to get Lady Montgomery's permission for me to mentor you."

I pretended to pout. "I thought she liked me."

"She does. Our relationship would be very much against the guild's rules, however, and I don't think either of us would want to go back to keeping our distance."

"I quite liked sneaking off for dates in coffee shops, but no thanks." I leaned in to brush my lips against his. "Speaking of. Want to go there now, before they drag us back in?"

"I'd like nothing more, Ilsa."

I took his hand and pulled him after me into daylight, where the sight of transparent ghosts hovering around couldn't kill my good mood. Even when they zoned in on the mark on my head.

River looked at me. "Are you sure you want to wear the mark everywhere?"

"I think it's going to be tricky to hide that I'm Gatekeeper by now." The book began to glow in my pocket, and I pulled it out. The swirling mark on the cover had changed... to a picture of a raven.

"Someone had to get the last word in." I rolled my eyes.

The bird winked.

ABOUT THE AUTHOR

Emma is the New York Times and USA Today Bestselling author of the Changeling Chronicles urban fantasy series.

Emma spent her childhood creating imaginary worlds to compensate for a disappointingly average reality, so it was probably inevitable that she ended up writing fantasy novels. When she's not immersed in her own fictional universes, Emma can be found with her head in a book or wandering around the world in search of adventure.

Find out more about Emma's books at
www.emmaladams.com.